PRAISE FOR GRA

M000017928

Beach Rental

DOUBLE WINNER IN THE 2012 GDRWA
BOOKSELLERS BEST AWARD

FINALIST IN THE 2012 GAYLE WILSON AWARD OF
EXCELLENCE

FINALIST IN THE 2012 PUBLISHED MAGGIE AWARD
FOR EXCELLENCE

"No author can come close to capturing the awe-inspiring essence of the North Carolina coast like Greene. Her debut novel seamlessly combines hope, love and faith, like the female equivalent of Nicholas Sparks. Her writing is meticulous and so finely detailed you'll hear the gulls overhead and the waves crashing onto shore. Grab a hanky, bury your toes in the sand and get ready to be swept away with this unforgettable beach read." —*RT Book Reviews 4.5 stars TOP PICK*

Beach Winds

FINALIST IN THE 2014 OKRWA INTERNATIONAL
DIGITAL AWARDS

FINALIST IN THE 2014 WISRA WRITE TOUCH
READERS' AWARD

"Greene's follow up to Beach Rental is exquisitely written with lots of emotion and tugging on the heartstrings. Returning to

Emerald Isle is like a warm reunion with an old friend and readers will be inspired by the captivating story where we get to meet new characters and reconnect with a few familiar faces, too. The author's perfect prose highlights family relationships which we may find similar to our own and will have you dreaming of strolling along the shore to rediscover yourself in no time at all. This novel will have one wondering about faith, hope and courage and you may be lucky enough to gain all three by the time Beach Winds last page is read." —*RT Book Reviews 4.5 stars TOP PICK*

A Light Last Seen and A Reader's View of Cub Creek

From a reader about Cub Creek and A Light Last Seen: "'In the heart of Virginia, where the forests hide secrets and the creeks run strong and deep,' is a place called Cub Creek. A place that has meadows filled with colorful flowers and butterflies to chase, and dirt roads and Cub Creek to jump over and disappear into the woods. A living and rural place that draws the reader to the setting and the characters who have stories to tell. A place with light and darkness and as unique as the characters who live there. When I opened the beautiful cover of this book, I stepped into the Cub Creek world and met the main character, Jaynie Highsmith. This is her story."—*Reader/Reviewer Bambi Rathman, February 2020*

A LIGHT LAST SEEN

A LIGHT LAST SEEN

By Grace Greene

Kersey Creek Books

This is a work of fiction. Names, characters, organizations, places, events, and incidents are either products of the author's imagination or are used fictitiously. Any resemblance to actual persons, living or dead, or actual events is purely coincidental.

Text copyright © 2020 by Grace Greene
All rights reserved.

No part of this book may be reproduced, or stored in a retrieval system, or transmitted in any form or by any means, electronic, mechanical, photocopying, recording, or otherwise, without express written permission of the publisher.

Published by Kersey Creek Books

Hardcover Release: November 2020
ISBN-13: 978-1732878549
Large Print Trade Paperback Release: February 2020
ISBN-13: 978-0-9907740-4-4
Trade Paperback Release: February 2020
ISBN-13: 978-1-7328785-0-1
Digital Release: February 2020
ISBN-13: 978-0-9996180-1-1

Cover design by Grace Greene
Printed in the United States of America

A Light Last Seen is dedicated to my beloved mom, Olivia, who gave birth to me, put up with me, and always believed—and made me believe—I could do anything I set my mind to.

She loved her family—all her family—however related. She loved her friends and cared about them deeply, especially her neighbors through the years, her friends in her church and the ladies in her Sunday School class.

She was sweet and gentle, but she could be fierce, particularly in defense of and in protection of her children.

We are blessed to have had her as our mother.

We lost her by degrees as Alzheimer's took her away from us, but it never altered the sweet and gentle courage with which she lived her life. Even when she was stubborn. When mom was stubborn, she could out-stubborn anyone. She was also a prayer-warrior—sometimes silently, sometimes loudly, but always with sincerity and faith.

When I received *A Light Last Seen* back from the editor in late December and began working on revisions, I never suspected Mom would be gone from us within days. She slipped away quietly soon after the new year began.
I continued working on the revisions because Mom loved to read and taught her children to love reading and she would expect me to keep my commitments, so this one's for you, Mom. *A Light Last Seen* is dedicated to you and the light and love you instilled in our hearts and left with us in our memories.

BOOKS BY GRACE GREENE

Emerald Isle, North Carolina Series
Beach Rental *(Book 1)*
Beach Winds *(Book 2)*
Beach Wedding *(Book 3)*
"Beach Towel" (A Short Story)
Beach Walk *(Christmas Novella)*

Barefoot Tides Two-Book Series
A Barefoot Tide *(Book 1)*
A Dancing Tide *(Book 2)*

Beach Single-Title Novellas
Beach Christmas *(Christmas Novella)*
Clair *(Beach Brides Novella Series)*

Cub Creek Novels ~ Series and Single Titles
Cub Creek *(Cub Creek Series, Book 1)*
Leaving Cub Creek *(Cub Creek Series, Book 2)*
The Happiness In Between
The Memory of Butterflies
A Light Last Seen

The Wildflower House Novels
Wildflower Heart *(Book 1)*
Wildflower Hope *(Book 2)*
Wildflower Christmas *(A Wildflower House Novella) (Book 3)*

Virginia Country Roads
Kincaid's Hope
A Stranger in Wynnedower

www.GraceGreene.com

BRIEF DESCRIPTION

Chasing happiness and finding joy are two very different things--as Jaynie Highsmith has discovered. Can she give up searching for the one and reclaim the other?

Jaynie Highsmith grows up in Cub Creek wanting nothing more than to escape from it and the chaos of her childhood. Desperate to leave her past behind and make a new life, she is determined to become the best version of herself she can create. But when she does take off, she also leaves ~ and forgets ~ important parts of her past and herself.

The new life is everything she wants, or so she thinks, until it begins to fall apart and she realizes she's been fooling herself.

Seventeen years after leaving home, Jaynie needs a *new* fresh start and returning to Cub Creek is critical, but she promises herself that the visit will be as short as possible and then she'll be out and free again. However, to have any chance of changing her destiny, Jaynie must reconcile the past she left behind with her present, and a longer stay may be vital to her hopes now and for the future.

A Light Last Seen

Prologue

Time and memories are fluid. Just when you think the artifacts of your past have been carefully packed away and left securely behind, the ghosts of them—the memories—grab you like quicksand and suck you right back into what you wanted to forget. The present is never free of the past.

I have a recurring dream. In fact, it's a memory masquerading as a dream, and it steals in as I sleep. In this memory-dream, Jaynie is almost six. Her big brother, Mitch, eleven and tall for his age, seems grown to her. He is standing at the front window in the living room—Mama calls it the picture window—and they hear the car door slam hard outside. Mitch says, "Mom's home from work too early. Go lay low for a while, kid."

It isn't the first time Jaynie's had to make herself scarce. Shoeless and wearing her favorite yellow cotton dress, she slips quietly out the kitchen door.

The sun is bright. The summer day is warm. Jaynie plays in the meadow for a while, chasing butterflies, and then skips along the dirt road to the woods. She'll hunt for pink lady's slippers. Pink and yellow are her favorite colors. But to get to where the flowers grow, she must cross the creek. She goes to the narrow spot where she can jump the flowing water if she gets a good running start. She makes the leap, slipping only a little when she hits a muddy spot upon landing.

On the far side, under the canopy of trees, it's shady and cool. The earth is alive. She feels it breathe and hum beneath her bare feet like a distant, whispered song. She sings and dances to its rhythm as she moves along. After enough time has passed, as best she can judge, she starts back home. She jumps the creek again, spreading her arms wide like she's flying. This time she lands as delicately as those butterflies lighting on flowers in the field.

As Jaynie leaves the shelter of the forest and walks along the dirt road that will take her back to the meadow path and home, she senses something skimming the air around her head. She tries to shoo it away, but it's close now and catches in her flyaway hair. She spins and ducks frantically. When the insect lands on her arm, she panics.

It's a dragonfly. Even the name is scary. Dragons have big teeth, sharp claws, and breathe fire. This one is little, but Mama has told her that dragonflies bite and sting. That she could be allergic. She could swell up and die.

Fearful, Jaynie takes a swipe at the insect. She feels its soft body give, and a wing detaches. Goo smears on her arm. The torn wing is stuck in it. Her stomach lurches. She screams and shakes her arm, but the goo and the broken wing are still there, maybe forever. Sudden tears obscure her sight. The sun itself dims. In that frantic moment, she thinks it is the end of all things, and it is caused by her. Her fault. She's too afraid to open her eyes, but then the dark area resolves into a person-shape. A woman. She is silhouetted by the sun, creating a rose-gold light against Jaynie's closed eyelids. A large woman.

She grabs Jaynie's flailing arms. She kneels and speaks in soothing tones, saying, "Jaynie, honey, are you hurt?"

The woman knows her name. Jaynie is surprised, and that dispels some of her panic. She says, "No, ma'am," as she rubs at her eyes, trying to clear her vision, because she knows this must be the woman who lives up the road, in the house Mama doesn't like.

"Calm down, child. Tell me what's wrong."

The woman keeps ahold of her, but gently. Jaynie feels her heart slowing. Calm and comfort flow from the woman's hands. Jaynie leans into them, into those strong arms, needing what they offer.

The woman says, "My name is Ruth Berry. I'm a neighbor and a grandma. You can trust me. Now tell me what's wrong."

Jaynie sniffles and whispers, "I killed it, ma'am. I killed it."

The dream ends, and I wake.

I lie in the dark for a while as sleep releases its hold on me, thinking about that child, Jaynie. Dirty feet. Snarled hair. Tears mixed with mucus. Me.

The memory-dream always feels like it ends too soon. Before it is done. Before I can grasp why it keeps returning.

It strikes me that it ends like life does—with too much left unseen after the last light is gone. I'm sure Ms. Ruth could have explained the memory and why it keeps coming back as a dream because, while I don't know much about some things, I know for certain sure that Ruth Berry knew everything about everything—at least about anything that mattered.

CHAPTER ONE

I slipped out of bed and went to the kitchen to make myself a cup of hot tea. Wearing a t-shirt and lightweight pajama pants, I carried my tea outside to the back porch. Ruth's porch. This house had been her home.

Was it ironic that the memory-dream had returned here with me? Or should it have been expected?

The white metal table where I set my mug was small, as was the porch, but roomy enough and the wicker chair was comfortable. I propped up my bare feet in the other chair. This table and chair set had not belonged to Ms. Ruth. Her grandson, Wyatt, had placed them here as part of staging the house for sale. I settled back, sipped my tea, and observed the night as I waited for dawn.

It was that time between dark and light when the stars were still visible above the tree line, but the insects had ceased their night music and the birds were not yet greeting the morning with song. The trees themselves were dark blocks of shadow. In these predawn hours, a person might wonder if she was the last living creature on earth. And if she was, what would she do with her life—alone?

At this hour, even the most introverted would be relieved to see kitchen lights flick on in neighboring houses and know the inhabitants were stirring. That the people you cared about would rise to greet another day. That civilization endured and loneliness—the actual reality of aloneness— was staved off for a while longer.

There were no lights on at Wyatt's house. Not yet. But there would be.

Soon the sky would change. The stars would begin to wink out as the sky lightened along the horizon. I was content to wait. What I didn't want to do was toss and turn for another hour or two hoping for sleep, knowing I'd find only frustration.

I was here in Cub Creek again—after almost twenty years away and despite my best efforts never to return. In fact, this house where I was staying was only two houses away from my childhood home, and between them was the house where Wyatt was sleeping. Wyatt, my sometime friend from childhood, who'd been my teenage crush but never my boyfriend.

Was Wyatt also awake? Was he restless too?

Thinking of him, I half expected to see his tall, dark shadow moving across the yard, coming to me, striding across that blank, empty stage of night.

I would welcome the interruption because beyond the memory-dream, and even thoughts of Wyatt, Ms. Ruth waited. I wanted a pleasant memory. There were many. For instance, on one long-ago day when I was eight or so, Ms. Ruth had brought home a flat of flowering plants with purple velvet leaves. I was outside, playing in the meadow behind Uncle Lou's house. She'd called to me from this very backyard, "Jaynie, girl! Quick! Come give me a hand?"

The flimsy plastic tray supporting the small peat pots

looked precarious as Ms. Ruth carried it from her car to the backyard.

"Yes, ma'am." I ran over to steady the flat. Together, we placed it on the ground next to her yard chair. Her chair was the usual webbed lawn furniture, but she always called outside seating yard chairs.

"Want to help, missy?"

"Sure."

It must've been a Saturday since I wasn't in school. Ms. Ruth settled in her chair to supervise, while I knelt on the earth itself. Her face was round with full, rosy cheeks—rosy with help, Mama had said. Ms. Ruth's black hair—long, thick, and curly—was piled up on her head, but much of it had escaped, and with the day being warm, the strands were stuck fast to her neck. Each time she tried to unstick her hair, pushing it back and away from the moist flesh, it snagged in her rings and in her dangly earrings and she'd grunt in annoyance. I looked up when she made that noise, and she said, "Dig that hole a little deeper, hon. Just a smidge."

I worked the garden trowel into the dirt until Ms. Ruth pronounced the depth right. She selected the next small plant and carefully placed it in my hands. I arranged the loose roots in the hole, then patted the dirt firmly around it until the flower was nice and snug.

"Pansies," I said.

"That's right. Can you spell it?"

"P-a-n-s . . ." I slowed to a stop. "Y-s?"

"That's for one pansy. If it's more than one—which it is—that y becomes i-e-s."

I nodded. Ms. Ruth nodded back, and we smiled.

"Good work, little miss. Time to give this baby pansy,

with a y, its own special sip of water." She gestured toward the green plastic watering can beside her chair. As I watered the plant, Ms. Ruth said, "Thank you for your help." She coughed.

"Can I fetch you a drink?"

"No need. We'll call it quits and finish up later. It's about lunchtime anyway, and I'm running on empty. I expect your brother will come looking for you if you don't head home soon."

"Mitch won't care."

I said it honestly, but perhaps with a touch of a pout because Ms. Ruth said, "Your brother does his best."

"He does. He's okay, I guess, as big brothers go."

"Says you in your vast experience." Ms. Ruth laughed.

Her laughter always got my attention because it was flat out laughing, like she was being tickled. Not a polite laugh or because someone had told a joke, and it was never cruel—it was laughter straight from her heart.

"What's so funny?" I asked.

"Nothing. And everything. You have a light, child. In you." She pointed her index finger at me and then drew an invisible circle in the air. "Extra strong. Inside you and around you."

I stared at her moving hand, then at my smaller one. Dirt was creased in the lines of my palm and caked under my fingernails. I shook my head. "I don't understand."

"Most people start with it. The light, that is. Some have the glow stronger than others. But most try to dim their own personal light so they can fit in, finally burying it beneath all the stuff—the rules, the griefs, the hungers of life—and forgetting the light was ever there."

"But why, Ms. Ruth?" I asked, feeling sad at the idea of the lost, unwanted light.

"It's human nature to want to belong, missy. That said, there's always a few who keep their light shining. You know them when you see them."

"Like movie stars? Rich people?" Mama always had something to say about the rich and famous. Oh gosh, yes, Mama noticed them for sure.

"No, child, though it's a human irony that people chase wealth and happiness thinking it will bring them joy, when it's really the lost light they're searching for. It's another human irony that we are all made different, yet it's not always a good thing to stand out. You can attract the wrong kind of attention."

I nodded, thinking of how Mama was always telling me to watch out for the wrong kind of attention. Because I was born with her good looks, she'd say. Because pretty girls had to be careful.

Ms. Ruth said, "You sad, missy?"

"No, ma'am. Just thinking."

She leaned over and touched my hair. "Don't worry, kiddo. For now, you focus on your education and your toolbox. Hone your life tools, girl, so you'll have them at the ready when you need 'em. One of these days, after you grow up a little more, you'll know what I mean about the light. And when you do, you'll think of what I said just now. You'll remember this warm, sunshiny day and those flowers you just helped me plant. And you'll remember not to hide your light because without it, you can't find joy."

"When I remember what you said, I'll think of you, Ms. Ruth."

I had a pretty good idea of what she was trying to tell me, but I pretended I didn't because she was wrong. I'd never had any kind of light, and I didn't want to see disappointment dawn in her eyes when she realized it.

But Ms. Ruth had the light. It was unmistakable and undeniable.

My dearest friend, Ruth Berry, was the brightest light in my entire small world.

Until she wasn't.

CHAPTER TWO

Bella Highsmith's daughter—that was me. Offspring of that same Bella who'd been the prettiest, most envied gal in high school. Who'd fallen in love with George Highsmith and had gotten her young man, had been the first among her friends to marry, and had then watched as her life devolved, slowly suffocating like a dying fish gasping in a vacuum, left wondering which of her choices had been the wrong one.

Bella's answer was none. It was all George's fault. And Mitch's. Mine too, apparently, even though Mama's personal die had been cast long before I came along.

One morning when I was eleven, Mama was raging because she couldn't find her car keys. Anyone out there in the wide world overhearing her racket would've thought she was under direct, vicious attack by evil forces bent on destroying her life. I stood in the kitchen filling her tall cup with coffee for her to take along to her newest job, which was at the gas station convenience store. She wouldn't drink their coffee because, as she said, she was one of the folks who washed the pots, and she knew how that went. No one was fooling her into drinking anything that came out of those nasty things. So I prepared her coffee and heard her raging and occasionally accusing me, along with other unnamed conspirators, of hiding her keys. Mitch was better at soothing Mama's rages, but he was off with friends. Seemed like I fed her temper somehow. Not intentionally. It just happened. Thus, when Mitch wasn't around and Mama was in a mood, I mostly kept my mouth shut and avoided eye contact.

I settled the lid onto the cup and pressed it securely in place.

After a few minutes of hearing nothing but silence, I was about to venture out of the kitchen to give her the coffee when suddenly she was in the doorway, all smiles, dressed and reaching for the cup in my hand.

"It's gonna be a fine day, Jaynie. Mitch will be home by noon. Stay out of trouble 'til then."

A person could go nuts trying to keep up with her moods. She'd been full to overflowing with hateful craziness, and now she was wearing that smiley face and acting all chirpy.

"Yes, ma'am," I said, but for reasons I never understood, I sometimes felt compelled to remark further, and I did today, asking, "Where'd you find your keys, Mama?"

Her face flushed; her expression darkened. "Are you confessing or accusing?"

She stepped closer. That cup of coffee in her hand was boiling hot. Wisps of steam trailed upward like a thin veil between our faces.

"You let me know, smart mouth, because I have an answer for you either way. Go ahead, Jaynie. You tell me where I found them."

I averted my eyes slowly.

"Smart mouth," she muttered, then added more strongly, "but sometimes you're also a smart girl. Keep it that way, Jaynie. You think I'm harsh? Trust me, the outside world is much crueler."

Keeping my mouth tightly shut this time, I nodded.

Mama put her finger under my chin and lifted it, forcing me to meet her eyes. "Remember this, Jaynie, whatever the world gives you, you have to make the best of it, or suck it up, because it's all you get. Just know that."

I hardly heard her words. They faded away as the edge of her fingernail dug into the soft flesh under my chin. Some nasty kind of dark energy was snapping between us like a live wire, and that sharp nail was its junction. She felt it too. I could see the energy flashing in her eyes, and she must've caught something similar in mine that gave her pause. I was indeed Bella Highsmith's daughter. We weren't anything alike, yet close enough in blood and proximity to share few virtues and numerous flaws.

After a long, tense moment, Mama withdrew her finger and stepped back. She stared at her coffee cup as if only just noticing it, and then with a dismissive glance my way she walked off. She collected her purse and keys from the chair by the door and was gone. I was still standing in the kitchen when her car came alive in the driveway and her tires crunched onto the gravel road.

I could've stayed in the house. I was alone now. Would be until Mitch came back from his friend's house. But. The air. The energy in the house. It sizzled. It had a smell wildly redolent of Mama and anger. Like singed hair. My end of the live wire was still twitching, keeping the energy active. I shook my head, my shoulders. I needed to be away. I needed fresh air and to run. So I did.

And I ended up at the Berry house.

Ms. Ruth opened the back door, took one look at me,

and asked if I was all right.

"Yes, ma'am."

"Well, you'd better come in for an ice-cold glass of sweet tea and a fresh-from-the-oven cookie because you look peaked, like you could use some sweetening up at this very instant."

Ms. Ruth knew Mama's temper. When Mama was really rolling, she could be heard clearly throughout our small patch of dwellings. Ruth knew that though Mama's ire could curdle fresh milk in a heartbeat, it was mostly just noise. Mama was like a big storm that rushed in and was gone again about as quick, leaving the yard furniture turned over and trash strewn about.

When I was little, I'd thought Mama didn't like this house. She'd point her finger at it and say, "Stay away from that place." Now I understood it was the woman who lived here, Ruth Berry, that Mama had no liking for. But Ms. Ruth and I enjoyed each other's company, and after a while—after careful watching and questioning and realizing Ms. Ruth never criticized her to me—Mama looked the other way.

I popped the last bit of cookie into my mouth before saying, "She couldn't find her keys. She was worried she'd be late to work. Again."

As we sat at her kitchen table, Ms. Ruth said, "Don't you worry overmuch about your mama's problems. You keep an eye on your own choices. Your mama went from being the gal who had everything to having job problems, cash problems, and man problems." She tapped the back of my hand. "Listen up, missy. Don't be confused by noise and chaos. That's all it is, and it passes." She took my hand and held it firmly. "This world we see, what we hear, everything we touch—our understanding of it is only as good as our senses. And our senses are limited by the filters of our experience, our hopes and our scars."

She broke off, probably noticing my gaping mouth and the confused look in my eyes. Her jaws flexed as if she wanted to say more but didn't. Finally, she said, "Actually, little lady, it was good timing you showed up today. You must've known I needed you. I have a task and could use the help of young, nimble fingers, not to mention someone who appreciates worthwhile conversation."

Ms. Ruth stood and walked to the counter. She selected a large plastic mixing bowl from the cabinet and put it on the table in front of me, then returned to the counter to pick up a huge jar of large coins which she carried braced against her stomach, half supporting it with her hip. When she reached the table, she twisted off the lid and poured the contents into the plastic mixing bowl. The sound of the coins spilling out into the bowl made me think of a waterfall. She set the jar aside and pointed at the bowl, now full of coins. Big tarnished ones.

"They're silver dollars," she said. "Take this bowl into the living room and put it by my chair. I'll find polish and rags." She laughed. "But don't drop it on your foot. Like as not, it'll break a few bones."

We settled in, Ms. Ruth with her comforts near at hand, and me cross-legged on the carpet, and she explained the cleaning process. She handed me a rag and a dark coin, and we went to work.

After a while, Ms. Ruth paused, sipped her drink, set it back on the side table, and picked up another tarnished coin. She looked at me directly and said, "Listen close, child. The world around us is like a collage. It's what we see, smell, and hear, missy. The world that we think is real isn't the actual real world. It's just how we see it."

I shook my head. "I don't get it. How come it's not real but I can still touch it?" I held up the coin I was cleaning as an example. "I can feel it and move it."

"It's like a magic trick. I'll tell you just like I learned it many years ago. Think of it this way: We are each the center of our own world, whether we like to think we are or not, because we can only see it with our own eyes and brains. What you see ain't exactly the same as what I'm seeing. It can't be. It's unique. My real isn't the same as your real." She took a breath and then asked sharply, "Are there two reals?"

"Unique?" I was stuck on that word and repeated it, savoring it and ignoring her question. "I like how that word sounds."

"Means different. One of a kind different." She laughed and relaxed again. "I guess that can be your word for the day."

I nodded. "My teacher says we always have to try to see things through the eyes of others."

"I dislike saying this because I'm sure she means well, but it's a cheat. We can't ever presume to see except through our own eyes, our own brain. What you can do is to empathize and respect what others see. Give credit to someone else's heart and life experience." She made an impatient noise. "Don't let the world define who you are. Don't take on your mama's troubles. They might inconvenience you, but they aren't yours. Don't color your life by her filters."

I digested that for a while as I worked my rag over the coin to shine it up. "It confuses me. How'd you learn all this?"

"I've had a bit of a checkered past." She laughed again, waggling her fingers so that the rings and jangly bracelets clattered. "And that don't mean I played a lot of checkers."

"It means you had adventures."

"True enough. Not to say whether such adventures were good or bad, but yes, I've had my time as a prodigal child. Adventures." She shrugged. "And my family was fond of loud discussions about theories and suppositions. But mostly I've always known. Sometimes you just know in your heart when you hear it or feel it that a thing is true. But you have to get past the noise out there to hear it." She waved her hand generally toward the outside. "Just like the prophets and soothsayers of old did, you have to listen inside your head instead of in the usual way." She reached up and tugged on her ear, which caused her earring to shimmy.

Ms. Ruth liked shiny, jangly, dangly jewelry.

"Tell me about the sheets again." I liked hearing about the sheets drying on the clothesline. I could get my head around that story pretty good. Plus, I loved the thought of fresh, clean sheets smelling of the woods and meadow and the breeze that came from all around the world.

"You mean like how a sheet hangs on the line to dry and billows in the wind? That the movement has nothing to do with any will or effort done by the sheet? Yes, the actual real stuff is going on behind the scenes. The billows are caused by the unseen wind. And like that sheet that's dancing courtesy of an unseen force, we have precious little control over what happens except in how we react to it and the choices we make as a result."

I asked her, "Does that mean when something goes wrong it's not my fault?" I was thinking of Mama fussing that morning, going on and on about her lost keys. That hadn't been my fault, but I'd suffered because of it anyway.

"Yes, but also no. The unseen is a swirl of the bad and good." She waved one hand in a circle. "It's always in motion around us, and we react without knowing and feed it. Like adding our portion or contribution of good or bad into the physical world, and if we aren't careful, and we react badly, or make bad choices, we add to the chaos."

That day we cleaned the bowlful of silver dollars. It was one day and one conversation among many that spanned years. They stood out like shiny days and bedazzled jewellike memories. Ms. Ruth didn't throw all that woo-woo stuff at me in one shot, thank goodness, but it was hard later to find the line between what Ruth told me and how I interpreted it back then and remembered it as an adult.

But when it came to the two of us talking—we could go on for hours. No doubt about that. And the topics fascinated me almost as much as the attention she paid me. I asked her, "Is that what they call philosophy, Ms. Ruth?"

"Not philosophy. Philosophy is just a bunch of people, mostly people who never cooked a good biscuit in their lives, yelling at each other and banging on tables to make a point. Nope, as far as I know it's just the truth."

"Banging on tables?" The rest of what she'd said sort of just evaporated in favor of the solid image. "Why would they be arguing and banging on tables? And what about biscuits? I like biscuits. My grandma used to make yummy ones."

Ruth laughed. When she was done, she took a long

drink, then said, "My two grandpas. One was a teacher, taught philosophy over at the university, and the other was a preacher, a theologian. I can't tell you how many great debates happened in my parents' living room every holiday while everyone else was just trying to decorate, eat, or whatever the holiday called for. Meanwhile, my grandma was in the kitchen creating heaven in the form of food. She fed us food, she fed us love. She welcomed us. But my two granddads? They welcomed each other, more interested in the adrenaline of the debate than touch football or a quick pickup game of softball or checkers." She went silent for a long moment, staring at the coin in her hand. "I knew which room I wanted to occupy. I wanted to be where the love was." She gave me an extra-long look, saying, "Follow your heart to the love. Put that in your toolbox, girl. Never can tell when you'll need that bit of guidance."

I had a notion that I might've enjoyed the show in the living room while munching on a biscuit from the kitchen. That said, if Ms. Ruth's grandpas were anything like my mama when it came to arguing, I'd have to pass.

All these long years later, I still see Ruth sitting there with a mixing bowl full of tarnished silver dollars on her lap and a half-used jar of silver polish on the arm of her easy chair, with both of us dipping our rags and polishing the coins as she told me we had to rise above that invisible crap swirling around us and through our world, so we could breathe and hear the truth. She said we must pay attention to the tasks at hand each day to keep the world spinning right. Pay attention to the day, get through it with the least damage possible, and with as much grace as we could, because we didn't want to add to the darker parts of the ether.

I understood the "pay attention to the task at hand and mind our own business." The rest of it was too murky. I must've looked glum because she asked, "What's wrong, girl?"

"I don't know about all that stuff, Ms. Ruth. It makes me dizzy to think about it too much. I'm sorry about your grandpas."

"Do you ever tell your mama what we talk about?"

I cast a quick, rather alarmed look at her and saw her eyes twinkling.

"It's okay, child. She and I have our own checkered history." She smiled. "Do you tell her about the ether and the swirls?"

"Not a chance."

"What does she say about you spending so much time over here with this old woman?"

"Old? You're not old." I felt compelled to say that, as if it would be bad manners or ungrateful to confirm that she was indeed old.

"It's okay, sissy. Young people don't understand old. I'm comfortable with it." She dried a newly cleaned coin. "So what does your mama say? Because I know Bella Highsmith, and I know she's asking."

"I tell her I help you around the house and yard because . . . ," I faltered.

"Because I'm old?"

I looked away, ashamed.

Ms. Ruth patted my hand. "Well, and you are helping, aren't you now?"

I looked up again, feeling braver. She nodded slowly, and her darker-than-dark eyes conveyed solemn dignity and deep wisdom.

"Yes, ma'am."

Her fingers were short and plump, and the backs of her hands had brown spots. I patted her hand right back.

Ruth Berry was not only my mentor when it came to deep thinking but was also a lover of words, and she set that as an unofficial price for admission. She asked, "What's a good word for that?"

"For what?"

"Old."

"Elderly?"

"Better than that."

I shrugged. "Senior?"

"Geriatric. Know that one?" When I didn't answer, she said, "Tomorrow you can spell it for me and use it in a sentence."

"Yes, ma'am." No one else—except in school, that is—required vocabulary from me, but somehow it never struck me as odd that Ms. Ruth did. I knew without doubt that she was special on uncounted levels, and I wanted to be on those special levels with her. I was proud to call her my friend.

The bowl of tarnished coins emptied as the shiny stacks of silver dollars grew. They were arranged on the end table next to her bottle of beer. It wasn't Ms. Ruth's preferred brand. When Ms. Ruth was flush, she bought mostly one brand, but when times were tight, she bought whatever was cheapest. If cash was really tight, she bought cheap wine. She didn't care much for wine, though, 'cause it gave her a headache. I wondered if low cash might be why we were cleaning the coins—because they were needed—but I didn't ask because that seemed rude. Ms. Ruth was particular about not being rude, and she'd promised me one shiny dollar for myself for helping her. I wanted that silver dollar, but I would've helped her without payment, because she was not only an old friend, my only true friend, but she treated me like no other adult ever had. She saw me. Me. I considered that ample reward.

When she told me to keep the last coin, I said, "No need to pay me. I'm happy to help."

"Always keep money on hand, little girl. Keep a bit on the side so you're less inclined to put up with being treated badly."

I laughed. "That's how Mama treats me now."

"At present you're a kid, so this is your learning time. Just take my advice. Remember it and put it right alongside all the other stuff you're learning as you grow so you'll have the right tools at the right time when you're done."

I stared at the coin in my hand. "I'll save it for when I need it." I looked up at her. "Is that what you do?"

This time, Ms. Ruth snorted when she laughed. "Child, I ain't never been that needy. What I need always seems to come along exactly when it's called for. That's the wonder of annuities." She stood, perhaps too fast, and stumbled before righting herself.

Ruth Berry—my sage, my mentor, lover of words and philosophy and bright colors—was a drunk, yes, but I didn't care. To me, the smell of alcohol on and around her was no more than her perfume. When she spoke, the way the hard consonants rolled out sounding soft and sort of merging together was hypnotic. If at times she focused on something unseen and grew lost in the gaze, I put it down to ethereal communications and the swirling ether. Her feet and lower legs were puffy and sometimes they pained her, but she rarely complained. I liked that she was always relaxed and never in a hurry. In a world where Mama was either freaking out over something or worrying herself sick about other stuff, Ms. Ruth stood out as kindness and reason itself.

That day I decided she'd probably made a good choice of which room to be in.

"I better head home and get supper cooking. In fact," I said, "if I can find my grandma Highsmith's old recipe, I might cook up some biscuits for supper."

CHAPTER THREE

One autumn afternoon when I was almost twelve, I caught the acrid smell of smoke through Mama's open kitchen window. I stepped out into the yard. Beyond Uncle Lou's barn, a thin white column was rising and dispersing through the nearby trees. My great-uncle—my father's uncle—had died before I was born. His small house, the patch of land it sat on, and the huge barn were neglected and looked deserted, except for when the property had tenants. Currently, the windows were dark, and the grass and weeds were high. Uncle Lou's property and then a wooden fence and a dirt road formed the buffer between Mama's house and the Berry house. Once, Mama had laughed and said it was literally a no-man's-land. When I'd asked her what that meant, she'd laughed louder and walked away.

Ms. Ruth must be burning leaves today, I thought. Sitting around a barrel of burning leaves and chatting was one of the things I loved best.

I yelled into the house, "I'll be back soon." Without waiting for a response, I let the screened door slam shut on its own and ran across our backyard and through the meadow of tall grass. I vaulted over the wooden fence and hit the dirt road hard with my bare feet, and there was Ruth Berry's house right in front of me. Same house I'd been coming to for years. It was no nicer in appearance than where I lived, certainly no bigger, but somehow neater outside and inside. And flowers. Ms. Ruth planted little spots of flowers around the yard. She'd laugh about it saying you didn't need flowerpots when you had flower spots. This time of year, they were gone—all but the dried-out brown stems she hadn't cut back yet—but the memory remained in my head, and I saw them there with my mind's eye as colorful as at the height of spring.

The tang of the smoke was stronger up close and tickled my nose. Ruth had pulled her yard chair near to the big, rusted drum. Her plump, bare feet were stretched toward its heat. She had a bucket of water beside her chair, and a stick rested aslant against her knees. She was watching the leaves burn and the smoke roiling up from the container. I pulled a white painter's bucket from a stack next to the shed, checked it for spiders, and upended it to sit on like a stool.

"Hey, missy." Ruth waved her hand and gave me a grin. Not so much with her mouth, but with the crinkles at the corners of her eyes. "Come to lend a hand? Or just to visit?"

I grabbed up an armful of leaves and held my breath against the smoke as I leaned over to drop them in. I stepped back quickly and brushed my hands off. "There. Did my part." I returned to my seat.

Ruth laughed.

Her laughter was musical.

"I came for a smile, Ms. Ruth."

"A smile?" She quirked up a dark, thick eyebrow. She'd twisted up her long, curly black hair—black by bottle, as Mama would say—but it always managed to escape and brush her shoulders. Ample shoulders. She shifted in her chair and leaned back, the metal frame and plastic webbing squeaked in its joints and gave a low groan. "Problems at home?"

"Nah. Nothing more than usual." I offered a one-shoulder shrug and flicked my fingers as if my problems were no more than a grain of dirt. "Miniscule," I said.

"That your word for the day, sissy?"

Sometimes she called me *missy*, sometimes *sissy*, and sometimes *kiddo* or *child*. For a long time, I thought it was because she couldn't remember my name, but I didn't correct her. Today seemed right for asking.

"Ms. Ruth, no offense intended, but why do you call me by different names?"

In a dramatic voice, she recited some line from a Shakespeare play about a rose by any other name smelling the same. "You ever heard that, honey?"

"Yes, ma'am. I think so."

"Might not've gotten it exactly right, but it's close enough to the point that the details don't matter." She waved her finger at me. "It's pertinent, that's the thing. After all, your mama might've named you any old thing, but you'd be the same person regardless. Am I right?"

Which, I supposed, had been Mr. Shakespeare's point, so I nodded.

"Besides," she said, "I never did think that name your mama gave you suited you. I'm still waiting to find out your real name."

Was she teasing? I thought it likely because of the way she tilted her head and squinted her right eye. The wrinkles around the eye grew deep, and her thick black lashes were so long they brushed her cheek.

"I should choose my own?"

"Not exactly. Maybe the name will choose you. It will fit, and you'll know it's right."

"Did you choose your own name?"

She shook her head. "No need. My ma got mine right the first time."

I nodded. I'd never especially liked my name, especially when Mama or Mitch were yelling it. So maybe Ruth had a point.

"Oh, wait," she said. "I almost forgot." She chuckled and shook her head as she hiked her skirt around to dig into a deep pocket, saying, "Don't make my mistake, little miss. Don't live so long that you get old. Losing your health *and* your memory are not for the faint of heart." She held up a closed fist. "Here it is. Open your hand, girl."

I did. Ruth placed a piece of silver jewelry with a red stone in it on my palm.

When I didn't immediately exclaim over it, Ruth asked, "You know what this is, don't you?"

"A dragonfly. It's pretty." The lack of enthusiasm so clear in my voice embarrassed me.

"Pretty? Is that all you have to say? What's up with you, kiddo?"

"Well, I appreciate it and all, but . . . it's a dragonfly. I don't much care for dragonflies."

"I've never been stung by one. Have you?"

"No."

"That's because they don't sting." Ms. Ruth shook her head slowly. Leaning toward me, she closed my fingers around the pendant. "Think on this, little girl—a fragile insect scares you years ago because of what someone told you, either to tease you or because they were misinformed, and you fear them still. To be honest, they can bite, but those little bitty teeth won't do much damage."

I'd believed for too long that they did sting. I'd accepted the fact of their malevolence. It was hard to shift my thinking. "Could hurt."

"True enough, it might. Life and love hurt you too."

"I guess." I was holding the silver dragonfly in my fist. I wanted to be grateful. To show my appreciation. But I wished it had been a firefly or maybe a bluebird or even a green frog with bulging eyes. But a dragonfly . . .

"Remember this, missy. Whether it's life or a dragonfly—you must own it. Pain or not. Own it or it will own you."

She uncurled my fingers. She picked the dragonfly up by the cord necklace and placed it over my head. It settled around my neck, and the pendant fell halfway to my waist.

Ruth said, "You don't need to be afraid of things, including things with teeth. A creature might nip at you, but one a nip will only be the hurt of a moment. Face it down and you'll conquer it."

"Yes, ma'am, Ms. Ruth." I hid my face so she couldn't read it. I intended to take the necklace off as soon as I got home. Thinking of dragonflies made me shudder inside, but I wouldn't hurt my friend for anything in the world.

I poked a stick through a hole in the side of the rusty barrel. Flames licked out, hungry for oxygen and fuel— always craving more. I said, "As for *miniscule* and my new word this week—no, ma'am. *Miniscule* is from a while ago. The word for this week is *detritus*."

"Woo-hoo," she exclaimed, stretching the word out for about five syllables as she shook her head in mock admiration. "Now that's a word."

"It is."

"Can you spell it for me?"

"*D-e-t-r-i-t-u-s*."

"And use it in a sentence?"

"I can." I changed my voice to be a little higher and sharper and wagged my finger. "Jaynie, you get that daggone detritus bag out of the kitchen right now before it attracts bugs."

Ruth put her head back and laughed like I was the most brilliant, funniest girl this side of Mineral.

In her presence, I often felt exactly that way. But what she said next brought me back down to ordinary.

"You put that in your toolbox, missy. There'll be people in your life who'll treat you like *d-e-t-r-i-t-u-s*. Remember that. Recognize when it happens, and don't allow it."

We both heard the boy arrive at the same time. Ruth turned her head and was on her feet so quickly she nearly knocked her chair over.

"Wyatt, what are you doing here? Where's your mother?"

"She's out front in the car. Said she'll be along."

The boy had black hair and coal-black eyes. Those eyes shifted back and forth between Ruth and me, darting, taking everything in as fast as possible—probably wanting to see whatever threats might be coming before they reached him.

Wyatt. Ms. Ruth had mentioned him before, but I hadn't given him any thought. Her grandson. I'd never considered her life beyond or before me at all. I remembered her talking about her grandparents. But a husband? Children? I had assumed she was a widow like my mother, but did I ever ask her? No. Hadn't given it a thought. I needed to be a better friend.

Wyatt must be about my age. He was a little taller than me but super scrawny, which was emphasized by the clothing that obviously hadn't fit him properly in quite a while—high-water jeans and a stretched-out T-shirt. Not that I was judging. I wasn't exactly fashionable myself. But I belonged here. He was new. It seemed to me that people should make an extra effort when they were new. Unless they couldn't. Which seemed all the sadder. And he looked tense, standing so rigid it hurt my own muscles.

Ms. Ruth was almost to the house, moving fast despite the barefooted limp, when a woman came rushing around the side. Wyatt's mother, was my guess. Ms. Ruth seemed either very happy or very angry to see the woman, who, herself, was clearly distressed. I looked away.

The boy's discomfort was obvious. I thought about it for a moment and about the way he'd stopped shifting his gaze and had settled his attention on the fire barrel. I understood he was embarrassed, and who could blame him?

I said, "Grab a bucket and have a seat. It's nicer near the fire. Not so damp and chill."

Those black eyes again—they stared at me like I was speaking Klingon or something. But then he moved forward and upended a bucket and took a seat—a careful four feet away from me or any other obstacle. I recognized he knew, as I did, to keep the tool of fast getaways handy. We met eyes. He didn't nod, not in actual fact, but I felt the connection.

"Your grandma and I are friends. She's a real nice lady."

Nothing. He sat like he was mired in misery.

I told myself I should go. Mama would be looking for me right about now to get supper fixed. A woman's voice came to us from the house. I couldn't make out her words, but the anger was pretty darn clear. I looked at the boy again and saw his slightly hunched shoulders. I couldn't leave him alone to listen to his mom and grandma fighting.

It wouldn't be the first time I'd made Mama angry. I knew how to duck around that.

I waited another minute—what seemed a decent delay—and asked, "Where're you from?"

He made a small movement with his mouth but didn't speak. I let him be, for the moment, while I considered again.

Maybe me staying wasn't helping? Maybe he felt like I was witnessing his embarrassment? This boy wasn't my responsibility. My responsibility was way over on the other side of my uncle's property. Anytime now Mama would be sending Mitch over for me. She'd be working up to a good fit if I wasn't home soon.

I sighed. "Guess I'll get on."

He didn't speak.

"Mama will be ticked that I'm not home to fix supper. No sense in making her angrier than she usually is."

He looked away, fixing his gaze on the barrel and the smoke. Still I sat.

He said, "Your feet are dirty." He looked away again. "No offense. I just meant that it's good you're barefoot." He looked down at his own shoes, which had traces of mud on the sides.

I shrugged. "Doesn't matter. I live barefoot mostly." I gave sociability another shot. "You must be from the city if you're worried over a little dirt."

He echoed my shrug. "We move around a lot, but mostly live in town. Mom says she can't find work out here in the country."

An extra-loud yell came from the house, and we both cringed reflexively. This whole time I hadn't heard Ms. Ruth's voice, and I was pretty sure most of the noise was coming from this boy's mother. No wonder I felt in tune with him.

"I guess you don't get out this way much, because I'm over here a lot and I've never seen you."

"They talk on the phone. Mom's always busy. We lived up in Pennsylvania for a while."

"Why are they angry?"

"I don't think she's mad at my grandmother."

"Sounds mad."

He shook his head and pushed his hair back out of his face. His dark eyes touched my heart.

"She's mad, but at my stepfather. He left."

"Oh. I'm sorry."

"Be sorry for her if you want, but not for me."

"Oh."

"So now Mom is deciding what to do next."

We weren't hearing voices now, so my guess was that the crying had started. Crying and hugging, maybe. Mama didn't hug much, but sometimes she cried.

In the silence, Mitch hollered across the empty field between my house and Ruth's house. "Jaynie? Mom says get in here right now."

"Who's that? Your dad?" the boy asked.

"My brother. He's sixteen." Didn't need more explanation than that. *Sixteen* pretty much said it all. I said,

"I better go."

"Are you in trouble?"

I grinned to show I was above it all, even though I wasn't. Believe it. See it. Make it real. My mask may have slipped a little, because the boy didn't seem to buy my bravado.

Mitch yelled again, "Now, Jaynie!"

"See ya, Wyatt."

I crossed the dirt road, climbed over the fence, and hot-footed it back across the field.

Mama wanted to know where I'd been.

As I washed my hands, I said, "Over at Ms. Berry's."

Her voice did a down shift from anger to "who cares" as she said, "Well, I guess I know that. Where else, right? I heard Dee was in town."

"Dee?" I glanced up from breaking up saltines, surprised by her change in tone.

"Ruth's daughter, Demaris. Heard she was seen in town with her boy." Mama shrugged. "I don't suppose she'll be showing up over at the Berry house, though. Not considering how she and her mother left it the last time she was there. I don't suppose her boy was more than a baby back then." Mama added casually, "Ms. Berry have any company over there besides you?"

"Yes, ma'am, she did. A woman came by." I broke off as I realized that Mama was pumping me for information. If she'd asked right out, I might've gone mum. I'd been tricked. At my affirming but brief response, Mama's eyes lit up. I played it cool and added the crackers to the ground beef, then began whisking the eggs. "Oh, sure. They were all chatty. Ms. Berry must'a been expecting her. She seemed real pleased to see her. All that hugging and stuff, you know."

Mama frowned. "That's surprising."

I smiled to show innocence. "Why's that?"

"She have her boy over there with her?"

"His name is Wyatt. Why?"

"Never mind. Just get supper cooked."

Mama's mood had soured. Which was good. It meant she'd go into the living room and leave me alone. I mixed the eggs into the ground beef and broken-up crackers.

"Get out of my way," Mom said, but not to me. Mitch was walking into the kitchen as she was leaving it.

Mitch glanced at her, but he didn't speak to her. He asked me, "How long 'til supper?"

"An hour. Maybe less."

"Making meatloaf?"

"Nah. That would need to cook too long. Chopped steak patties."

"Hamburgers."

"Not hamburgers, 'cause we got no buns."

"Same either way. Buns or not."

His words reminded me of the name discussion with Ruth. "Yeah, maybe so. Some things are just what they are, no matter what we call them. But what I know is this—while you're eating hamburgers without buns, I'll be enjoying chopped steak." And I laughed.

Mitch wasn't a bad guy. He was almost grown now, almost seventeen. He should already have a job after school and on weekends, but he seemed to consider school as optional. He gave no thought to his future. In my mind, he was lazy, and Mama let him be that way because she liked having him around the house for company. She'd used him as a sitter to watch me when she was at work or out with friends, but I was long past needing that. In fact, now he was more necessary to me than to Mama because he was the buffer between me and Mama's moods. I was grateful to him for that.

I sprinkled salt in the bottom of the frying pan. I didn't know why I needed to sprinkle salt in the pan, but only that my grandmother had done it that way when I was little bitty. As I was taught, so did I do. At least as far as cooking. When the pan was hot, I laid each of the meat patties in, flipped them to sear them on each side, then put the lid on the pan. I turned my attention to opening the can of green beans.

Mama could've cooked, but she was lousy at it, never being able to focus on anything for more than a minute or two—unless it involved someone else's private business. She'd drill right down into that. Or Mitch could've cooked, I supposed, but I'd never seen him do it. I didn't mind so much. At least, being the cook meant I could choose what we'd eat and how to cook it. More often than not, Mama and Mitch carried their plates into the living room and ate there in front of whatever TV show was on. Sometimes I joined them, and sometimes I sat at the kitchen table and read while I ate. I was always on the lookout for a word—a special word that I could present to Ms. Ruth. It mattered to Ruth Berry, so it mattered to me. A rare day went by without us seeing each other, and I knew she was always there for me.

I cleaned the kitchen after supper. Sometimes Mama or Mitch would lend a hand, but I mostly preferred to do it myself. My brain was always full of whatever book I was reading. Sometimes I'd prop the book on the kitchen windowsill and read it as I was washing dishes. Mama didn't like me reading that way because one time the book fell into the dishwater. I did a lot of mopping, of both the book and the floor. Ended up that I had to pay the library for the damaged book. So now I only read that way when she was watching one of her favorite shows. It was unlikely she'd come into the kitchen and risk missing something in the program.

My bedroom was small, and the furnishings were simple. A bed and a dresser. Whatever didn't fit in the drawers or the closet was stacked on the floor in the corners. I couldn't keep personal items in my room because Mama would find them. She'd search. Not in front of me, but she didn't hide the fact of the search either. I'd find my books out of order, or my sheets would be disturbed where she'd checked under the mattress. My guess was that she was checking for drugs or evidence that I had a boyfriend. Some of the girls my age had school boyfriends—meaning boys they held hands with at school and built a lot of personal drama around with their other friends. I didn't fit in with them. Bottom line—Mama didn't want to end up with a drug-addicted kid or an unwanted grandbaby on her hands. *My* bottom line was that anything I wanted to keep private couldn't be kept here in this house.

Mostly I hid the private things only in my heart. When I needed a hiding space for something more substantial than a memory, I took it into the woods and up to my rock and stashed it there. I'd found that rock so long ago I hardly remembered. I'd been going there ever since. Sometimes it was a refuge. Sometimes I went just to read or be alone to think or hear the birdsong or listen to the sound of Cub Creek flowing by.

That evening, after meeting Wyatt, I sat on my bed with my sketchpad on my crossed legs and leaned back against the wall and drew his dark eyes, the shape of his face, jaw, and mouth. His brows were black, and I was heavy-handed, so I had to apply the eraser over them and redo. It was a small picture, and if it didn't look much like him, then that might be for the best. Even so, I wasn't willing to risk that someone else—someone snooping—might recognize him too. I tore the page neatly from the drawing pad and slipped the paper carefully into a book and put it in my backpack. I'd go up to the rock tomorrow when no one was paying attention, and I'd tuck the picture of Wyatt into my toolbox.

~~~~

The year I turned twelve was a year of change, including getting to know Wyatt. We were still young enough to be friends without the boy-girl thing getting in the way too much, especially with no other kids around complicating things. His mom parked him at his grandmother's house for days at a time, especially during holidays and over the summer. We played board games at the kitchen table with his grandma, and when she and I followed our natural bent for conversation and got too far out into the ether, Wyatt would look mystified and then confused and annoyed. I tried to include him, but he didn't get it. Even just the joy of a willing conversation with someone who liked talking to you was a treasure he didn't understand, so when we started to wander down those philosophical alleys, I pulled us back when Wyatt was around. I didn't want us to bore him, nor did I want to seem odd in his eyes. Ms. Ruth would cast a look at me, a questioning glance, but she'd go along, and we'd keep our attention on the game and other mundane topics.

It was over a Monopoly board, and while Ms. Ruth was on a bathroom break, that Wyatt mentioned his mom was seeing a guy and it seemed serious.

"Is that good or bad?"

"He seems okay." He shrugged. "Hard to really know, though, until you see them every day over a long time, and by then, if it's not good, it's too late." He picked up a game piece and gave it a close examination as he added, "The good thing is that we're staying in the area, at least for a while. So I'll be around, and I'll see you in school."

That summer was extra special to me. It was a sadness to discover that Wyatt was not only a year older but also a year ahead of me in school, so when the summer ended and his visits went back to occasional days, it was disappointing that we wouldn't be in any of the same classes. Still, I'd see him there in the hallways and maybe the lunchroom. It wasn't what I wanted, but I suspected it was as much as I could handle. I could never have withstood the scrutiny of the popular kids, who'd be all nosy and curious about me, that scroungy-looking girl, hanging around him. Passing in the hallways and occasional waves weren't much but still a consolation of a sort.

CHAPTER FOUR

By the time I was thirteen and in middle school, I'd figured out school wasn't for me. Mitch had mostly given up on it, and I understood why. We were an awkward fit with the teachers and most of the other students. I was pretty enough and smart enough to mix for a while, but I didn't have the right clothes or haircut. Or style—that kind of personal style and home breeding that shows the instant you walk into a room and the other kids look at you—and they *know*. A lot of them already knew who my mother was and the truth of how my life was. All it took was one look for them to take my measure and find me lacking.

I was thirteen, so I didn't expect much. Thirteen was an unlucky number, Mama said. Always had been.

So I didn't care much for school, but I stuck with it because if I was ever going to get out of this place, I had to get an education. It was a help that home, on the other hand, was generally tolerable these days. I'd gathered the tools I needed to manage within the Bella Highsmith landscape, and I knew the dangers to avoid there.

Until Mama got a new boyfriend. And she brought this one home with her.

His name was Boone. He was tall and lean, with a hungry look as if he needed a few good meals. His shaggy hair seemed to emphasize that. He had a drawl that wouldn't quit and he grinned a lot but I noticed right away that he lacked a socially acceptable sense of humor. One thing was for sure, he didn't like Mitch hanging around the house. Mitch looked too much like a grown man, which kind of cramped Boone's style. Mitch had stopped going to school and showed no signs of planning to resume. He picked up work where he could, mostly to pay for the gas to keep his clunker car running. Boone hassled Mitch about not having a real job and a steady girlfriend. Mama would shush him, but he kept at it, and after a while she stopped shushing so much. As Boone hung out at our house more, Mitch began staying away. He didn't tell me where he went or what he was up to. One day he packed a bag. On the way out, he gently tousled my hair and hit my shoulder with a fake blow.

"I'll get you my phone number when I have one, Jaynie. Stay away from Boone, and if he bothers you, you find me or tell Ms. Ruth."

"But Mitch, just stay. Boone will move on soon."

He picked up his bag. "I don't know, sis. This one might be different from Mom's other boyfriends." With a last wave, he was out the door.

Boone hardly ever said a word to me, but sometimes I felt his eyes on me, full of speculation. I didn't like to think about what. I spent more time at the Berry house or out at my rock in the woods.

"Where are you going now, Jaynie?" Mama asked.

"Over to Ms. Ruth's house. She's feeling poorly. I'm going to see if I can help her . . . see if she needs anything."

"Boone is coming over in a while."

Why else am I getting out of the house, right? But I didn't say those words aloud. After a long pause, I asked,

"You need me to fix you two a meal?"

After an even longer pause, Mama said, "No need. He's bringing something with him. No reason to rush home." She kept her eyes fixed on mine for an extra-long moment. I could read that look without difficulty.

I didn't go directly to Ms. Ruth's house. I sat on the fence alongside Uncle Lou's old field, hugging my sweater to me. Fall was here, and there was a chill in the air this afternoon. I might be only thirteen, but I wasn't a kid anymore. Somehow with Boone arriving and Mitch leaving, my last bit of childhood had fled, and I'd become aware. I understood Boone's stare in my gut. But I didn't feel flattered. It made me feel hunted. Mitch, for all his flaws, would've protected me. Always had, as best as he could.

Mama had been telling me for as long as I could remember that I took after her—that I had her looks. Beautiful from the time I was a baby, just like her, she'd said. She worried about it. A lot. Mostly, that men would be persistent, and I might not be careful enough. These days I wanted to ask her why—if she was so worried about keeping me pure, why was she bringing Boone around so much? But that might be pushing her too far. She thought Boone was hers. I wasn't so sure. He seemed more like the tomcats who wailed in the night, always on the lookout, on the hunt, but too lazy to go too far afield.

With Mitch gone, all Mama's unhappy energy now tended to descend upon my head, especially when Boone wasn't around. So instead of fighting Mama over it, it was better to just avoid Boone. And Mama too. Eventually, he'd move on.

I missed my brother, but I was happy for him. In this,

Boone was right, even if for the wrong reasons. It was time for Mitch to be on his own. Mama should've encouraged him to find his own life sooner. And one day, I'd find mine too, but I wouldn't need anyone's urging.

But not until after high school. I'd get a job and a small place, or maybe I'd luck into college somehow. I didn't like public school. The guidance counselor tried to get me to stay after for extra activities, but of course, I couldn't. She seemed to think there was more to me than bad attitude and fancy words. That said, she did make me think about the future. I had an idea that being in college would be different. I'd be a different person there. Remake myself. Maybe find my real name, as Ruth might say.

"Hey, Jaynie."

"Wyatt. Whatcha doing here?"

He climbed onto the wooden fence and settled beside me. Since I'd first met him, he'd grown. His legs and arms were longer, and his clothes were better. His hair was longish but clean and trimmed. Though we attended the same school, we moved in different circles. He was a natural at sports and had a friendly manner. That made a difference.

We'd wave or nod if we passed in the hallway, but that was all. His mom had remarried, and sometimes he stayed with her and the new husband, and other times he stayed at his grandma's house. He was his regular self at times like this when we saw each other away from school.

"You back at your grandmother's house for a visit?"

"No. Mom dropped by to bring her something, and they're visiting. Thought I'd take a walk. Hoped maybe I'd run into you."

I hugged my sweater tighter.

"How are you, Jaynie? I see you at school, but we never talk."

And whose fault is that? I could've said that I didn't fit into his circle. We were a mismatch. Didn't mean we couldn't be friends, though, at least outside of school, and I could've said that I'd be happy to talk if he showed the least sign of wanting to in front of the other kids. But I didn't say those things. I wouldn't beg him or any other living person to talk to me or show kindness or respect. I'd learned that if you had to ask for it, what you'd receive would only be a pale version of what you were hoping for. It had to come naturally.

When I didn't answer, he said, "I saw you talking to Tommy the other day. You and he hanging out together now?"

"Tommy? No." I even managed a small laugh. "He's a good guy, but no."

Wyatt nodded. "Yeah. He's okay."

"You're dating that girl still?"

He shrugged. "That girl?" He laughed a little. "Sherry's mom won't let her date officially—being fourteen and all—so we hang out with the group."

"That's probably good."

"I don't really care anyway." His voice was strong and suddenly bold. "I don't care about any of this."

His vehemence jolted me. I looked at him.

We happened to meet eyes—by chance since we seemed to be working so hard to look elsewhere—and I saw desperation in his. "I hate school. I need to get out, Jaynie."

"I feel that way a lot too. Any reason in particular?"

"No. Yes." He leaned against the post. "Mom calls it

being restless. I just need to get my feet moving. Leave this place behind."

And leave me too, apparently. But it wasn't as if he figured big in my life these days. Besides, I knew that even if he did kick the dust of this place from his shoes, he'd be back. I just knew.

"How's your stepdad?" I asked.

"He tries. It's not his fault. Mom worries over everything we say or do—as if she's the only one capable of keeping the peace, and instead she's just setting off the . . . Never mind."

"Maybe go somewhere this summer. To a camp or something."

He looked at me like I was stupid.

I shrugged. "Suit yourself, then."

"Don't you want to leave?"

"Yes," I said. "More than anything. But I have nowhere to go. And when I leave, I'm not coming back. Except maybe to visit Ruth occasionally."

"Not your mom?"

"Mama has Boone now. She's let Mitch go his own way. He's gone, and I expect she'd be happy to see me gone too."

Wyatt asked. "Why's that?"

I shrugged and didn't say.

"Because she has a boyfriend?" He sounded surprised.

"Maybe so."

Wyatt said, "It was tricky at first when Mom got married, but Bill's not a bad guy. I just wish she'd relax and let us find our way around each other."

"It's not like that with Boone. He's stayed over a few nights. I don't want them to get married. I want him to go."

"Has he done anything? I mean, you know . . . anything to you?"

I knew what he was asking. I shook my head. "He just creeps me out. Totally."

"What does your mom say?"

This time I laughed, but not happily. "She tells me to get lost for a while."

We chatted on about family and such, and then out of nowhere, Wyatt gave me an extra-long look, one that seemed almost puzzled.

"You have red hair."

I thought of that day when we first met, when he'd told me I had dirty feet and then had quickly apologized.

"So what?" I asked. I ran my fingers through it and flipped it so that the tresses settled back around my shoulders. "Not really red, anyway. Just looks that way in strong light. More auburn."

"Auburn?" he repeated after me. "Looks red. I like it."

My heart responded, even though my words failed me.

Wyatt's mom yelled for him.

He grimaced. "Mom."

"Yeah," I said.

"Better go." And he was off, almost running, but he turned back briefly and gave me a grin and a wave.

I didn't move from that fence for a long while.

That was the day I began to focus seriously on leaving. Not immediately. I'd watched enough reality TV to know that stuff didn't end well for teenage girls who ended up on the street. I might not be happy where I was, but Ruth would advise me to check my toolbox and see what was needed to get ready for the day I could. I'd have to learn marketable skills and save all the money I could. I needed a specific plan to help me get from the here and now to the life I wanted.

As for Boone . . . a few times over the years when things got super tense with Mama, I wondered if I might move in with Ms. Ruth. She had a spare bedroom. But despite knowing my situation, she never made the offer. Plus, she and Mama had some sort of truce going on between them. It had held for a long time, but likely it wouldn't survive Bella's daughter moving in with the enemy.

I jumped down from the fence and walked along the dirt road, hands in my pockets, skirting the potholes and kicking a few rocks. *Earn what I could, save it and plan a strategy for my future.* Being an essential optimist, I could believe that with a little luck Boone would leave and I'd just have Mama to deal with. Mama wasn't easy, but I knew her triggers. And I was still flexible and fast. I knew how to make myself scarce.

Yes, with a little luck and diligence and focus, I could last four years, graduate, and get out of this place and begin my real life.

CHAPTER FIVE

A few months later, Boone was still coming around, and I was getting worried. He stayed over more nights than not, and just that morning I'd tripped over his spare shoes—shoes he'd left behind when he went to work. I was seeing more and more of his personal items lying about. I'd turned fourteen, but sometimes I felt like the only adult in the house. I remarked to Mama that her boyfriend might be a little too cozy around here and acting as if he belonged here, like he thought he owned the place. And maybe owned us too.

She threw out, "You don't like his manners. But let me tell you that fine words and a polished manner ain't no indicator of who a person really is, nor what they are capable of."

What was I supposed to say to that? "Manners do count. But that isn't what I'm talking about."

She dismissed my look of doubt. "Never mind. Boone isn't the marrying kind anyway, so you needn't worry he'll overstay his welcome. Like every other man, he'll move on one day—probably when he's needed most."

"Dad didn't, right? Dad didn't leave on purpose."

Mama harrumphed. She drummed her fingers on the kitchen counter. She shook her head, then said in a disappointed voice, "No, Jaynie. Your daddy didn't leave because he wanted to." Then she laughed harshly and added,

"But likely he would have. That's what men do, both husbands and daddies." She stalked out of the room.

My dear Mama.

I sighed. At least I now had the kitchen to myself. It was just as well, because it was time to start cooking. I banged a few bowls and pans around.

"Jaynie, stop sulking and breaking all the dishes. If you're mad, just say so."

She was back, standing in the kitchen doorway. I considered whether I wanted to escalate this or defuse it. She would've liked me to take it up a violent notch—Mama thrived in chaos. In this case she'd use the hullaballoo to silence her doubts or gloom. I was pretty sure she preferred that route because there was no accountability in chaos—it was enough to simply participate. I wasn't a crowd chaos person, and even if I had been, I was contrary enough to withhold from Mama what she wanted most.

I smiled sweetly and apologized for disturbing her.

She waited another long minute, perhaps hoping I'd change my mind about choosing peace, before walking off. I returned to fixing supper.

Boone arrived shortly before the food hit the table. He acted extra glad to see me and made a big show of sniffing the air and saying how good my cooking smelled. He said it all with a big smile—his big wolf's smile. I smiled back, showing just as many teeth as he did. Mama might be as wild as a coyote, but she tended to surround herself with wolves.

Boone tried to be charming at the supper table. Mom had only just started joining me at the supper table—at Boone's insistence.

"It isn't healthy to eat in front of the TV, Bella. Smart

woman like you should know that." He gave Mama a hug, and she giggled. "Besides, it's not polite to leave the cook to eat in here all alone." He winked at me and released Mama.

"I don't mind," I was quick to respond. I touched the book I'd set beside my plate.

"No, ma'am. No substitute for family. For the real thing," he said as he put both his and Mama's plates on the table. Then he picked up my book, gave it a dismissive glance, and tossed it onto the far counter where I kept the cookbooks and such.

"Boone, honey, Jaynie enjoys eating alone and reading."

"Well, let's see if we can fix that. Mealtime is family time." He pulled out his chair, and it scraped against the floor.

It was Mitch's seat. Of course, he'd rarely sat in here with me before and not at all since he'd moved out several months ago. But he still showed up from time to time, especially when he had laundry to do, so it was his chair. Mitch was family. Boone was not and never would be. My stomach burned a little, and then I reminded myself that this would pass. Mama wouldn't put up with losing her suppertime entertainment for long. For right now, Boone was still shiny in her eyes. That too would pass.

I saw nothing shiny about him—not in his yellowed eyes or his scruffy hair. His teeth were his best feature. When he smiled, he almost looked reasonable—so long as you didn't notice how big his teeth were, how they overfilled his mouth—and didn't look him in the eyes. Eyeball to eyeball, there was something disquieting about him. We never exchanged a glance that didn't leave me feeling a strong need to wash.

"Damn, girl, this chicken is good. You've got skills." He turned to Mama. "You hear that, Bella? Jaynie's a fine cook."

"I guess I *do* know. She's my daughter. She's almost as good a cook as my mother was. With a little more practice, she'll be as good. I never had the ability."

"You have other talents, Bella." He snickered, and then his voice changed. "What are you gonna do when she leaves home? Starve?" He laughed his loud, raucous laugh that made me want to cringe. But I didn't. I stayed in my seat with my back straight and my head high and focused on my food. In a different tone, he added, "She sure is growing up fast. Practically grown already. Bet you already have a boyfriend, right, Jaynie?" He winked.

Mama said, "She's a child, Boone. You leave her alone." She said to me, "Don't pay any attention to his teasing."

He laughed louder. In a teasing, almost singsong voice, he said, "Your mama is jealous of you, Jaynie. Yes, I believe she is." He winked again. "Of your cooking, I mean."

I was about done with this, so when Mama blew up, I didn't mind. Anything to interrupt him. To stop this.

Mama yelled, picked up her plate and threw it. Boone ducked, though to be fair, she'd never had good aim. As the plate hit the wall and shattered, his chair tipped back, and his arms flailed before he grabbed the table edge and barely stopped his fall. It pissed him off. His face turned beet red, and he bared his teeth. Boone jumped to his feet and shoved the table, moving it several feet. More dishes fell. My favorite drinking glass nearly went flying, but I grabbed it in time and stepped away, pressing back against the sink counter.

Mama screamed at him, "Get out of here." She grabbed her dinette chair by its back, picked it up and heaved it at him, then ran out of the room.

Boone took no notice of me now. He'd dodged the chair, and his attention was fixed solely on Mama as he followed directly after her. I heard them both shouting—which decreased somewhat when the bedroom door slammed shut.

I felt small. Like a child—the child I hadn't been in years. And shaky. When the noises started—it sounded like furniture being tossed around—I broke. I was fourteen and old enough to deal with crap like this, I told myself. Ignore it. Or throw a few things of my own. But instead I dumped the contents of my plate into one of the plastic leftover containers, tossed in a fork and slapped the lid on, and went out the door.

Halfway to my spot in the woods, I realized I was still clutching my glass of iced tea. The glass had been one of my grandmother's, from her wedding set, she'd told me. It was old and discolored from decades of use. But mine. And not a drop had spilled, either in the contretemps or in my flight.

I settled on the rock. *Contretemps*, I repeated, listening to the rhythm of the word. It was French, I thought. At least the root of it was French. My heart settled into a respectable rhythm too as I rubbed my fingers long the smooth, sculpted flowers etched in the glass and remembered when *contretemps* had been the word of the day and Ms. Ruth had teased me about venturing into foreign territory and had told me about France.

C-o-n-t-r-e-t-e-m-p-s. I spelled it aloud.

Ms. Ruth said she'd never been to France, but she'd

always had a mind to go. I'd told her that maybe we could go together one day. We could learn French. She'd laughed and offered me a soda.

It was a pleasant memory that chased away the ugly stuff.

The rock was surprisingly warm, its broad surface having absorbed the sun all day. Winter was coming. We'd be stuck in the house more. Our small house. If Mama was still having Boone over, it would feel a whole lot smaller. I might not be able to stay.

Ms. Ruth had that spare room. We'd get along well as housemates, no doubt of that. But Mama would never allow it. Even if Mama chose Boone over me, such a move would surely kill the détente. *Hah, another French word.* I needed to tell Ms. Ruth about it. But I couldn't. I sobered quickly. Because she'd either invite me to live with her or refuse to invite me . . . and that would destroy us all, one way or the other.

The chicken breast and the noodles, now drying out, no longer looked appetizing. I took the biscuit to nibble on while I drank my tea. I'd donate the rest to the deer and bunnies.

I eased the toolbox out from under the moss and the small rock it was secured under. I brushed the dirt off but didn't open it. Instead, I lay back on the rock. The stone was hard against my head with only my hair to cushion it. But the rock felt friendly, like an old companion, which was a really stupid way to think of a rock, but there it was. I rested my hand on the toolbox, thinking about my life as contained therein. *Contained therein.* I'd heard that phrase somewhere and I liked it. It was controlled, precise. It indicated a world that didn't know chaos.

My savings. A picture of my dad. The sketch of Wyatt. A green feather I'd kept from a parakeet that Ms. Ruth had had when I was a kid. A tiger's-eye marble I'd stolen from Mitch out of petulance over some argument or other. I'd kept it hidden because the only thing that would've made him madder than losing it would be to discover that I'd taken it. There were other small odds and ends, including a memento from my mother. An earring. She'd lost them, and I'd found one. Giving her the one I'd found would've been guaranteed to set her off. She'd suspect me of messing with her stuff, so I tucked it away. If the other earring ever turned up, maybe I'd give them back to her. Maybe I wouldn't.

Days were shorter this time of year, and the light would soon be gone. I could find my way home blind if I needed to, but it wouldn't be my first choice. By now, Boone would either be gone or sitting with Mama on the sofa watching a movie or such. I could slip in quietly and get the kitchen cleaned up. Better yet, maybe Boone would've gone to his own home or to work a late shift or wherever. I could deal with Mama's tantrums.

Tossing the food into nearby bushes, I fitted the lid back onto the dish, picked up my grandma's glass, and after securing the toolbox back in its hiding place, I headed home. I pushed Boone's nonsense and Mama's foibles out of my mind and concentrated on the quiet of the forest, and then I was passing through Uncle Lou's old field. An interior light gave a yellow cast to Mama's kitchen window. Almost a welcoming glow. A deceptive promise.

I tried to peek in through the window, but the view was limited, so as stealthily as I could, I eased the kitchen door open. The chairs were back to upright, and someone had stacked some of the dishes. The broken dishes had been pushed into a pile on the floor.

Detritus, I thought. Trash, for sure. But who? Mama might've done that much if she was feeling sufficiently regretful. I stepped quietly into the room. The lamp was on in the living room. I moved forward for a look through the open doorway and saw Mitch. He was seated on the sofa with a view of both the front door and the kitchen.

I shot him a silent look—a question.

"It's okay, Jaynie. Mom and Boone left for a while. When Mom comes back, she won't bring Boone with her."

"How's that?"

"I explained it to her," he said, with his typical even and certain tone.

I shook my head but crossed my arms. "Thanks for picking up in the kitchen."

"What happened?"

"Boone pissed Mama off. He said some stuff, and she lost it."

"Did he say or do anything to you, Jaynie?"

It was a charged question.

"He's creepy, that's all. I don't like him."

"I agree." He shifted forward to sit on the edge of the cushion. "I'm not fooling myself into thinking that me kicking him out today will keep him away indefinitely—not if Mom wants him here—but it might help for a while." He stood but stayed there in the fringes of the lamplight.

I said, "He's why you left, right?"

"Better to leave than do murder," Mitch said with a half smile.

"How'd you happen to come back today?"

"To get some things I'd left behind. Decided to make a surprise visit." He waved an arm. "And I saw all this."

Mitch wasn't just talking about the mess in the kitchen. He was also talking about the general mess that Mama and Boone left in their wake wherever they went—the empty cans and bottles and full-over ashtrays, among other stuff.

He moved closer to the kitchen doorway and to me, and I saw what the dim light had obscured before—the red area on his cheekbone. It was quickly going to swelling and bruising.

"Took some persuading, I see."

"Not a big deal. It will be a big deal if he comes back or if Mom replaces him with someone else."

"She never brought anyone over to stay the night until Boone."

"Mom has problems." He shook his head. "So, I wanted to tell you that Boone is gone, at least for a few days. He knows I could walk back in here anytime. If he comes back, you let me know. If he bothers you or tries to mess with you in any way, you tell me. I'll figure something out, regardless." He held out a scrap of paper. "Here's my number. Tuck it away and don't lose it."

"Where are you living?"

He put his hands on my shoulders. "I've got nowhere for you, Jaynie. If I did, I'd take you out of here." He squeezed my shoulders before dropping his hands. He lifted his face and seemed to be looking somewhere above my head, his nose testing the air. "I feel bad coming, Jaynie. I don't know why or when or how, but it's there." Then he shook it off. He smiled and said, "Let me know." He scanned the kitchen. "I made a start on this mess. You need help getting it finished up?"

"Nah. I got it. Thanks, Mitch."

He nodded. He retrieved a backpack he'd stashed in the corner, and with a reminder to me not to lose his number, he left.

I finished the kitchen cleanup in quiet, occasionally even humming a tune and thinking that one day I would have my own life. I'd be in charge, and I wouldn't screw things up with bad habits or toxic people. One of my teachers called it *living an intentional life*. Ms. Ruth called it *living in each moment*. I had a stash of bills and coins that I was saving for the day when I'd be able to leave. To have my own kitchen to clean. Or maybe be rich enough to hire someone to do it when I didn't want to. Have a maid. Maybe hire people to clean up the yard instead of dragging our ancient lawn mower out of the shed every few weeks to tackle the growth.

I looked at my surroundings, at the dingy paint and the worn furniture. Some of the furniture had new cracks and chips, and we'd lost a few dishes today. It was a disorderly life, lived among people who chose chaos and drama over dignity and creativity and . . . and . . . I needed a new word. One I'd share with Ms. Ruth the next time I saw her. Before I was finished with the kitchen, the exhaustion—emotional exhaustion—had settled in and around me.

Still no sign of Mama.

She came home late that night. I'd given up waiting and had finally gone on to bed after having pushed my dresser in front of my bedroom door, just in case. But I slept undisturbed until two a.m. when I needed to go to the bathroom. I moved the dresser a few inches and slipped out into the hallway. Lamplight was still coming from the living room, and Mama was on the sofa, sound asleep and smelling strongly of smoke and drink. I searched the house and found no one else.

So Boone was gone. At least temporarily. I left Mama asleep and returned to bed, and after a short pause, I went ahead and pushed the dresser back against my bedroom door. Just because.

~~~~

The next morning, while I was in the kitchen fixing our coffee, Mama came to the doorway and said, "I put him out. I didn't like the way Boone was talking to you. I'm your mother, and it's my job to protect you."

The words rolled out stilted and sounded like someone else's. Maybe Mitch's?

She resumed, "But I have a right to my own life too, so no promises. You'll be out of here in no time anyway—I know you want to leave. No secret about that. But when you do, remember when I did right by you. As your mama."

"Thank you?" I heard the unintended question in my tone and quickly amended, "*Thank you.*"

She grunted and walked away.

What did that mean? I suspected it meant that I was going to be punished for her having to do the right thing when it wasn't what she wanted. Remember *when* I did right by you—not remember I did right by you. So my mother had done the right thing, whether she wanted to or not, because Mitch had insisted. He couldn't have made her kick Boone out, though, so she must've seen the necessity. But she didn't like it. Not one little bit.

On my next trip up to the rock, I dug out my toolbox and

unwrapped the plastic cover protecting it from water and insects. I pulled the rubber-banded bills and the baggie of coins out, which also included my silver dollar. I laid it all out on the rock and counted it again. Not enough. Not even near. And hardly growing at all. I had nothing I could sell, but maybe I could find jobs, babysitting or such, but there weren't any kids within close walking distance and no way to get to such jobs otherwise unless the person I was working for would fetch me and take me back home after.

My focus redoubled. When Ms. Ruth decided to go with her sister on a bus trip to Atlantic City, she asked me to check on the house while she was gone and said she'd pay me. Frankly, in this case, the money didn't matter. It was a relief to go over there and watch TV or read one of her magazines. Ruth had a taste for the salacious—another word of the day—and she'd laugh like a loon over the more outrageous stories. I spent a lot of time over at her house that week. Even with her gone, the echo of her laughter was strong in my head. But while I was enjoying the solitude at Ruth's, I should've been paying more attention to Mama. If I had, I would've noticed she was simmering with a restless tension. She was often absent and out late most nights.

One morning Mama said, "You'd rather hang out at that drunk's house. Is it because her grandson is there? Are you meeting him over there? Sneaking around with him?" She came up close to me, face to face. "Because if you are, you'd better tell me right now."

"No, Mama," I said, backing off a step. "His name is Wyatt, and he doesn't live there." She already knew all that, but I felt like it was important to restate it because I didn't like the way she was tossing the facts around like some sort of garbage that didn't matter. Plus, I didn't want her to mistake my silence as an indication of guilt—something for her to pick at whenever she was in the mood to take emotional bites out of me. "Since his mom got married and moved clear out to the other side of Louisa, I only ever see him in school."

"You two hang out at school?"

"No. We have different friends."

I couldn't read her eyes. Was it pity? Or satisfaction?

"Good. You've got plans for your life, Jaynie. That's a good thing. Stay focused." And she walked away. I stood there amazed. She'd never said anything remotely like that except for when she got on a tear about me not getting pregnant. Sometimes I thought that if I heard "And don't be thinking you can get caught and bring some baby home for me to support, for me to raise. I already did my part in populating the country," one more time, I'd scream. Or better yet, shove a pillow up my blouse and scare the crap out of her.

I needed fresh air and to be alone. I gave the back door just enough of a slam to give Mama a little satisfaction that she'd gotten under my skin, but not enough to make her feel disrespected or challenged. But I wasn't leaving to sulk. I'd heard the distant sound of a lawn mower.

Wyatt was mowing his grandmother's yard. He did odd jobs for her from time to time. I crossed the pasture and stopped at the fence. I sat on the top rail to watch.

What Mama had said was wrong, but not all the way wrong. I'd never in a trillion years admit it to her 'cause it was all imagining and daydreaming. We were at that age. Hadn't I seen it play out over and over, all around me, in school? The girls would be grouped together whispering and keeping watch for whatever boy the girl at the center was crushing on. The next day it would be some other guy they'd all be whispering about. And the boys strolled the hallways acting like they didn't care, but they were watching from the corner of their eye for that special girl who'd caught their attention. How many times had I imagined Wyatt looking at me in that way, fastening his eyes on my face? Perhaps even declaring his feelings? He'd be brash, but then he'd get shy because of course he couldn't be sure how I might respond. And how would he tell Sherry and break her heart because, he'd declare as he stared deeply into my eyes, he'd given his to me?

All that imagining was so strong that it almost felt real, but when he turned the mower near Ms. Ruth's shed and came back into view, I remembered how pretty and upbeat Sherry was and how her family had money and a good reputation and how they both had lots of friends in common. My imagining evaporated.

As he reached the burn barrel, he caught sight of me. His hand went to his chest as he apparently remembered he'd ditched his shirt. He ducked his head and put all his effort into moving that mower. I smiled but let him alone. Sometimes imagining was better than reality.

He wasn't over this way a lot these days, and if moments of friendship away from the rest of the world was what I had to settle for, then it was still something.

The highlight of that year was the night we danced with the fireflies. I'd spied the light given off by Ms. Ruth's barrel—not a high burn but perfect for a late spring/early summer evening—a companionable light without too much heat. Just right for pulling up a seat next to Ms. Ruth and watching the stars overhead and creatures rustling in the night. But when I arrived, all set to tell her my newest word, there she sat with Wyatt. I paused a few yards away.

Ms. Ruth leaned forward, put her hands on the armrests, and pushed herself up. She stood for a moment staring into nothing, then said to the dark, "Why don't you join us, missy? I'm about to go in, but I'll be right back out." She walked away. By then, Wyatt was looking over at me, and I could hardly run away, so I joined him.

Wyatt and I heard the screened door connect as it closed. The fire was at a low burn, a companionable burn. It was a warmish night, and the fireflies were lighting up amid the trees.

We looked at each other as if only just realizing we were alone. We'd been alone before, but it had never felt quite like this. The night was not to blame; the change was in us. We were no longer little kids, and it seemed a little dangerous in a delicious sort of way.

I smiled, and as I stared at Wyatt, the flamelets from the barrel cast a flickering light across his face and revealed he was smiling back.

CHAPTER SIX

While Wyatt and I were smiling at each other by the flickering light of the barrel, back beyond the tall grass was the ever-present hulk of Lou's barn. It had been there long before I arrived on this earth, and during my short lifetime it had been rarely used—at least, seldom used as intended. It was odd how things like that huge, almost forgotten building became part of the landscape. A landmark of sorts, like a mountain peak or an ancient oak might be.

A few years before, Mitch had told Mama that I'd gone in there snooping. She'd yelled at me, saying she wasn't about to waste money on doctor bills if the thing came down on my head—or alternatively, someone might see me messing around the building and then blame me if it burned down. Mitch had told on me, but not because he was worried about me. He'd told because he wanted me to stay away from it. Mitch had his own secrets, including what he'd been up to in the barn with his girlfriend that Saturday night. I gave Mitch an evil look, but otherwise let it go and promised Mama that I'd stay away from what she called a deathtrap.

On this warm night in the turning point of spring into summer—when I was almost fifteen and Wyatt was nearly sixteen—Ms. Ruth had excused herself and said she'd be back out shortly, but she hadn't returned. I wondered if she'd found herself too thirsty. I knew Wyatt's mom had forbidden her mother to drink alcohol when Wyatt was around. But Wyatt wasn't in the house, so maybe she'd found a needed loophole.

After a while without conversation but being acutely aware that Wyatt and I were here alone, I blurted out, "I'd better get on home myself." Why I was aware, I didn't know. We'd been alone before. But we were also older now. And while my brain was whirling like crazy, I couldn't think of a thing to say to him.

Wyatt said, "I'll walk you."

I almost joked about whether he thought I might get lost, then pulled it back. "Thanks."

We only got as far as the fence. Somehow, about halfway over, our forward progress stalled. We hadn't had much to say, but that might have been due more to not knowing how to quantify what we were feeling.

"It's a nice night, isn't it?" I said. "The stars are big and bright. The katydids are calling. It's peaceful."

"Too quiet for me. I need more going on. A little excitement."

"Like a party?"

"Not that. I'm not sure how to explain it."

I watched him talk. I saw his profile. I felt the energy coming from him and connecting with my own. And I thought of that barn nearby.

The walls loomed tall in the dark night, black except for the bright flicks of light where the fireflies danced in the tall damp grass. They darted and floated among the boughs of the pines, hollies, and oaks and other deciduous trees. The fire in Ms. Ruth's barrel was burning low, and it couldn't cast its light that far. It barely touched us here on our fence.

The barn was beyond its glow. I remembered how in prior years I'd seen Mitch and his girlfriend coming out of that barn. And maybe that was on my mind just a little when I laughed, smiled at Wyatt like a dare, and reached forward to snare a firefly in my hands, nearly falling off the fence.

One came close, lighting up, and Wyatt leaned too far forward, holding out both hands, and lost his balance. I laughed so hard, I lost mine too. That evening, feeling a little drunk with our age—a giddiness that played into our moods and as we might have done as four-year-olds—if we'd known each other then—but now we were dangerous because we were fourteen instead of four—and we galloped, laughing like loons, after the bright, flashing lights, cupping our hands to catch them—and releasing them in the same instant—because we both knew the game wasn't to catch the fireflies but to race beyond the fire with its flames licking through the holes in the rusted metal, beyond the stage-lit world in our little corner of the universe, and chase a more elusive fire—despite the risk of getting burned. Racing, laughing, colliding in the darkness by the barn—feeling that night like a temptation and a shield—and caught in each other's arms, we kissed.

Our intended endgame was uncertain and remained so because a sharp beam of light hit our eyes. We flinched and peered from between our fingers as our eyes adjusted. Mitch waved a large flashlight beam back and forth between us, saying, "Get home, Jaynie. Right now."

"You have no right to boss me around, Mitch Highsmith. No right. Just because you come home to wash your dirty laundry doesn't give you rights. Besides, we weren't doing anything wrong." I shielded my eyes from the light he was directing in them.

"If it wasn't wrong, then why did you have to run off into the dark to do it?"

"The fireflies. We were chasing—"

"Home. Go home." And he moved the beam back and forth between both our faces.

"You can't tell me what to do. You're not in charge of me. I don't need you."

I gave Wyatt a hard-eyed glare, expecting him to back me up. But at this age the difference between him being not quite sixteen and Mitch being twenty was pretty big. Wyatt looked defiant and embarrassed all at once. I felt disappointed. I told myself it didn't matter. Mitch had spoiled the fun anyway.

"See ya," I said, and walked away. When I neared Mitch, I gave him a look that could've killed, but he probably didn't see it because he was still focused on Wyatt. I bumped his arm, hard, and he lost his grip on the flashlight. He scrambled for it in the grass, saying, "Enough, Jaynie. Go."

"You leave Wyatt alone."

"You're my sister, and you don't have a dad to speak for you, so Wyatt and I will have a few words." He trained the light in Wyatt's direction again. "You okay with that?"

Wyatt said, "I am."

Embarrassment suddenly overwhelmed me. I ran through the dark field and left my brother and Wyatt to have their talk. I was furious with them both.

~~~~

I was even angrier the next morning when I knocked on Ms. Ruth's door.

She gave me a funny look. "What's your word for today, girl?"

Sensing something different in her voice and seeing a message in her eyes that I couldn't read, I frowned. Was that pity?

"Wyatt. That's my word. And my sentence is, 'Is Wyatt here?'"

She shook her head slowly. "No, he isn't, I'm sorry to say. He's a pleasure to have around, don't you agree?"

My face grew hot. I may have blushed, but I refused to acknowledge it. "Yes, ma'am, I do."

"His mother thinks so too. She needed him back home sooner than expected and picked him up first thing this morning."

I was shocked. In Ms. Ruth's eyes I read that it might be my fault. I was desolate and couldn't hide it. But I kept from spouting dramatic demands or poor-me lamentations. I held my anguish in and felt the warmth of my face fade to pale. And I broke. I ran.

Ruth called after me, even using my real name, "Jaynie, come back." She was soon distant from me, still yelling from her kitchen door, but her dark eyes filled my head, the twinkle long gone and sadness etched all around them.

I wasn't good enough. I knew it. She'd sent him away. So I ignored her and kicked my feet into the dirt of the road all the harder and faster, past Lou's old field and his ramshackle barn, and jumped the creek where the woods began. I ran. My chest hurt, the gasping breaths tore at my throat, and when I reached my rock I knelt and tried to recover. As my breathing eased, I lay on my side and then rolled over onto my back and cried.

That evening in the kitchen as I spooned the hamburger-and-noodle casserole I'd concocted onto our plates, Mitch walked in. It hit me suddenly that Ruth couldn't have seen Wyatt and me kissing, so Mitch must've said something . . . either to Ruth or to Mama. Mid-serving, heedless that the spoon was about to drip, I stopped and glared at him.

He shook his head ever so slightly and put his finger to his lips. He nodded toward the back door. I set the pan and spoon on the stove and followed him out. Grabbing my arm, he led me over to the old concrete bench Dad had made, and Mitch said, "Mom followed me out last night because she was curious. I didn't know." He gave a low, frustrated groan. "She thought I was maybe going out to meet a girlfriend. You know how Mom is about one of us bringing home a baby."

I nodded.

"She saw the flashlight waving and came close enough to see you run past and then Wyatt leaving. She called Wyatt's mom and told her you two needed to spend some time apart."

I gasped. I tried to yank my arm free of Mitch's hand, but he tightened his grip.

"You aren't going to like me saying this, Jaynie, but you have Mom's temper. You two go at each other awful, and I'm not sure it can ever be fixed. You have to hold your tongue on this one."

"No." I spit the word at him.

"Yes," he said, and gave me a shake. "Yes, because if you act like you don't care, she'll decide she got worked up over nothing. I told her you were both chasing fireflies like stupid toddlers. If you act like him being gone is nothing to you, she'll decide it's okay and that she overreacted, and she'll let it go. Understand?"

"I do."

"And?"

"She'll never know she got to me."

"Good enough. And, Jaynie? One thing you've got to learn is that you're too young to mess with boys, even with a friend like Wyatt, and . . ."

Annoyed, I tossed out, "And what else?"

"You gotta learn to be more discreet." With that, he gave me a brotherly shove and followed me back into the house.

~~~~~

After two nights on Mama's sofa, Mitch moved on again to share an apartment with a couple of friends. I rarely saw Wyatt after that. No one kept us apart—not openly—and maybe I blamed the wrong people. Maybe Wyatt himself got busy with life. When I saw him at school, he was always talking to his friends, had an arm slung around some girl's shoulders, or was digging in his locker. If he noticed me, he'd nod or wave, but nothing more. When he was at his grandmother's house, she was always there with us. It felt awkward now, and the three of us being together seemed to cause pain instead of delighting her.

Or maybe it was no one's fault. Maybe Wyatt and I were each so focused on getting out that we forgot to pay attention to each other.

~~~~~

Mitch was gone. Wyatt was gone too, for all practical purposes. Boone had stayed gone, thank goodness. Mama would go out in the evenings. She never mentioned who she was seeing or what she was doing, but it wasn't wearing well on her. She looked tired. But not hard-work tired. More like bad-choices tired. It seemed to me that if she put half as much energy into work or just being happy, she'd feel less need to go hunting for it every evening.

Life was often weird, and that was about all the sense I could make of it.

I woke in the middle of the night. I heard pacing, then footsteps, jerky and awkward. I slipped quietly out of bed and eased my door open wider, mindful of the squeaky spots, and stepped into the hallway so I could see into the living room.

Mama. She was muttering and stumbling around. Her arms were held strangely out to her sides, one sort of crooked up and the other forward. Her hips swayed wildly. I got the distinct impression that she was dancing and had a partner as she stepped and twirled. It would've been almost amusing if it had been anyone but my mother. It had been a long time since I'd seen her this far gone. There was an almost empty bottle of whiskey on the end table. She didn't drink a lot in recent times because it interacted badly with the "mood" pills the doctor had prescribed. Sometimes, though, life just overwhelmed her, and she couldn't help herself. Another irony was that at those times, even though I might fear her a little more, I also felt more sympathy for her. Mama wasn't made for this world or this life. I felt guilty since I had a part in that—especially in keeping her tied to it.

Wanting to avoid a scene, I stepped back, but a board made a noise as my foot pressed upon it. A tiny noise. Maybe she'd also felt my eyes on her, because she spun around— her absent partner forgotten—and came toward me. She gripped my shoulders, her eyes blazing crazy. They held me spellbound.

"When is it my turn? Will you tell me that? That's what I want to know." She pushed me, and as I stumbled backward, she staggered in the opposite direction. I wanted to go hide in my room but felt paralyzed. Mesmerized, maybe. Hiding wouldn't have mattered anyway—not if she really wanted to fight with me.

"My turn." She hit her chest with her fist. "First it was Mitch. Then George drowns his stupid self in a damn fishpond. A fishpond! And you. At least Mitch is useful. Ruined my life, that's what. Kids, kids, kids. What about me? Me? Where's my life?" She covered her face with her hands and swayed back and forth.

For lack of a better option, I left my mama to her misery and took my useless self back to bed, but before I climbed in, I slid the dresser across to block the closed door. Mama was petite but wiry. If she was determined to get in, she could— perhaps to continue that lovely conversation—but I'd have warning. And there was always the window as an exit option if I chose to take it.

Sleep was hard to find, and every noise and creak in the house made me jump, but finally I dozed off. This wasn't my first time dealing with Mama's problems, though they weren't often this bad, thank goodness.

I thought briefly of calling someone, but who? And if some well-meaning person told the authorities and they carted Mama off, or perhaps took me instead, I could end up in a far worse situation than this one. At least I knew the perils of my life with my dear mother. I understood the landscape I lived in. And it wouldn't be forever. I would be fifteen soon. Three more years and I'd be out of here and making my new life.

~~~~~

In the morning, Mama was up and moving a little slow but seemed more bemused than anything else.

"I got such a headache, Jaynie. Fix me some coffee, will you?"

"I'll miss the bus, Mama." I said it softly and stayed on the far side of the room.

Mama walked slowly over to me, giving me a long look, and then she patted my cheek. "Poor Jaynie. You look as peaked as I feel. We both had bad nights, I think."

"I hope you'll have a good day, Mama."

"That's my sweet girl, Jaynie. You fix me that coffee and maybe an egg over-easy too on top of a slice of toast to settle my stomach. I'll give you a ride to school. We'll tell 'em you had a touch of flu. You're such a good student, they'll never think twice about it."

Mama's latest storm had passed. Might be for a while, or the lull might only last until the next irritation hit her. This one, though, stuck with me. However much she might have yelled or fussed before, she'd never said outright that I was unwanted—as if I'd ruined her life by the very fact of my existence.

I remembered the year when I turned from fourteen to fifteen as the year when no one was happy. Despite some good moments and no one dying or going to jail, it was a year that no one wanted to redo. Not anyone.

But unexpectedly, and amazingly, fifteen showed promise.

CHAPTER SEVEN

One sunny Saturday when I was fifteen going on sixteen, Wyatt found me sitting in a yard chair in my backyard. It had been a block patio in better days. Now the weeds and moss had pushed up between the patio blocks, making them uneven and somewhat overgrown, but in its own wild way it attracted butterflies and birds and was a pleasant place to sit and think or read. Today, I had a sketchbook against my propped-up legs and a medium-lead pencil, working on a drawing for art class. I'd chosen to sketch how the weeds lay up against the old brick of the disused fireplace. Someone must've once used it for cookouts, but before my time. Now it wasn't much more than a pile of old, scorched bricks with only parts of the original structure remaining. I was focused on what I was doing and didn't see Wyatt's wave. Finally, he called out in a low voice, and I looked up.

Wyatt was standing in Uncle Lou's yard so that the house hid him from view should Mama be looking out the window. He motioned to me to join him.

I did.

Time seemed to be working some sort of magic on Wyatt. Over the last few months he'd grown taller and slimmer, but not skinny. Maybe he looked slim because his shoulders were so wide. He was looking older. Noticeably. If I'd been outclassed by his appearance before, I was totally buried by his looks now.

On the other hand, my legs were longer too and had gotten some shape. They looked pretty darn good. I'd washed my hair just that morning, and it was long and shiny. Wyatt might be more striking, more confident, and better dressed, but I reminded myself that I had Bella Highsmith's good looks and, thank goodness, a better disposition.

The most recent tenant had moved out of Lou's house just days before after a remarkably short stay, so the grass wasn't too high yet. We sat together on the back steps.

Wyatt said, "Are you going to the school dance?"

Was that a trick question? Had I ever gone to any of the dances?

"Not as of this moment."

"I thought you might be going with Steve."

I laughed and then regretted it. Steve had asked me out once. It wasn't his fault that me having to deal with Mama had made it not worth the effort. "No, not Steve. Nice guy, though."

"Would you like to go?"

Again, my first inside-my-head thought was, *Trick question?* But I kept the words in me. I looked at my hands. "Why? What are you saying, Wyatt?"

"Go with me."

"What about Sherry?"

"We're off. We broke up."

"So you're asking me? To go to the dance?"

He grimaced and shrugged. "Decided I'd better while the time was right. Seems like our timing is always off. We're always just missing each other."

"Our mothers aren't likely to be in favor of us going

together."

"Mine won't make trouble. I'm sure of it."

I shook my head. "I don't know. I don't want to be sneaking around. If Mama finds out . . ."

"Tell her. Just tell her like an adult. That's what I did."

The idea stunned me. Talk to her like an adult? Did Wyatt have any concept of my reality? Of my mother? I reconsidered my initial reaction as I entwined my fingers and stretched them out. Mama did have her good moments. She'd stopped complaining about me spending time with Ms. Ruth long ago. She worried I might sneak around with boys, so I mostly avoided friendships because it became unpleasant with Mama and awkward to pretend with the would-be friends that my life was normal. But in this case, if I was upfront about it . . . I had an idea of how to phrase it too. Bella Highsmith could be difficult, but she was also competitive.

"You're sure your mom's okay with us going together?"

"Yes. She won't be a problem."

I grinned. "I'm thinking if I tell Mama that your mom is okay with it and act like it's no big deal, she'll want to one-up her and . . ."

Wyatt laughed. He put his arm around me, hugged me closer, and laughed again. He took his arm back too quickly. The warmth lingered, along with his scent.

We heard his mother's voice calling from the direction of the Berry house.

"See you in school," Wyatt said, and walked away, pausing to wave from the fence before vaulting over.

Reality hit me.

He'd asked. I'd said yes.

Mama.

That evening it was just Mama and me at supper. As I spooned the food onto her plate—and before she made her getaway to the sofa and the TV—I looked at her squarely and tried so very hard to sound nonconfrontational, and reasonable without wheedling. I said, "Wyatt asked me to go to the school dance with him."

Her expression hardened, and her eyes got that glitter-look going.

I kept my own demeanor and voice even. "He cleared it with his mother before asking me. She said she was fine with it."

A slight frown crossed her face. I fancied that shadow of a frown was her instinctive reaction fighting with what I'd said. Maybe they struggled to a standstill, because she said, "Demaris is okay with it?"

"Yes, ma'am."

She took her plate from me, holding it in both her hands. "Well, then, that's fine, I guess. You'll have a curfew. And no drinking or other stuff. Plus, I can't afford a fancy dress."

"No worries, Mama. I'll work out what to wear."

"Well, then."

I fought the urge to get in the last word. And failed. "Thanks, Mama. I'm glad you don't mind." But they must've been the right last words because her face relaxed.

"Supper looks good, Jaynie."

This time, I did keep my mouth shut, leaving well enough alone, and gave her a pleasant smile.

There was something happening in my chest. I couldn't quite identify it. It was unaccustomed. An almost fuzzy feeling. I pressed my hand over it, wondering if it might be good. If it wasn't such a happy, ticklish feeling, I might be worried my heart was failing. I pressed my hand harder, wanting to keep the emotion in and hidden. Perhaps cherish it. Like a tiny pansy that needed a little soil and a tiny drink of water, but whose survival was always in question. One positive moment was only that. One moment. The next could be a killer.

I asked Ms. Ruth if I could ride into town with her when next she went. She agreed. I wanted to check out a consignment shop in the town of Louisa that sold other people's clothing at reduced prices. *Consignment* sounded so much nicer than *secondhand* or *thrift*, but I wasn't proud. If they had what I needed at a price I could manage, I'd call 'em whatever they preferred.

I hiked out to the rock and dug up my toolbox. I counted out my savings and tucked the bills inside the lining of my jacket through a slit where the stitches had come undone. It wasn't a lot of money, but I might get lucky and find the right outfit. Impulsively, I grabbed up that little picture I'd drawn of Wyatt and gave it a quick, light kiss and giggled. I took a long look around to make sure no one was spying before I put the picture back into the toolbox and returned it to its hiding place.

Now my toolbox stash was cashless. I'd taken my savings to spend on a dress. For a date. A pain hit me. I told it to get lost. I was going to the dance with Wyatt, no matter what.

Ms. Ruth drove us into Louisa, the town and county seat of Louisa County. We each took off on our own business, but it wasn't long before she caught back up with me. She found me in the consignment shop checking the racks. The store clerk was watching me like I might grab an armful and run. I'd found one dress that was okay, not great, but better than what I had, and I was wondering if I could stitch it where it looked a little big under the arms when Ms. Ruth walked in.

"That for the dance?" she asked.

"Yes, ma'am."

"Put it back."

There was no nonsense in her voice.

"You have a problem with Wyatt and me going to the dance together?"

"If I did, you'd already know. Mind you, don't take that to mean I'm without worries about it, but mind? No, I don't mind. What I do mind is you wasting your money on this bit of frippery."

I held it close to me. "It's not so bad."

"We can do better," she said.

"We can?"

"Put it back on the rack and come with me."

I did, but reluctantly. I couldn't imagine where we'd do better.

She said, "If you want vintage, I am overflowing with vintage."

She drove us back to her house.

The closet in the second bedroom wasn't big, but it was chock-full of garments and managed to swallow up almost all of Ms. Ruth as she dove in among them. I sat on the twin bed and watched the backs of her legs. She was wearing her blue pantsuit today. It was one of her going-to-town outfits. She left most of her jangly jewelry at home on those days but made up for the lack of flair with her scarves and pins. She called them brooches.

"Was this your daughter's bedroom?"

"It was."

"Sometimes I forget that Mama didn't grow up here, in this neighborhood."

"*Neighborhood* is a bit grand of a word, I'd say."

"You knew my daddy and his people? The Highsmiths?"

"I did. Not well." She emerged from the closet holding a garment bag. "I fell in between generations. Of the Highsmith's, your great uncle Lou was the one I knew best. Course he was right across the road from me. He'd help me out with this and that. We got along. Your father, George, and my girl, Demaris, were good friends growing up. 'Til Bella came into the picture, anyway."

Ouch. I sat up, all attention. Bella and Demaris had been friends in school until they weren't. Was the break because of George?

While I was thinking, Ms. Ruth unzipped the bag. A gauzy dress in a soft lemon-yellow color slipped out.

Gauzy but not billowy. Shaping with folds and a satiny underskirt. This dress would come to my knees. Sleeveless except for tiny little caps at the arm holes.

"Bought this for her. She never wore it. I forget why not, but it's yours now. Styles like this don't ever change. Always good, if you're comfortable carrying if off." She held it by the hanger so the dress was free of interference. It swayed slowly, gracefully, moved by the air current. "What do you think?"

"It's beautiful."

Suddenly the dress was in my arms and Ruth was heading to the door. "Try it on and let's see if we need to fix anything."

It fit perfectly. The skirt fell a little below my knees. Mama had a pair of flats that should work reasonably well if she was willing to let me borrow them. I stood in front of Ruth's mirror and considered that heels would look so good—but I wasn't accustomed to them and would likely wipe out trying to walk in them.

I looked like a princess. I spun, and as the soft folds of the skirt settled back around my hips and thighs, I felt like a princess.

When we were satisfied that the dress would work, Ms. Ruth put it back into the zippered bag and handed it to me.

"Did your mother know where you were going today?"

"I told her I was going to see if the thrift shop had any cheap dresses."

"Good. Just let her think you got this dress there. No need to mention where it came from or who it was originally intended for. Understand?"

"I guess."

"Your mama and I, we have a kind of truce, mostly because of you."

I'd always kind of known, but it had been unspoken. "Me? Why?"

"Because we both care about you." After a moment of silence, she added, "And there's no point in upsetting the balance."

"I'll return the dress to you after the dance. Should I wash it first?"

"No, you keep it, Jaynie. It's yours now."

It wasn't until later that I realized she'd called me Jaynie.

By my name. Not *missy* or *sissy* or *kiddo*.

I must've looked grown up. As if I'd finally grown into my name—maybe had had the right name all along.

~~~~

As we drew closer to the evening of the dance, I walked on eggshells, mindful of the balance that Ruth had mentioned. Mama and I existed and interacted within our own special emotional balance too. *Our* truce. I took care to be cooperative without being too nice or too challenging so that Mama wouldn't get suspicious or vindictive.

"Where'd you get that dress?"

"At the thrift store."

"What did it cost?"

I did a quick check of my memory and the dress I'd been looking at there and told her that price. Something sharp flickered in her eyes, and I added, "But I talked her down some. I had enough from the money I'd saved up."

"You had that much?"

I shrugged. "Christmas and birthday monies and the chores I've done for Ms. Ruth."

Mama nodded. "Okay. Yeah. It's only right that she gives you a little money from time to time, you always being over there and helping her." She nodded one more time. "Okay, then."

And that seemed to be it. I hung the dress in my closet and then took it out and hooked the hanger over the door trim. It swung there, and I saw it every time I walked into my room.

A princess. Going to a dance. Going with Wyatt. That girl was me.

Even at night when I lay in bed, I left the curtains open so the moonlight could stream in and silhouette the dress. It was the last thing I saw before sleep and the first thing I saw when I woke.

Wyatt didn't come back to his grandmother's house, but we passed each other in the school hallways between classes and shared a special smile. Later that day, I was digging in my locker and suddenly he was there next to me. I wanted to cast a quick look around and see if anyone was noticing, but I didn't want them to see my own hot face.

"We're still on?" Wyatt asked.

"I have my dress."

He grinned so big my heart nearly exploded. I fought the urge to either climb into that locker, as if I could, or throw my arms around him. Since I could do neither, I settled for my own silly grin.

"Later, Jaynie."

"Later, Wyatt."

He walked away, and as the rose-colored fog cleared from my eyes, I saw Sherry standing several yards away. Just standing and staring. Just that.

I turned away to close my locker. Having seen that anger-glitter look in Sherry's eyes, I knew nothing was going to be simple. It wasn't going to end as *just that*.

~~~~

The next day, the first drive-by happened. It was a squealing of breaks, a revving motor, and lots of dust left in the truck's wake.

Mama asked, "Who's that?"

I was standing at the picture window. "No one I know.

Didn't recognize the truck. Must've been lost."

No one drove here unless they knew who they were coming to visit or if they were lost.

They hadn't been lost. I'd caught a glimpse of a couple of teenage boys in that truck.

Heaven help me if Mama knew. I could forget that dance.

I didn't fool myself. This had happened because Wyatt had shown interest in me in front of the school body. The question was whether it was connected to Sherry.

And there was another question. Would they be back?

I hoped not. I gripped the windowsill. The dust had pretty much cleared from the road.

If Wyatt came by, I might tell him. Just to see what he thought.

~~~~

Wyatt didn't come over to see me or his grandmother, but Mitch showed up. It was a couple of days after my uninvited visitors, a Sunday afternoon. Mitch had come to wash his laundry. He was in the living room when they returned, and after the truck raced by, we heard it do a doughnut at the end of the road. Just that quick, Mitch was beside me there at the window. We watched the truck as it came back our way. It slowed, and some fool leaned out and yelled something about me coming out there to see them and then laughed as the driver leaned on the gas pedal again, nearly tossing the boy out on his head.

My face burned.

Mitch didn't rush out. He stood still, staring, taking in every detail before they were gone from view.

"What's that about, Jaynie?"

His voice was low, but not soft. Maybe a little dangerous sounding.

"Stupid kids. That's all."

"From your high school."

"Yeah."

"Why are they messing with you? How long?"

"Just the last few days. This is the second time."

"Mama?"

"She was here the first time, but they didn't yell, so she thought it was someone who was lost."

"Do you recognize them or the truck?"

"No. Too quick and not my friends."

His eyebrows went up at that. "Whose friends?"

"Not sure. Maybe friends of Wyatt's old girlfriend."

"Why would she care about you and Wyatt?"

I shrugged and looked away. "Wyatt and I are going to the dance together."

We stood there silently staring out the window for a few long minutes before Mitch spoke again.

"If they come back, you don't run out there. Stay inside. They can't be sure you've even seen them. Don't make it bigger than it needs to be."

Annoyed, I said, "They're the ones making trouble, not me."

"No worries, Jaynie. You stay out of it. If you see me in the school parking lot, don't say anything. Just pretend I was never there. I'll recognize that truck and its dents when I see it again. Had a sticker on the back window too. I'll have a word with the owner."

"No, Mitch. It means nothing. Just a couple of fools."

He ruffled my hair. He hadn't done that in a long time.

"I'll just have a little chat with whoever shows up. If that doesn't do it, then I'll have a chat with the sheriff." He shook his head. "If Mama realizes what's going on, you'll have hell to pay. You know that. Worse than any hassle in school."

He was right.

"Okay. But be careful and don't get yourself in trouble."

~~~~

Mitch must've found the truck and had that chat with the driver, because the vehicle didn't return to our little road. A couple of boys I hardly knew looked askance at me when we passed in the hallways. As usual, I kept my head up and my eyes straight ahead or just plain blind as I'd always made my way through my school days. I was just marking time anyway. Instead of marking time until graduation, though, I was now counting down to the dance.

I did keep my eyes peeled for Wyatt but rarely saw him, and that was from a distance. Considering the negative attention, I decided that was probably good. After the dance, it would be different. It would be official.

After the dance, Wyatt and I could openly be a couple. People would look at me differently then, and I'd be smiling.

~~~~

On the evening of the dance, Wyatt didn't show up at five p.m. as planned. I kept my eyes on Hope Road, looking to see the dust puff up as he drove along.

Mama said, "Come back inside, Jaynie. You don't want him to see you out here looking all desperate. He's not worried about making a good impression, that's for sure."

"He'll be here, Mama. He's late, but he's coming."

"Come in anyway."

I did. I stood at the picture window so I was near the phone. I didn't have a cell phone yet, but I knew Wyatt had the number for the house phone. It didn't ring. It rarely rang anyway, and when it did, it was almost always a telemarketer or for Mama, but I watched both the window and that beige push-button phone, ready to pounce.

Mama hovered nearby, pretending to be busy in the kitchen, and then she sat in front of the TV to watch a show. I stayed at the window. Mama's shoes were pinching my feet, but I kept watch anyway. After a while, Mama said, "It's late, Jaynie. He's not coming." She walked to her bedroom and shut the door.

My fingers and lips tingled. A humming sound filled my ears until the pressure was so high that I thought my head might explode. I wanted to be angry, but there was also worry. Since he hadn't called, I was inclined to think he might've had a flat tire or such and was still on his way.

I reached for the phone, then pulled my hand back. I wasn't going to chase him. To beg him for an explanation. To ask if he was coming or not.

So I waited. I still had hope he'd drive up any moment now. He'd explain. But hope or just plain lying to myself didn't change the *stood-up* sensation that wrapped itself around me and branded me. My living room had never looked so small, so drab, so . . . inadequate. Same as me.

Mama didn't come back out of her room, and I decided I didn't want to be standing here when she did. I went to my room and shut the door. But when I lay down, I did so fully dressed, just in case . . . Wyatt might yet show up.

CHAPTER EIGHT

I needed an acceptable explanation from Wyatt for why he left me hanging that evening, but the weekend passed, and he didn't show up with an apology or come begging for forgiveness. On Monday morning I went to school glad that no one knew I'd expected to be attending the dance with Wyatt. Part of me wanted him to see my face, to understand what he'd done to me and how he'd hurt me. Between second and third period that happened. I saw him coming up the hallway, and as he neared me, he passed me a note. I stopped as he slipped the paper into my hand, but he kept going.

I moved out of the between-class people crush before reading the note.

Meet me at the bleachers after last class.

The school bus was my ride home. If he was all that serious about talking to me, he could do it at *my* convenience. I crumpled the note and tossed it into the trash can.

Wyatt came to Ruth's house the next day acting all annoyed because I hadn't gone to the sports field as instructed. As if I'd stood *him* up.

The fence was there between us like a referee of sorts.

"I was all dressed up and waiting, Wyatt. Not a call from you. Nothing. Not even a message passed to me through your grandmother."

His face flushed, but he looked more angry than

embarrassed. "That's what I wanted to explain to you yesterday."

"Don't you dare give me a hard time. You know I can't stay after. I have to catch the bus home." I shook my head and dismissed him. "I'm easy enough to find anytime you want to chat."

"You're angry. I don't blame you. Things blew up at home. Mom changed her mind—I don't know why—and then my stepdad got involved and . . . Anyway. I couldn't leave. I'm sorry. I did call. I called your house phone over and over."

"You didn't. I stood there right beside that phone, sure you'd call any minute."

"I did. I tried. I called and called. You don't have voice mail." He crossed his arms too. "Then I had to take Bill to the emergency room. We thought he might be having a heart attack. He wasn't. But he thought . . . anyway, I had to drive him while Mom rode in the back with him."

I wanted to believe him. I didn't want to harden my heart. But two adults—and one almost adult—and none of them thought to call an ambulance? Nope, sounded to me like just more chaos. Maybe his mom hadn't been so willing after all.

In addition to my crossed arms, I now took a step back. "Well, I appreciate you making all this effort to explain it to me, Wyatt. Now, if you'll excuse me, I have things to do." I turned and stalked off.

He could've called out. He could've jumped over that fence and chased after me. But he didn't. I was sorry he chose not to, but I didn't blame him. He knew as well as I did that we had no business trying to be anything more than whatever it was we already were. Sometime friends—that's all we'd ever been.

When I entered the house, the phone drew me like a magnet. I stood there staring at it. Unable to resist, I picked up the receiver.

Hah. He'd lied. The dial tone was strong.

I cradled the receiver. After a moment, on impulse, I picked up the base and checked the switch on the side. The ringer was turned off.

How long? Who knew? There was no question as to who had turned the ringer off because it wasn't me. Why? Was it to sabotage my date?

Probably not. When had I last heard it ring? Not a clue. Besides, I was pretty sure that in her own way and for her own reasons Mama was disappointed that the date hadn't happened. Disappointed for me or for herself? Who knew? I surely did not.

I could've called Wyatt on the night of the dance. I had his number. I hadn't because of pride. And, truly, it wouldn't have made a difference anyway. I would still have been all dressed up and going nowhere.

I went to my bedroom and fell across my bed and cried myself to sleep.

~~~~

A month or two later, as I prepared to get off the school bus where our private dirt road met the main road, I pushed up the collar of my coat, hunched my shoulders, and had my umbrella ready to deploy. I was grateful that my backpack was almost empty, so I'd be able to move faster. Heavy-looking, dark banks of clouds moved across the sky, and blustery showers had been blowing through on and off all day. I tried to hurry, to run along the dirt—now mud—road and to the house to beat the next squall. A few fat warning drops fell. Head down, shoulders hunched, and one hand hanging tight to the loose strap of my book bag, I picked up my pace. An unfamiliar truck was parked in front of the house. Not Mama's car. Someone may have had to give her a ride home.

At least it's not Boone's wreck, I thought. He hadn't been around in a long time. I was pretty sure he was still seeing Mama, but she hadn't brought him home again.

I entered swiftly, grateful the door was unlocked, but just inside, I came to a dead stop. Boone *was* here.

He was in my living room, sitting at one end of the sofa. A stranger was seated at the other end. Boone's legs and arms were sprawled out like he belonged here. No lights were on. The living room, the kitchen . . . they were dark. My eyes adjusted slowly. Given the already dim light outside, there wasn't much for them to adjust to.

"What are you doing here? Where's my mom?"

Boone pulled in his big feet and sat forward. "We were invited here by your mom. She still owns this place, don't she?" He held up a shiny bit of metal and gave that short laugh intended to show no hard feelings. "She gave me this too."

A key. Our house key?

Who was that other man? He had black hair and very long fingers, and I couldn't read his face. My head began to spin a little.

Boone said, "Bella went on a quick run for beer and snacks. We ran out—so she ran out." He laughed again.

"She'll be back anytime now. Come inside and close that door before the rain blows in and wets everything." He gestured at the two of them sitting there. "Come visit with us. This here is—"

I closed the front door reflexively. My mind was momentarily blank, feeling only Boone's thoughts. Toying with me, angry with me. The other man's eyes were harder to read, but I felt expectation in his manner, perhaps in the way his hand moved on the armrest, his fingers toying with the fringe of the pillow as if his brain was busy. Were they predators? I didn't know, but I felt like the prey, and that was *all* I needed to know. There wasn't any logic in my thought. Just the ether that Ruth had spoken of, and it was telling me . . . *Not here. Don't be here.*

I didn't stay for the introduction. They thought I was cowed or stupid or who knew what, but I went straight to the kitchen. In one smooth move, I flipped the back-door lock to open and left.

It was full-out raining now. I lowered my face against the rain and ran, my backpack jouncing on my back. I should've tried kicking them out. I felt miserable, cowardly, and I was furious. I reached Ruth's back door and knocked hard. There was no answer, but I still had her key from when she'd gone out of town. I fished it out of the zipped pocket on my pack and opened the door.

I walked inside and closed the door against the rain. The house seemed dark and empty.

"Ms. Ruth?"

There was no answer. I set my backpack on the linoleum, closed the door, then leaned back against it, feeling almost plastered to the door and too weak to move.

It was Wednesday. Ruth usually met friends for lunch on Wednesdays. Instead of wearing her stretchy pants or one of those full skirts she liked, she'd dress up in her pantsuit and wrap a scarf around her shoulders and pin it with a bejeweled creation of flowers and butterflies. It was my favorite. She often did her grocery shopping on the way home, so it was reasonable that she might not be home yet, especially given the weather.

I sighed. A part of me had wanted to unburden my heart of its fear and anger, maybe even to cry on her shoulder and enjoy the luxury of showing weakness and need. But the other part of me—the Bella part—didn't want anyone to know the truth, that some people—those men—might have seen me as prey, a victim. Their victim. As if it cast a stain on me instead of them. On the other hand, if they'd just had the bad manners or bad timing to be in my house when I came home and I'd overreacted, then maybe they hadn't done anything wrong, but I still didn't owe them the opportunity to prove otherwise.

Was I making something out of nothing? Again, I felt that voice or whatever it was that inhabited the ether and swirls, telling me to lie low for a while. To breathe and relax. That I was safe now.

Might as well relax. I had nowhere to go but home, and I wasn't gonna go there right now.

The jar was sitting on the counter full of its treasure—the silver dollars that Ruth and I had cleaned four years earlier.

I picked up the jar and hugged it. It was heavy. It wasn't mine, but I pretended for a few minutes, standing there with my eyes closed and feeling the weight of that jar, that with it

I could buy any future I wanted. My sodden hair dripped on the lid. I put the jar back on the counter. I snagged my backpack from where I'd left it near the door and unzipped it. Still pretending, I put the jar in. It weighed a ton. In actual dollars, there was probably only two hundred or so, but I wondered if they might fetch more from a collector. If they were mine, that is.

They weren't, of course. In a moment, I'd take that jar out of my backpack. I'd return it to the counter before anyone was the wiser. They wouldn't understand I was pretending. No one would understand that or believe it.

I was reaching back to the zipper and saw I'd made a wet puddle on the floor with my dripping wet clothing. I kicked off my shoes, shrugged off my coat, left it on the floor next to the backpack, and went to the bathroom to grab a towel. Ruth had left the bathroom light on. I switched it off. I toweled my hair as I walked back to the kitchen and then mopped up the puddle. In the midst of all that, Ruth's phone rang.

Ruth had a push-button phone on an end table beside the front window. Of course, the call wouldn't be for me, and so I let it ring. When it started ringing again, it occurred to me that Mama might have returned home and assumed I'd be over here. Last thing I wanted was for her to come looking for me. Would she? Not likely, but who knew what was going on with her? Look at the filth she'd brought home today. I grabbed the phone.

"Hello?"

"Ruth, honey?"

"This is Jaynie, Ruth's neighbor."

"Of course, Jaynie, Ruth has spoken of you. Is she okay?

I was worried when she didn't show up for lunch and didn't answer the phone. Is she there with you?"

That ether hit me again. It slammed me like a hard, cold fist in the pit of my stomach and grew so big it even stopped my lungs from working. Through the curtains, I saw Ruth's car parked outside. I hadn't noticed it before.

Distantly, I heard the voice say, "You okay, Jaynie? Are you still there?" I set the phone receiver down on the table.

She was in her bedroom, facedown on the floor. She was wearing her strawberry housecoat but had lost one pink terrycloth slipper. It was nearby.

Something had happened. It didn't look violent. It just looked final.

I knelt and touched the side of her face, her cheek, just to be sure. It was cool, too cool for living flesh. She must've passed hours ago. I reached for the blanket on the bed, instinctively needing to cover her swollen calves, her defenseless state, and that one bare foot. But I stopped short as I remembered that Ruth was past caring.

I backed out of the room. I suppose my intention was to return to the phone, but instead my eyes focused on a framed photo of Ruth and me from a year or so ago. Ruth was laughing as she often did, and we stood there with locked arms, my cheek resting on her shoulder. A sweet moment. It was one of my favorite pictures. Wrapped around it were the memories of the times we'd shared. The laughter. The crazy talk. The ether.

I held the picture to my cheek, then hugged the frame. The glass over the photo protected it from my general dampness. The image of Ruth on the bedroom floor was already receding, being replaced by this picture of her laughing.

The phone began making a loud beeping noise—a fast beep intended to alert someone that the call had been disconnected and the receiver wasn't properly reset in its cradle. Reflexively, I picked up the receiver and hung it up and saw a car—the sheriff's car pulling up in front of the house. The sheriff climbed out of his car wearing his brimmed hat and a transparent slicker over his uniform. I recognized him, though I didn't know him well. When you had a mama like mine, you tended to know a lot of people connected to trouble one way or another. I went to the door and opened it wide as he came up the steps. He stopped at the open door and stood there as if trying to interpret the mystery written on my face. Then he knelt on one knee such that he was now looking up at me.

"Jayne? Jayne Highsmith? Is Ms. Ruth here?"

Squeezing my eyes shut, I pretended I was five—maybe even six—and of no importance and with no accountability. But the forced denial couldn't last. That kind of hiding was beyond me now because I was nearly grown.

I nodded.

"Is she okay?"

I shook my head, but now I was trying to find my voice. It came out like a harsh, wet blubbery sound. "In the bedroom."

He moved me aside—it was done gently and adroitly—and I stepped away into the background with gratitude. I found myself in the kitchen next to my pile of wet shoes, coat, and backpack. I heard the sheriff speaking into a black walkie-talkie type of radio as he walked out of the bedroom and into the living room, and then he saw me standing in the kitchen.

"Some officers will be coming over here in a very few minutes. I'd like to ask you a question or two. Can you tell me how you came to be here?"

"I came over after school. I have a key. Ms. Ruth usually shops on Wednesday afternoon, so I wasn't surprised that she wasn't home yet."

"I see. What do you have there?"

He was staring at the frame in my arms. I handed it to him. He looked at it, looked at me. I saw his eyes were moist. A lot like mine. Silently, he handed the frame back to me. He said, "I reckon this is as much yours as hers." He stood. "Is your mom at home?"

His question caught me unawares. Might've been just as well, as it turned out. "No, sir. Or, rather she wasn't when I got home from school, but two men were—" I broke off suddenly, realizing that I was about to say something embarrassing, and not sure who it would've embarrassed. Me? My mother?

"Two men? Did you know them?"

That misty look in his eyes was gone now, but something else, a harder look, was in his face. I was pretty sure that whatever had spoken to me from the ether—well, he might be hearing it too.

Softly, I said, "I know one of them. Boone. Mama's boyfriend. He was there with another man. He said they were waiting for Mama to come back from a run . . . from the store. I didn't want to wait there alone with them, so I came over here to visit . . ."

"Are you okay, Jayne?"

I couldn't help but glance in the direction of the

bedroom. And I shrugged because there were no words appropriate to answer him. We heard vehicles crunching gravel and the motors and doors slamming, and he said, "Hang out here for a while, okay?"

"Sure."

He left me there in the kitchen. I shook out my crumpled coat and put my shoes back on. But when I grabbed the straps of my backpack, I nearly dropped it again. Heavy. Very heavy. And I remembered what I'd done. In that moment, my chest seized up, my face—my whole body probably—flushed hot and red. Prayers I didn't even know I knew flew up into heaven and into the ether, hoping to be heard.

Men and women in uniforms—deputies and EMTs maybe—filled the living room. Almost every one of them cast at least one curious glance at me. If they knew what I'd stashed in my backpack, they would believe I'd stolen Ruth's money. My fingers were frozen on the straps.

If I waited, there might be a moment when I was alone. When I could unzip my pack and pull out that jar and set it back on the counter.

If I was caught? Oh, dear Lord. If I was caught, they'd think I'd stolen it and had maybe hurt Ruth for it. No, not that. They couldn't believe that. But even if they didn't think I'd had anything to do with her passing, they'd see me as someone so low that she'd steal from her own best friend—her own dear, dead, defenseless friend. My fingers released the strap and flew back to hugging the picture frame to my chest even more tightly. *Now what?*

I might go to jail . . . At the very least, I'd be arrested.

I didn't see that an emergency vehicle had blocked access to our dirt road such that no one could drive away from my house, even if Boone or his buddy caught a glimpse of the official activity happening up the road. And I didn't notice the deputy who, after a quick chat with the sheriff, went on down the road to my house.

People were still milling around, focused on what they were doing. I was in the way. I couldn't just leave. Someone might question me trying to take my own stuff from the house—for instance, if there was going to be an investigation.

In an unobserved moment, I moved my backpack nearer the back door. I opened the door and saw the rain had abated.

A deputy was in the living room. I said, "Mind if I wait outside?"

He gave me a wave. "That's fine."

That was my ticket out. I picked up my backpack and stepped outside and headed to the woods. That was still outside, wasn't it? I hadn't said *where* outside.

I was well out of sight before I stopped to put the backpack on my shoulders. As heavy and awkward as it was, it was really the only way I could manage it. I wouldn't think about anything else. Nothing. Not the sheriff, not Mama, not Boone, not . . . Ms. Ruth. For now, it was just me and my backpack heading to the rock, putting one foot in front of the other.

But before I got there, I started thinking about Wyatt. Ruth was his grandmother. She meant so much to me—like the mother of my heart—but she was his actual grandmother. This would hurt him badly. I bit my lip to keep it from quivering and walked faster.

The rock was wet but already drying where the sunlight peeked out from between the clouds and hit its surface. I sat with my backpack situated between my legs, unzipped it, and pulled out the jar. It was my mark of shame. However unintended the theft (it had been unintended, right?), it was stealing. Ruth would be so disappointed . . . No, Ruth wouldn't because she wasn't here. She was past caring about that, or anything, I reminded myself.

Even having seen her lying on the floor, there was a big part of my brain that rejected the truth. I couldn't quite hold on to the reality. It wanted to slip away. It was more possible to imagine Wyatt's grief than my own.

At some point I had to go back. Or go home. I couldn't count on being able to return the jar to Ruth's house before heading home. And I couldn't take the jar home. Therefore . . .

I lay down on my side with one arm crooked between my head and the damp rock. A few tears ran down my cheek onto the stone. I brought my other arm up so I could cover my face with my free hand.

I didn't know how long I lay there. Not really asleep. Just not present. After a while, I felt the breath moving in and out of my lungs. The slight stinging of salty tears in my eyes. And a tiny prickling feeling on my arm—the arm that wasn't pillowing my head. I felt the prickling on my forearm as if the fine, tiny hairs were moving. Ever so slowly, I opened my eyes.

A dragonfly. It had landed on the narrow area of my wrist exposed by the turned-up cuff of my coat. The insect was light, and its legs were as thin as the thinnest hair on my arm. It moved slightly, almost as if to get a better look at me with its protruding insect eyes. It fluttered its fragile, lacy wings but didn't leave me. I squeezed my eyes shut, and when I opened them again, it was still there. I blinked and it was gone.

Dragonfly season had ended months ago. There were no dragonflies around now.

I pressed my hand to my chest. I hadn't worn the necklace in a long, long time.

It was getting late. With the cloud cover, it seemed dark earlier than usual. By now, Mama must surely be aware of what had happened. She might be looking for me. If she was in the mood for drama, she might be screaming at the sheriff to form a search party. I surely didn't want that.

I buried Ruth's jar near the rock, near to the toolbox. When everyone left Ruth's house—probably tomorrow—I'd fetch the jar of silver dollars and return it. I'd put it back in her house and walk away. Whoever came along later to sort things out, probably Wyatt's mom, would never even know it had been missing.

Thoughts of the dragonfly and Ruth's long-ago words seemed to entwine—*own it or it will own you.*

All will be well, I told myself. *One way or another.* I had the know-how and the tools, thanks to Ms. Ruth.

As it turned out, when I walked into my kitchen, I saw Mama through the door to the living room. She was sitting on the sofa. I stood, my backpack still in hand, and looked around. No one else. Only Mama.

"Hi, Mama," I said, and went past to put my backpack in my bedroom and hang my coat on the bedpost. I took the opportunity to slip into the bathroom and wash the dirt from my hands. When I returned to the living room, Mama was still sitting there, silent and looking lost.

I said, "Ms. Ruth is gone. I guess you know."

She shot me a look. "I guess I do. Sheriff's deputy told me himself. Frank Helms. Did you know he was a friend of your father's? Long time gone." She added in a low voice, "Guess that's why he felt free to tell me how to manage my family. Like I don't already know. Telling me who should be coming round here, here in my own home." She sighed and resumed her normal voice. "Did you know your daddy was a deputy? Did I ever tell you that? Probably not. It was all he ever wanted. More even than he wanted me. There I was, stuck at home, pregnant. Mitch was too young to be useful but young enough to be getting into everything. And where was your father? He was out chasing after that deputy job when he already had good-paying work at the lumber mill." She went silent again and then shook her head, which seemed to restart her. "He finally got the job. He was oh so proud. He had a uniform and a hat and all that stuff. To celebrate, he went fishing with his Uncle Lou, and they got themselves drowned in a stupid pond. He left me with his son and a baby about to be born any day."

No, I hadn't known about the deputy part.

"I did my best, Jaynie. Not good enough, I'm sure. But a woman alone . . . with kids. Did you know I was once a beauty? That's what they called me in school. Beauty. Men and women both. Somewhere along the way, I lost that. But you look a lot like me. You watch out for the world, Jaynie girl, because when you're not looking, it'll chew you up and spit you out."

Mama looked at me speculatively. "I guess you'll want to go to the funeral." She paused to gnaw on a rough cuticle. "No one would think twice about it, with you and Ruth being so close."

I thought of a casket and of seeing Ruth Berry laid out in it. Flowers would be arranged all around. People would be speaking in soft voices. And then I saw Ruth's face but without the life in it. Her dark but very warm eyes, cold and hidden behind closed lids. Closed forever.

My stomach twisted, and I felt light-headed. "I guess not, Mama. I think I'll skip it."

She seemed surprised, and her mouth hung open for a second while she sorted it out in her mind. She said, "Your choice. I never have understood you, Jaynie. Never." She shook her head. "It'll be easier on me, for sure. Folks would be mighty curious to see me at that woman's service, plus me and Demaris in the same room together . . . We had a big fallout long ago. I don't suppose you know about that. But whew, it was the talk of the town for a while." She touched her hair. "Come to think of it, I might just go after all. Get me some satisfaction. You let me know if you change your mind."

She rose, that speculative light in her eyes, and went down the short hallway to her bedroom and shut the door.

Later, I regretted saying I didn't want to go. I would have liked to pay my respects and could even have been there as support for Wyatt. It was a missed opportunity, but he would surely have other friends there with him, or he'd be tending to his mom.

As for Ms. Ruth, I had some of the best parts of her, including the memories of her goodness to me and the lessons she'd taught me, tucked securely in my heart where no one could steal or soil them.

CHAPTER NINE

Long ago, Ms. Ruth said, "Some choices are ours to make, and some are forced upon us. It's what you do with those choices that turns them into opportunities."

When I was almost eighteen, I made my first big life choices. While the other kids in my graduating class were tossing their caps in the air and hugging and crying over how they were all going to miss those golden days—golden in their minds, not mine—I was on my way out of the high school stadium to catch my ride north. Mrs. Styles had helped me find a small room to rent in Fairfax within walking distance of public transportation, and a job, lowly though it was, that would keep me housed and fed if I restricted my diet to noodles and spent nothing on entertainment. But the morning I walked into the lobby of the high-rise on that first day of the job, I got stuck on the threshold, afraid to step onto those glossy marble floors.

My impression was of a vast lobby filled with brass fixtures, plush leather chairs, and lots of glass and lights. So grand. But other people walked through the luxurious space like it was nothing. I stepped out of their way and stood with my back pressed hard against the wall as I gathered my nerves.

My art teacher had been working on my confidence and

goals since my sophomore year in high school. She'd done her best to convince me that college was a possibility. But at the start of my junior year, Wyatt moved a few counties away with his mom and stepdad. He spent his senior year in a school many miles away. There were renters in Ms. Ruth's house, and apparently Wyatt had no reason whatsoever to be dropping by to visit anyone on Hope Road, because I certainly never saw him.

I missed passing him in the school corridors and exchanging an occasional word or smile. I began leaving early and skipping occasional classes—not too much, but noticeable enough for my art teacher to enlist the help of the high school guidance counselor, Mrs. Mary Styles. Mrs. Styles was a smart, bighearted woman. She and my art teacher tagged-teamed me and kept at it until I began to listen. I did try to get back on track, but the changes in me, along with dealing with Mama, made it difficult.

The day after Wyatt graduated, he finally drove over. He was standing in the dirt road by the fence, staring at his grandmother's house, and when he turned in my direction, he didn't motion toward me, but I knew he was waiting for me. As I'd done countless times through the years, I crossed the old, overgrown pasture behind Uncle Lou's house and met Wyatt at the fence.

"I'm leaving, Jaynie."

My breath caught. I tried to hide it by clearing my throat. "Not immediately, right? You just graduated yesterday."

He nodded. "Now. I'm taking off, just like I always said I would."

"But . . ." I stammered to a stop. Really, if he could leave like this then what was there to be said? But I had to say something. "I wish you well, Wyatt."

"I—" He broke off. He looked left and right and even rocked back and forth on his feet. Clearly, he had more to say.

"What? Go ahead and say whatever."

"I—" He stopped, breathed deeply, and then sighed. His voice sounded surer as he said, "I'll be in touch. I'll let you know how things go. Focus on school and don't get distracted. Graduate, Jaynie. The world is out there waiting for you."

"You too." I rushed to add, "I mean, don't you get distracted either." I wanted to move to him, touch him. But he stayed rigidly in place. Was that it? No hugs? No friendly arm bumps? It seemed so. "Travel safely, Wyatt."

His hands stayed firmly in his pockets. "Goodbye, Jaynie."

I couldn't say it. The G-word wouldn't come. I stared at him as I accepted what was happening. He nodded again, turned away, and all but ran to his car.

Disappointment was a word that had degrees but not sufficient depths to describe my pain.

I went home and sat in front of Mama's TV for the rest of the day and never even knew what was showing.

~~~~

My encouragers resumed their efforts at the start of my senior year. And I tried, for them, if not for me. But something inside me was broken. I didn't know how to explain it. I only knew that my toolbox didn't have what was required to fix it. I didn't bother trekking out to my rock. If my heart was repairable, then the fix was miles away from this place.

By November, both the art teacher and the guidance counselor accepted that college wasn't in my future at this time. *Later*, they said. I could get a degree later. For now, I needed to focus on a successful senior year. Mrs. Styles called me into her office.

"Jaynie," she said, "stick with it. Hang in here and get your diploma. You have the opportunity for a bright future. Don't let it slip away."

"For what?" I asked. "So that the day after graduation I can get a job at the convenience store with my mother?" I laughed harshly and waved a finger in the air. "Woo-hoo. Maybe we can even get on the same shift and carpool." I made a disgusted noise, shook my head, and stared out of the window beyond her. I thought of Wyatt. He was out there somewhere. He'd left—pretty much as he'd said he was going to do when we were kids sitting on the fence and wishing for happiness. I'd made plans too, but none of them were working out.

Mrs. Styles rapid-tapped her pen on the desktop. "You're right."

I gave her a look.

"With that attitude, all you'll find is the future you claim you want to avoid."

"So tell me where I'm wrong." I made a rude sound. "Staying in school was supposed to teach me how to get a job and a decent life, wasn't it? Nope. Not seeing any proof of that."

"Maybe it's in how you're looking at things. Even now, your grades are good. But you must keep your grade point average up and graduate for it to help you."

I didn't respond. I stared at the window beyond her, thinking that I'd walk out to the nearby woods and sit in the shade. Go read or sketch. This place . . . it was hard to breathe in here—as if each breath brought me closer to a real life that was even more suffocating than this one was. I needed a car. With a car, I wouldn't be stuck waiting for transportation out of here every day. I could leave at will. I could turn the key, press the accelerator, and keep going.

"Jaynie?" She spoke sharply.

"What?"

"You were a million miles away."

I shrugged and gave her a small smile. "Guess I was."

"I know your homelife is difficult, but that's not your permanent state. You have options, a choice, about your future. What would you say if I told you I could help you get a fresh start elsewhere?"

Suddenly I was listening.

"I have a friend in Fairfax. If I ask him, if I vouch for you, he'll find a place for you in his contracting firm."

Now I was sitting upright—hadn't even been aware of slouching until now that I wasn't.

"It's clerical. Administrative. Entry level. It won't be exciting, but it will be a change of scene and an opportunity."

The words spilled out before I knew I was saying them. "I'll do anything. Whatever."

"If I pull strings . . . if I ask him for this favor, I need to believe that you won't let him or me down. You must keep up your grades and get that diploma. And when you get that job, you'll have to work hard. Can you do that?"

"Yes." Then the doubt rolled in right on cue. I'd never been good enough. Why would that change? Being inadequate wasn't dependent on location.

"I see what's written on your face, Jayne." She came and sat in the chair next to mine. "Don't ever give in to fear—not fear of falling short, fear of failing, or of embarrassment. Don't give in to fear and feeling less than."

For a moment, I couldn't breathe. It was almost as if Ms. Ruth had come and set herself down next to me—had given those words to this woman for express delivery to me. I shivered. "Yes, ma'am."

"You do your part. Show me you are serious about this, and I'll talk to my friend. This could be your chance, Jayne. Once you get work experience, you can take that farther, whether with that employer or with another. Work for firms that have benefits, both health and education. Opportunities well used lead to other opportunities."

And I did work hard. Every time I felt that brokenness gaining strength over me, I doubled down on my schoolwork. But every evening I was back home with Mama. The highlights of our days were the rare occasions when Mitch dropped by, still needing to do his laundry. He lived his life from job to job, had the occasional girlfriend, but was a nice guy. The kind of guy everyone got along with. And he'd always be here in this place. We had nothing in common anymore. Mama spent a lot of time out, but she didn't bring anyone home, so I was grateful.

I waited until we were near graduation before I told her that the guidance counselor had found me a job. That I'd be leaving soon after the ceremony.

"That so?" Her face was pale, drained.

I could read her mind. She was thinking of her lonely home—all the lonelier with me gone. I didn't believe she'd keep the boyfriend or boyfriends away for long. She couldn't have handled being alone. I ached a little for her, surprised to feel sympathy.

"Well," she said. "I guess I did the right thing then after all. You doing so good in school and all and getting a good job proves it. Not like any of these crap, dead-end jobs I've had to work for years. And now you're going off to start a whole new life."

"Mama—"

"Oh, but that's just life, right? A person can only do her best . . ." She shook her head. "I know I wasn't a good mother. I do know. But I tried." She laughed and raised her glass, waving it like a toast to heaven. "Once I saw an old headstone, and you know what was engraved on it? *She hath done what she could*. I always wondered about that, right? Like not that she did well, or even that she did her best, just what she could. I guess that's what I did. What I could."

She'd been drinking all afternoon, and it was showing. I smiled, deciding not to argue with her. I'd be gone soon anyway. She turned to put her glass in the sink.

"But I did one thing right. Always felt like I should say something, but no mother, even a bad one, wants to break her daughter's heart."

She had my attention.

"So I didn't tell you that Demaris always suspected her boy was fathered by Georgie. Good old George. They had an affair. Demaris was never sure whether Wyatt belonged to her husband or to mine. Because of the timing, you know."

Mama kept her back turned and pretended to be busy at the kitchen sink. "Course she didn't tell me anything about the affair until after George was drowned and you were born.

One day she broke bad on me and told me what they'd done."

I heard myself gasping, felt the gasp as if my whole body were reacting to a sudden loss of oxygen, but Mama didn't notice. She kept on talking.

"I told her that we couldn't have you two palling around—being a boy and girl, I mean, and getting a little too friendly when maybe you shouldn't. Shouldn't be, you know? *Because.*"

She shook her head. "I told Dee, you keep your boy away from my Jaynie. When she agreed to you two going to that dance, I thought she'd figured the daddy part out somehow. But maybe she hadn't, since she made sure the date didn't happen." She made an odd noise. "Likely that boy of hers backed her into a corner over it. She couldn't come out and tell him without . . . well, without *telling* him."

My chest hurt, but I forced the words out. "You should've told me." My voice sounded wrong. Low and rough.

She turned toward me. "I've thought that many a time. But as it turned out, it didn't matter, did it, honey? Jaynie girl, you and Wyatt were never that close. Just friends from time to time. No harm done." She laughed again. "Except to me. And maybe to Demaris. For lo, these many years. Heaven knows, when I told her husband about the affair, he took off like a shot. Left her and the boy high and dry. Served her right." As she stumbled out of the kitchen and headed toward her bedroom, I heard her singing, "She hath done what she could."

She hath done what she could.

Numb, I left the house and wandered blindly through the field. When I reached the fence, I fell against it and dropped my head onto my arms and tried to breathe.

Mama had done what she could to contribute to the chaos. She didn't know what the words meant but I did. I'd learned it from a sermon during one of those church visits with Ms. Ruth.

It was a story about a woman who'd done something nice for Jesus. Not because she was asked and not for show. She wasn't even getting paid for the oil she used up. In fact, some of the folks there criticized her. But she did it because it seemed to her the right thing to do.

I thought I'd like to be that kind of person.

Not like my mother who'd just made certain sure that any tiny hope I might've continued to cherish about Wyatt and me having a future, especially after the way he'd left, had been fully extinguished.

~~~~

In the days that followed, Mama seemed to forget she'd told me that Wyatt, my Wyatt, might actually be my half brother. I made it through my exams in a fog with no idea how I passed them. Over and over, in my head I saw Mitch at the picture window. Tall. Slim. Dark haired and almost black eyes. And I saw Wyatt standing by the fence. Tall. Slim. Dark haired. Coal-black eyes.

And me. Standing alone.

I couldn't get out of town fast enough. And when I did, I left those people behind, including all thoughts of the people in my past—Wyatt among them.

~~~~

Still standing with my back against the wall of that fancy lobby, I heard Mrs. Styles's voice again warning me not to give in to fear. She'd said everyone felt intimidated at first, until they learned to hide it or the newness wore off. She said I could too. And she was right. As I stepped onto that glossy marble and moved from the wall into the lobby, I reminded myself that I could indeed do that. Whatever Mama had or hadn't taught me, she'd taught me stubbornness, persistence, and how to control my reactions and when to pick my fights. Mrs. Styles had helped me choose clothing at the consignment shop that would be appropriate for the job, and together we'd selected what I should wear to my first day on the job. She'd coached me to hold my head up and—not in an arrogant way—to move and walk as if I belonged here.

I crossed the last few yards to the reception desk, hoping I was, in fact, dressed right and would speak right and not trip over my shoes. Shoes. I couldn't help a swift glance down to check for dirty ankles or feet, even though I knew they wouldn't be. Dirt wasn't like tattoos. Washing cured dirt. And my hair was pulled back into a neat, all-business ponytail. I tried to breathe in a relaxed way and not sweat through my blouse.

The receptionist asked my name, and I said, "Ruth."

Stunned. Shocked. I stammered, "Jayne Highsmith, actually." I added quickly, "My friends call me Ruth. I'm looking for Simmons and Baker, please."

The receptionist's expression went from blank to a thin smile. "Certainly," she said as she checked a list. She pointed toward the elevators and added, "Third floor. Turn right."

"Thank you." I made it to the elevator slightly dazed. What on earth had come over me? How stupid had I sounded? *My friends call me Ruth.* Had I really said that?

It was my nerves speaking. It wouldn't happen again.

But when I stepped off the elevator on the third floor and the man at that desk asked my name, I said, "Jayne Highsmith, but my friends call me Ruth." This time the lie came out as smooth as warm butter.

The man's smile was broad and genuine as he replied, "Hello, Ruth. Welcome."

He'd taken my remark as an invitation to be friends. I faked a smile and nodded back at him, hiding my embarrassment.

I was stunned by my outrageous claiming of Ruth's name. It didn't require any deep thought to understand my impulse. I hadn't wanted to hear Jayne or Jaynie from the lips of these people. This was my new life. I'd left the girl I used to be behind. Hearing them say Ruth's name brought home the sweetness of the memories of my lost friend. Of the summer days and autumn leaves and chewing over conversations about life and its mysteries. I preferred to hear "Ruth," and to feel like that person, than to have them calling me by my given name and hear my mother's scolding voice or her harsh teasing.

No emotional tantrums or capricious emotional storms were allowed in my new life. And this time I was the one setting the rules.

~~~~~

From my first day at Simmons and Baker, a defense contracting firm, I worked hard and smart, even though the entry-level work was boring and my starting salary was meager. I was treated with respect by my coworkers and managers and received good performance ratings, promotions, and regular raises that allowed me to improve my standard of living. While my jobs weren't high-powered or glamorous, I knew my dedication was appreciated, and I appreciated that attitude and gave it right back to them. I held my head high and I was Ruth, but minus the shiny bangles and her philosophical bent.

Simmons was an established, respected firm that contracted specific services with the government, and we were known for delivering staff and accounting services as contracted and ahead of schedule. Both in and out of the workplace I had friends, all congenial. Civility. Courtesy. These things were very important to me. I had lacked those in my life. But also lacking in my life was the deeper comfort of having the *ONE*—of knowing that I was someone's particular person and that that person was mine beyond any other human being. I'd never had that kind of relationship, though I knew a little of what it should feel like because I'd come close to it as a child when Ruth had taken pity on me, a dusty, heading-for-wild child, and had gifted me with her love and concern.

Twelve years after graduation and my big getaway, I made new choices—undoing most of what I'd worked so hard to accomplish—when Justin Hale, with his sun-brushed hair and striking blue eyes, came into my life.

The owner and CEO of Simmons was Rob Baker. Not that I knew him, even after a dozen years in his employ. I didn't work on the executive floor and rarely caught sight of him, but he had a good reputation among the staff. Justin had joined the company just over a year ago, and we crossed paths in meetings. He was a handful of years older than me, but with much more influence. People listened to him, not only because he was an executive on the way up, but rumor had it that he was personal friends with the CEO, who'd courted him to come on board.

Justin wasn't the first man to pay attention to me, and a couple of my former boyfriends had been nice guys. They'd been determined, too, because I was, after all, breathing, healthy, employed, and—as Mama had often said—I had inherited her looks. But Justin was different. He made me feel special.

He began showing up near my work area, apparently there on business with my manager's manager, but he'd shoot me a glance and a quick grin. I was tripped up by love or something like it. Perhaps his power and increasingly obvious interest and approval attracted me. That's the most reasonable explanation I can come up with for why I would willingly allow him—or anyone—to turn my carefully crafted life upside down.

I basked in the glow of his perfect smile but kept my outward response cool. I was sure no one suspected our tiny, harmless flirtation.

At home in my apartment, I allowed myself to daydream about a future with him, not necessarily wanting this specific relationship to happen but imagining a life of romance and ease. Later, I blamed myself for that—wondering if I'd sent messages to the ether or the cosmos. Had those hopes been received and answered? What did the sages say? Be careful what you wish for because you might get it? Ms. Ruth had certainly warned me more than once to be aware of what you were contributing to the ether.

When Justin and I finally connected and that igniting spark shot between us, the rest was inevitable. In those rare, private moments with Justin, I relished his arms around me and our hurried, passionate kisses. I anticipated the small but expensive gifts he bought me—a flower sealed in amber, a silver bracelet with a heart charm, and such things as that. Soon we were finding discreet restaurants we both enjoyed or working late together but getting little work done. When the CEO showed up at Justin's office unexpectedly, we were nearly caught. But Justin was smooth, inviting him in and thanking me for something or other as I slipped out the door with a flushed face and embarrassed expression. We laughed about it later, but Justin said we needed to be more careful.

"There isn't a rule about employees dating," I said, thinking that as much as I liked Justin—and was apparently falling for him—I didn't want to risk my job. After all, I was my sole support. I'd worked hard to get where I was.

"No rule." Justin put his arms around me. "But Rob doesn't like soap opera in the workplace."

A.k.a. chaos. "I agree with him."

"You are gorgeous, Ruth." His fingertips brushed my temple and cheek and went on to touch my hair.

Gorgeous. No one had ever called me gorgeous. I remembered Mama's voice telling me pretty girls had to be careful of men.

"But this," he said as he kissed me softly on the lips, "this is not soap opera. This is very real. And it's just between you and me. Trust me, Ruth."

I kissed him back to show I did agree and that I trusted him.

Our restaurant. Our song. We loved the excitement of sneaking moments together in offices and empty meeting rooms for a quick embrace. It all added up to romance. I was single, and Justin's divorce was recent. He was open about it. His wife had wanted the divorce because she couldn't continue being married to someone who was too dedicated to his work. He said his first wife had had similar complaints. I was dedicated to my job too, so that could be in our favor.

Maybe my need for a special someone of my own made me easy pickings. Even so, I'd held back part of myself—that part I'd worked so hard to leave behind on Hope Road—and it piped up now to warn me. I ignored it.

It was inevitable that a couple of my closer coworkers would notice something going on. They warned me that getting involved with Justin wasn't good for my career or my heart. I refused any suggestion that his prior marriages predicted anything whatsoever about our future happiness.

The first time Justin took me to his home I was floored. These large brick houses were fairly typical in Northern Virginia, imposing homes with small but perfect lawns, in pocket subdivisions where the streets were always freshly paved and a pothole wouldn't last a day.

Justin's home was elegant. The furnishings were perfect but had an impersonal quality. I mused over that unlived-in quality as I walked on the block-and-concrete patio that adjoined the inground pool and a small bathhouse. Justin had excused himself to take a call. While I waited, I wandered up the steps to the covered, raised grill area, which was almost as well appointed as the interior rooms, but as I checked it out, it was clear that the grill had never been used.

This home lacked a family.

I heard no sounds and saw no one from the nearest houses. It was a quiet area . . . Maybe everyone here worked to pay these huge mortgages? Well, that was also true of Justin, right? He was a businessperson on the way up, and the circles he traveled in were far different from my own. I couldn't begin to imagine Bella or Mitch Highsmith fitting in here. Nor Jaynie, not as she'd—I'd—been before.

Did the upgraded version of me fit in better? I wasn't sure. Maybe my friends were right to warn me not to commit.

But at night when I was alone in my apartment, I would remember the polished leathered granite I'd run my fingers over while in the guest bathroom and the mirrorlike marble floors and draperies and window treatments in the large dining room. Those alone cost more than I made in a year, maybe two years. I knew people lived like this, but I'd never, ever envisioned that I might. I wouldn't sell myself for luxury and security. Security obtained through someone else's success was ephemeral at best. And each morning when I woke and dressed for work, grabbing a cup of coffee and a toasted English muffin as I left and headed for the metro, I laughed, remembering I'd already gotten everything I'd wanted. I didn't need the frills of Justin's world, and I didn't belong there.

Yet Justin thought I was gorgeous. He said he loved me.

One day, he asked me to move in with him.

Chapter Ten

"Move in?" I asked. "What does that mean?"

"I'll be traveling a lot in the coming year. Come with me. We'll see the world together."

"Great for your job. Not for mine."

Justin took my hand in his. "If I didn't know you better, I'd think you were playing hard to get. You are a mystery to me. I want to know the Ruth behind the controlled exterior. I want to know your secrets." He tightened his arms around me. "Besides, I've married and failed twice. I won't lie to you, Ruth. I wouldn't be interested in jumping back into marriage—if not for you." He put his arm around me and pulled me close. "If it's important to you, then it means the world to me."

It sounded so good. When I was in his presence, when I was with him and he focused on me as if I were truly his entire world, I melted.

A week later, I walked into work and found roses in a vase on my desk and balloons tied to my chair. A small black jewelry box was front and center on my desk. The attention of everyone in the office was focused on me.

I stopped several feet away from the desk. Now what? I hadn't lived through anything like this before. I felt like an actress on opening night who hadn't seen the script yet. It was surprisingly difficult to breathe. In that long silent moment, I heard, "Ruth," spoken softly. I looked toward the voice. It was Justin. Right there in front of everyone around us, he moved forward, picked up the small case, and reached for my hand.

"Marry me, Ruth."

He looked so handsome, so distinguished, despite the overhead fluorescent lighting. I touched my hair and wished I'd taken more care with my makeup and my outfit. If I'd had warning or if the proposal had been private . . .

"Of course, Justin." I gave him my hand.

Everyone clapped and cheered. It felt unreal, like a movie set.

Someone shouted, "When's the date?"

Justin put an arm around me and laughed, saying, "As soon as possible." With a change of tone, he said, "Thank you, everyone, for sharing this moment with us. I know that many of you were aware of the growing relationship between us, and many were cheering us on from the sidelines. I appreciate you sharing this special event with us." After a quick glance at me, he added, "Now I don't know about you all, but for me? It's back to work. Please excuse us." And he drew me away.

When we were alone, he said, "I hope you'll forgive me for doing it that way. There was talk. You and I deserve better than gossip, so now it's all out in the open." He clasped my hands in his. "And if you accepted my proposal because I put you on the spot, then you are free to let me know. I will be sad, but I'll do whatever makes you happy."

I threw my arms around his neck, and he grabbed me in a hug that lifted my feet clear of the floor, and we sealed the proposal and the acceptance with a kiss. A long kiss. Finally, we parted because this was our workplace, and whatever else occurred, the workday show must go on.

But having started the day with an over-the-top, life-altering moment, it was tough to resume the ordinary. Uneasiness weighed on me all day. I looked forward to supper with Justin. I felt caught in a weird time shift between the reality of one moment and the next, and I couldn't complete the transition. I'd feel better after talking to Justin. I always did. And as usual, sharing dinner with him that evening did dispel my doubts.

Two days later, I was walking down a long hallway to a meeting when I saw several men and women walking toward me. They were grouped around a man I recognized as Rob, our CEO. I moved to the side to make way for them, but Rob saw me and stopped. The others paused with him, but he motioned for them to continue, and with a swift glance at me in passing, they did.

Rob walked over to me. "Congratulations on your engagement?"

Yes, I heard it as a question.

"Thank you?" I said.

He smiled. I saw kindness in his expression. "I meant, are you happy . . . ?" He broke off, then resumed. "I hear it was very public."

"It was." I shrugged. "Justin surprised me."

Rob nodded. "You didn't feel pressured? You're good with this?"

How odd, I thought. *How exceptionally odd.*

"Yes."

"Good. I like a happy, drama-free work environment, but I'd never stand in the way of true love. Congratulations to you both."

He walked on.

I stood there, feeling that shift again. Caught between things out of place, suddenly re-sorting and me not knowing which way to go.

"Ruth?"

It was Sara. She asked, "You okay? You had the oddest look on your face. Are you ill?"

I forced a smile. "I'm fine."

"Was that Rob Baker?"

"It was. He offered congratulations on the engagement."

"Wow."

I asked, "Are you headed to the logistics meeting?"

"I am."

"Great. I wanted to mention a few things. Let's chat on the way?"

"Excellent."

And off we went. It was a relief to put that strange exchange with Rob out of my mind and think only about business.

That evening over dinner with Justin, I mentioned the encounter with Rob.

"Nice of him to express interest."

"Was it? It seemed odd."

"Offering congratulations?"

"Yes, but . . . he asked me if I was happy about it. Then he tried to make it sound as if he was speaking about the public nature of the proposal, but . . ."

"Then it's even nicer that he was concerned about your happiness. Rob is a great guy and an old friend of mine. He wants things to work out for us, of course, but—being real here, Ruth—Rob doesn't want problems in the workplace, and certainly nothing that would reflect negatively on the company. Reputation is more important than ever. Adverse allegations can come out of nowhere."

I nodded. He was right. I said, "Still, it was nice that he took the opportunity to speak to me personally."

"Rob is a good guy."

Justin always had a way of explaining things that made sense.

~~~~~

He'd mentioned his children before. Edward and Sylvan. Both were from his first marriage. Justin said he was on good terms with that wife, and that they worked to keep the relationship good for the children.

"I want you to meet them. I held off before because . . . well, introducing new people into their lives can be disruptive, especially if they turn out to be temporary."

"And I'm not."

"Most definitely not."

Justin thought meeting over a meal would be best. But it was a fancy place. I would've chosen somewhere more relaxed. Maybe a Dave & Buster's or a pizza restaurant. Edward, thirteen years old, had dark hair and nothing to say to me. He didn't look like Justin, so I presumed he took after his mother. Sylvan was about to turn twelve. She was quiet too, but she gave me many shy smiles. Her hair was almost white-blonde, and her eyes were blue, almost as blue as her father's. Her smiles encouraged me to suggest that she and her brother should be part of the wedding party.

"What do you think? Would you two stand with us at

our wedding?"

"Ruth," Justin warned. "It will be a small ceremony. Small and soon. That's what we both said we wanted."

"But it won't feel complete without your children there."

Justin's face looked flushed. Embarrassed? Annoyed? "I wish you'd spoken to me first."

I wanted to kick him under the table. The children shouldn't be hearing this. They wouldn't understand. They'd think they weren't wanted.

"I'd like that," Sylvan said.

Her light, high voice overruled her father's annoyance. I couldn't have stopped the smile that bloomed on my own face even if I'd wanted to.

Later, after we dropped the children off at their home, I said, "I can't help but feel we've missed an opportunity. I could've walked the children to the door. It would have been the perfect time to meet Sharon, to introduce myself."

"About that," Justin said. "Don't rush it. As for the children being part of the wedding, you should've let me check with her first. She might object. Now she'll hear about it from Sylvan, probably within the first ten seconds of her walking in the door. If Sharon's inclined to object, she'll be all the more unhappy about it."

"Wouldn't she assume that her children should take part in such an important day for their father? Especially since you two are on such good terms."

"But that doesn't include you." He caught my reaction. "Wait, that isn't what I meant. She doesn't *know* you. She's protective. Divorce is hard on kids. When she sees how happy and well grounded we are, she'll feel better about the children spending time with us."

"I hope so. I want to include them in our lives. Summers. Holidays. They can even travel with us."

"Wait, Ruth. Don't get ahead of things. We'll take it easy and let them become part of our lives naturally."

"Fine, but Sylvan wants to be part of the wedding, and I insist we do everything we can to make good on that."

"Agreed. I'll talk to Sharon."

"Good."

Justin sighed as he pulled into a parking space at my apartment complex. "Are you sure this is what you want? Marriage? With me? I'm afraid I'll let you down."

I touched his cheek. "Never."

He put his arm around me and pulled me closer, planting a kiss on my forehead. "Trust me, Ruth?"

"I do." I added, "Thanks for understanding about the children. I won't push with Edward, but I'd love to help Sylvan choose a dress for the ceremony."

"Ruth. I can't promise that. Her mother may have other ideas. But I'll do my best."

I laughed. "Your best? Then I'm sure you'll manage it."

"Should I walk you to the door? I wish I could stay."

"I wish you didn't have to go back to the office, but I understand." I laughed. "Get business handled. We have a honeymoon coming up in three weeks, and we're going whether your desk is clear or not."

"It's a deal."

~~~~

Frankly, I didn't plan to invite Mama and Mitch to the wedding. Justin didn't ask about them either. Staying in touch worked both ways, I told myself. Mama and I spoke on birthdays and some holidays, but it was never satisfying for either of us. We never stayed on the phone one moment longer than necessary. We communicated out of duty. Or guilt. I couldn't imagine Bella and Mitch Highsmith in the same room as Justin Hale and the friends I expected to invite to the ceremony. In the end, though, I did. Because . . . because, in the end, a person had to be able to look herself in the face.

Mama answered her phone. I explained.

"You're getting married?" she echoed.

"I am. It's going to be a very small ceremony. Just Justin and his children. A couple of friends. Would you like to attend?" I told her the date and time.

"That's quick," she said. "Are you pregnant?"

I closed my eyes and leaned my forehead against the cool wall. "No, I'm not."

"Well, then. I'll tell Mitch, and I'll get back to you."

She didn't, though. Mitch called me a few days later.

"Heard you're getting married," he said.

"I am. Will you and Mama be able to join us? I'm sure she told you it's a small ceremony."

"Is he a good guy, Jaynie? Someone who'll make you happy?"

"He is."

"Mama wants to come but she got a little . . . well, you know how she gets . . . after she told me. Probably not a good idea."

"What about you, Mitch? You're welcome without her." And he was. I kind of liked that idea.

"No, sis. I'd better hang here with her that day. I think

it brings back memories for her."

"I understand." I did, and I couldn't deny I felt relief that I'd made the offer and it had been declined.

~~~~~

A week and a half after meeting Justin's children, he texted me a photo. Sylvan was wearing a long, lovely white dress, embroidered with tiny rosebuds across the bodice.

I texted back, *It's beautiful. She's perfect. Thank you.*
See you at supper.
See you then.

~~~~~

At supper, at a restaurant Justin preferred to go to when he wanted a quiet meal—one where he wasn't likely to run into people from work or acquaintances—he said, "Edward will wear a suit. Sharon wants to be cooperative."

"That's wonderful."

"It is." After the waiter had taken our orders and left us, Justin said, "But nothing is ever simple, is it?"

"It can be, depending on how we choose to react and respond."

"You're my philosopher, aren't you? I should bring my troubles to you more often."

"I'm too earthbound, too practical, to be a philosopher, but when it comes to troubles and other problems, yes, you should bring them to me. And I should bring mine to you. That's an important part of marriage."

"I'm afraid you'll be hurt or angry."

"When do I get angry? Never."

"You do. I see the lights flashing in your eyes like warning signals. But you never *act* angry. There's a difference."

"Okay." I had to laugh a little. "You're right. But you can tell me anything."

He shifted in his chair, clearly uncomfortable. "Sharon reminded me I was forgetting something important."

Wedding arrangements flitted through my mind. *Flowers?* Check. *Rings?* Check. *What else?*

Justin said, "Sharon wishes us all the best and is willing for us to have the children in our lives, but she's worried about their future."

"What? She can trust me."

"Not like that. She's worried about what happens to them if something happens to me. She's concerned about the children's future security."

I shook my head, bemused.

"She asked if you'd signed a prenup."

I didn't know what to say.

He cleared his throat. "Jodi agreed to one, and it wasn't a big deal. But you and I haven't discussed it. I hadn't even thought of it—not in relation to you and our marriage. Sharon caught me off guard."

Jodi was his second wife. That marriage had been short-lived.

"She feels it's her duty to look out for the children's future."

"Of course." I had to stop and clear my throat too. "She's watching out for the interests and well-being of Edward and Sylvan. But, Justin, I wouldn't take anything from them. I wouldn't."

"Of course not." He grasped my hand. "That's not who you are. That's why a premarriage contract never occurred to me. Will you mind? I need to do this for everyone's peace of mind, so we can put it all behind us and move forward without worries, including a mother's worry for her children. Could you do that?"

Words flew through my head. *Of course I could. No, I shouldn't.*

How mean was I? How selfish. We were practically on the eve of the wedding. Could I refuse? What then? Would Justin tell Sharon to forget about it? Would I be interfering between a father and his children?

It all flashed through my head in seconds, but either my silence or my expression must've prompted Justin to say, "I'll tell Sharon to mind her own business."

"No," I said. "I respect her desire to protect her children, especially since she's open to us having an active relationship with them."

He nodded. "She is. I think the children must've said wonderful things about you, because she seems comfortable about you being in their lives."

"Okay, then. Should I have an attorney look over the document? I should, right?"

"You can. It's pretty basic. Standard language. It doesn't put any obligation on you to provide for the children, of course, and it says that whatever we each bring to the marriage doesn't fall into the marriage pot should something happen between us. The children will inherit whatever I have left of my assets. It also protects your premarital property for your heirs."

I fell silent. I wanted to be nice and agreeable, and his reasoning made sense, but there was a core of hurt in me.

In a low voice, Justin said, "Trust me, Ruth. You do trust

me, don't you?"

"Of course. I wouldn't marry you if I didn't."

"Precisely. What I have is yours. But if something happens to me, I have to ensure that my children will be provided for."

We ate our meal, but I couldn't quite shake that low, subdued feeling. When we left and Justin suggested we go to his house or he could hang out at my apartment with me for a while, I said, "It's been a long day, and I think I'd like to get to sleep early."

"I know you were surprised about the prenup thing. If you need time to think . . . If you're having doubts . . ."

"No, it's okay. But yes, I was surprised."

"I'm sorry, Ruth. I wouldn't hurt you for anything in the world."

"I'll see you tomorrow, Justin."

"Good night."

~~~~

That night as I slipped into bed, I asked myself, *What does the question of a prenup really change?*

Nothing. I had my own money and a job. I loved Justin and he loved me.

It was the unexpectedness of the request that had unsettled me.

In a few days, we'd marry—with the support of his children and even his former wife. That was huge. What could go wrong? After all, this was love, and Justin and I had years of happiness ahead of us.

CHAPTER ELEVEN

Flanked by Justin's children and a small gathering of well-wishers, we stood in front of the minister and exchanged our vows. I looked at those two kids with their carefully schooled expressions and closed faces and knew I could make a difference in their lives. I remembered being their ages. I fancied I could connect to the worries that must be troubling them about their father having a new wife. I would be a healing factor in their lives, I thought, as I recited the vows pledging my love and my future to Justin.

We took several trips during our first two years of marriage. Most were within the mainland United States, but we took one delightful trip to Paris—personal, not business—and I knew I'd made the right decision. I could never have seen so many new sights on my own budget, and Justin was always considerate and loving. In the beginning, I'd taken a leave of absence from Simmons and Baker so I could travel, and after a while, I realized I wasn't looking forward to going back to the cubicle environment, so I resigned. Justin was pleased. By then, it was obvious that he hated traveling alone, and I just plain loved traveling, so this suited both of us. Wherever we went, when I was alone during the day, I wandered the streets with a camera and even purchased a sketch book and drawing pencils and sketched many of the scenes.

I knew why Justin's house had seemed so unlived in— because it was. We were always on the road or in the air. As much as I loved the travel, I felt something was missing for me. We were in our second year of marriage, and it was one of those rare time when we were at home between trips, when I mentioned to Justin that I was in my thirties. Early, but there.

He was focused on something business related. I was hesitant. To suggest, practically out of nowhere, that perhaps we could consider a baby . . . seemed almost like I was breaking a contract. Ridiculous, of course, but still I eased the words out delicately.

"I was late, by the way. Only a few days." I shrugged to indicate the concern was now past. "But it got me to thinking that maybe we should talk about whether we might want a baby."

He heard me. He looked up. "A baby?"

"Well?"

"We have Edward and Sylvan."

"Well, not really. I mean, I thought we'd see more of them."

"Edward is off at boarding school."

"True, but even Sylvan . . ."

"Ruth, I'm doing the best I can. Sharon isn't always as cooperative as she could be."

"Also, Justin, they are your children and older than . . . a baby. I care about them and wish we had more time with them, but wouldn't it be lovely to have one of our own?"

"You never mentioned wanting to have a child."

"I never gave it much thought before marrying you. We're doing so well, having so much fun. Wouldn't it be even more fun . . ."

"I don't want another child."

"Children, even babies, travel with their parents every day. It could work out beautifully."

"Listen to me, Ruth. I don't want another child."

"Oh." Stunned, I tried to think of something to say.

"We should've discussed it before we took our vows, but I knew how I felt about it, and I thought, assumed, I knew how you felt."

I stood in place, shocked. Yes, we should've discussed this. That was my fault as much as his. I kept my tone even and calm. "Will you at least consider it, Justin? I respect your feelings, but I have discovered this is important to me." I went to his desk and touched his cheek. "Just think about it." I left, walking into the foyer and out to the patio, where I sat for a while, alone.

In fairness, I could hardly blame Justin for his reaction when I, myself, had never particularly wanted to have a baby. Motherhood was...problematical, as least as far as my experience had been growing up. With Justin's children, I'd viewed myself as more of a friend and mentor than a mothering figure.

But things could change. And maybe this—wanting a baby—had changed for me.

Justin joined me out there a short time later. He didn't sit with me but stood beside the table. Without mincing words, he said, "I had a vasectomy soon after Sylvan was born. So long ago that I never think of it. If we'd talked about having children, I would've told you, but we didn't. I don't want more children, but what I will do is go see my doctor and find out whether a reversal is even possible. No promises, Ruth, but if it *is* possible, then we'll discuss it."

I jumped to my feet and threw my arms around him. "Oh, my dearest Justin, thank you, thank you." I closed my eyes and pressed my face against his chest. "Thank you, not just for being willing to consider it, but for caring that it's important to me."

~~~~

One day in June, Mitch called. Mama had died.

"A car crash," he said.

I was numb. I didn't know how to feel. When Mitch and I ended our call, I dialed Justin. He'd flown out to Houston to meet with a potential customer for Simmons and Baker for both manpower and services. It was expected to be a lucrative account, and this was an important meeting. It was one of the rare trips he'd taken without me, and it seemed good that I'd stayed behind this time.

He answered, sounding distracted.

"I'm sorry. Did I call at a bad time?"

"No, it's good. What's wrong? I can hear it in your voice."

"My brother called. My mother died."

After a long, empty pause, he asked, "Was she sick or what?"

"Car crash. A tree, I think. No one else was hurt. No other cars involved. But my brother needs help with the funeral. Plus, I should be there."

After another long pause, he said, "Of course. Sorry, it's just that you rarely speak of them. I'd all but forgotten they existed. Where do they live? In Virginia, I recall that. But where?"

"In the country. It's before you get to Charlottesville."

"Okay. Do you need me to come home? I'll try to reschedule. The timing is tricky, but this isn't something anyone can plan for, so everyone will have to understand."

Did I want his help? In a way, maybe, but mostly no.

"You've only just gotten there, and I know this meeting is important. I'll be fine. Mitch and I can handle it."

"I'm sorry I'm not there, Ruth. Let me know if anything changes and you need me."

I met with Mitch and the funeral home via phone. We agreed on cremation, and by the time I arrived in town the next day, there was only an urn to stare at. I couldn't find Mama in its sleek, metallic form. Mama hadn't been a churchgoing person, and her friends . . . well, they were her friends and not ours. Mitch said he and the funeral home representative would see that the urn was interred next to our father, and he'd put the word out to her coworkers about that in case they wanted to pay their respects at that time.

We walked together out of the funeral home and into the sunshine.

"Mitch, let's go grab a bite."

"Do you want to go by the house?"

"No," I answered so swiftly and emphatically that I was embarrassed.

"We could just swing by. There's some changes going on in the neighborhood."

"No, but thanks for asking. I need to get back home. Appointments and such, you know?"

"Oh, sure. I understand."

We each got into our cars and drove over, separately but together, to the diner. I was rethinking what we'd done and hadn't. I'd had enough in my savings to cover the cremation and interment costs, thank goodness. But I could see that Mitch himself needed help. Our conversation over lunch confirmed that. Not that he asked, but it was clear enough to see.

Halfway through the meal, I sat back. "I'm stuffed, Mitch. The food was good, but I've gotten used to salads and lighter meals." I made a show of looking at my phone. "Do you mind if I step out and call Justin while you finish? Take your time. I may try a piece of that cherry pie. Will you order me a slice?" I smiled. "I'll be right back."

"Sure."

I went out to the parking lot and called Justin. "How'd the meeting go?" I asked him.

"Part one went well. Part two is tomorrow. It's looking like I'll be here the full week. Maybe a few days longer. What about you and your family?" He sighed. "Still feels odd that I didn't come home for support."

"Actually, I need to discuss something with you. Mitch needs some help. I'm thinking about buying his interest in the house." I hastened to add, "As houses go, it's not much money. It's old and run-down."

"Why not just sell it?"

"Well, he wants to live there. I could let him rent it back from me or something."

"So what he really needs is money. Is he working?"

"On and off. He works when he can get it."

"You sound defensive. Please don't. Family is family, I understand that. But when it comes to money, no, I strongly advise against it. Bad investment. It's always tricky doing business with relatives and close friends."

"But we could . . ."

"Not right now, Ruth. Seriously. You're talking about a significant impact to our cash flow."

"Okay," I said. "I'll call you later."

I hung up but stayed where I was, thinking.

Mitch had aged a lot over the intervening years. I'd been away for fifteen years, including my two years of marriage. Mitch was closing in on forty now. Same as Justin. I'd caught Justin by surprise about wanting to help Mitch. I shouldn't have spoken so impulsively to him about helping my brother, but poor Mitch was bone-thin, and his eyes looked beyond worn.

How could I go back into the restaurant and ignore that Mitch needed help—help I could afford to give but wouldn't because my husband considered him an unnecessary financial risk?

I couldn't.

Back inside, I returned to our table and settled into my seat, feeling energized. "Mitch, I have an idea. It will take me maybe a week or so to work it out, but this is what we'll do . . ."

As soon as I returned home, I cashed out my 401(k). With that money I could afford to buy Mitch's interest in the house and would replenish my bank account with what was left. Justin didn't need to know until tax time. By then, I'd find a way to explain my decision.

~~~~

It was less than two years later, just short of our fourth anniversary, that I acknowledged things had changed between Justin and me. In retrospect, I could see the changes had been in progress for a while but they'd been subtle and were easily explained away. Had Justin's ego taken a hit when he'd found out I'd gone against his advice regarding Mitch's situation? Justin had seemed supportive after the fact, and it was my personal funds that had taken the hit— not our joint monies. But things weren't quite the same after.

Justin began going on more trips without me. He'd suggested I stay home because the trips were short or the cities weren't good for sightseeing on my own. The first few times, I didn't fuss, but after several, I said I didn't mind hanging out at the hotel. We'd still have our time together in the evening. He replied that the meetings would run late.

"Is there a problem?" I asked.

"What do you mean?"

"A problem, Justin. With us or with work?"

"Not really a problem, but there's some changes at the company. This particular trip is very important for a venture Rob wants. He's expecting me to make it happen."

"Are you and Rob not getting along as well as before?" I had to ask because I had no idea. I was totally cut out of his work life.

"No, it's all good. No worries. Politically, defense contracting is having some hiccups, and we just want to stay ahead of any problems."

I heard a lot of clichés in his explanation. That worried me all the more.

"Justin—"

"What?" He almost yelled the word. "What's next? Are you going to start up again over whether I'm going to the doctor to see if the reversal was successful? Or maybe you want to talk about Sharon and the kids again and why they aren't around?"

"No, Justin. I'm sorry if I've been pushing too hard. But no." I had wanted to ask, though, about both those things. I wouldn't have minded staying behind if I'd had a little one or even stepchildren around to love on.

He rubbed his face. "I didn't mean to take my frustration out on you."

My stubborn persistence had intrigued him when we were dating. Now it irritated him. And hearing myself ask the same or similar questions over and over, I could hardly blame him. I was responsible for my life and happiness, even in a marriage partnership. "Maybe it's time for me to reenter the workforce."

He sent a quick look my way before turning back to zip up the tote bag. "That's up to you."

That's when I knew for sure. Whether between Justin and me, or with forces outside our marriage . . . something was very wrong.

He added, "I'm reluctant to say this. I don't want to hurt you, but the kids complained to their mother. Edward just wants to do his thing. It's not personal. He spends most of his time at school, and when he's home, he doesn't want to leave to come over here. As for Sylvan—I'm sorry, but children can be manipulative. They say stuff. Evidently Sylvan complained to her mother after her last visit and won't be coming back here anytime soon."

"What did she say?"

"Sharon wouldn't tell me. She insisted I not ask Sylvan."

"What? Not ask? Not tell? What is this? Some kind of game?" I was shocked at the unfairness, more so than about

Sylvan. Of course children were manipulative. They began to develop those skills after being told no for the first time. It was a negotiating skill, a life tool, and Ruth would've told me to put it in my virtual toolbox for when I needed it. But right next to it in that toolbox were love and respect. With love and respect present, manipulation was never the tool of first choice. Adults should understand this.

"Drop it, Ruth. Let it go. Don't be tedious."

He picked up his tote bag and grabbed the handle of his rolling case.

"Are you leaving now?"

"I am." He stared at me. "Rob left some files he wants me to review back at the office, and then I'm heading to the airport."

"When will you be back?"

"Three days. Could drag out a few days beyond. I'll let you know." He stopped to give me a hug and a kiss. "I'm sorry we're having this disagreement. Not great timing. We'll talk about it when I get back." He continued as we walked down the stairs, "I don't blame you for not wanting to be stuck here alone, but don't make the jump back into the workforce yet. Things will settle down at work, and we'll get our schedules back on track. A little patience." Before he walked out the door, he gave me a reassuring smile, saying, "Trust me."

I stood in that vast, empty foyer. Justin's office door was to my right, and I knew without touching it that the door was locked. I tried the knob anyway to confirm it. It annoyed me. Justin claimed that he kept it locked to secure our private business safe from the curiosity of maids or service people, not from me. But keeping it locked took the worry off my shoulders . . .

Every other door in this house was open to me, and more and more, mine was the only beating heart within these walls, and it felt lonely.

An expensive vase was displayed on a nearby pedestal. The painting on the wall had discreet but perfectly contrived lighting trained on it. The floral arrangement on the center table was changed with the seasons. The rug on the floor looked so expensively luxurious that I never stepped on it, always walking around it. It would serve him right if I rearranged the whole works while he was gone. Undo his perfect décor. Disturb his museum.

A bit passive-aggressive, wouldn't you say? Yes, and I was better than that. And if I did dare, the maids would sweep in and have it all set to rights as soon as Justin returned from wherever he was going.

I needed to be more assertive with Justin, but in a way that didn't come across as nagging.

As for Sylvan's mother . . . she didn't want her daughter around me? It hurt. No disputing that. And it was her right. Perhaps I should reach out to Sharon? Get to know her myself?

It would make Justin angry if I approached Sharon directly, but I might do it anyway. I could make a positive change for all of us, given time. Make a better future. It might take some time for me to win his ex over, but in the end, he'd be glad.

We were still early in our marriage, I assured myself. Not even four years in. It was normal for a relationship to have hiccups.

But three days later he returned home, and it was the

same. Perhaps worse.

We'd had more than three amazing years together before this. What had changed?

I stood in front of the mirror, examining my face for flaws. Mama was right. I had looks. I wasn't flashy, but Justin had seemed to like me as I was. There'd been no false promises from my end. So what was wrong? Justin was courteous, almost distant. And he was gone more often. Even when in town, he worked later.

Had I become boring? Had that mystery he'd imagined in my flashing eyes proven to be a dud?

I was home for the maid to come in and clean. I ran errands. I cooked. When Justin was home, I cooked more. Once upon a time, I'd dreamed of having my own kitchen but never dared to hope it could be as lovely as this one, and yet I ate most meals alone. I took some evening art and graphics classes at the community college, and that helped, but only a little. As my days filled up with mostly busywork, I grew alarmed. One morning, while watching Justin pack his suitcase for the next trip with no invitation for me to join him on it, I made my decision.

After he left, I dressed for business and drove to Simmons and Baker. I didn't call ahead. I didn't ask for permission because I didn't want to hear "no" or "wait." I was playing this out on instinct.

The time when fancy lobbies had intimidated me was long past. I walked into the building and past the reception desk, feeling like almost no time had passed since I'd last been here as an employee. As I entered the elevator, I knew I'd be seeing familiar faces and also strangers. And while I didn't want to return to my old job, it would surely be an easier transition back here than to a new work environment.

If by some slim chance it worked out, wouldn't Justin be surprised?

The person at the third-floor reception desk was a stranger. I said I was there to see Rob Baker. He called up, and after a pause, someone must've okay'd it because he gave me a badge.

"Wave the keycard at the scanner in the elevator, and it will allow you onto the fifth floor."

"Thanks." This felt almost too easy.

~~~~

I pushed through the double glass doors and went straight to Sue's desk. After being away for so long, I was delighted she was still there. She smiled, seeing me. We exchanged quick greetings, and I was asking her if Rob might be available to see me when he came out of his office and welcomed me himself. He ushered me in and offered me a seat near his desk.

The ease, the welcome, felt a little too good to be true. Plus, the expression on Sue's face when she'd seen me had been one of surprise, but also more.

Rob said, "It's good to see you, Ruth. It's been how long?"

"More than three years."

"You look well."

"Thank you. I appreciate you making time for me without notice."

"I'm glad I could. What's up?"

Deep breath. "I wanted to find out if there was an opportunity for me to return. I'm home alone a lot and miss being around people, plus you know how I loved working here."

I sensed hesitation from him.

"Unless you're worried because Justin and I are married. It didn't seem to be a problem before, but maybe things have changed . . ."

Rob stood. "Do you mind if I close the door?"

I hadn't noticed that he'd left it partway open. The way of the world now, I thought. I said, "Please do."

He closed the door and returned to his desk, but instead of sitting he stared out of the window for a long moment. Finally, he turned back to me.

"It is a problem—your being married to Justin—but not in the way you may think."

"I don't understand." And a part of me didn't want to hear.

"I can see you aren't aware that Justin no longer works here."

My brain went blank.

"As of about six months ago."

I opened my mouth. Some word, something, cried to be said, but my world had in the space of a moment ceased to make sense.

"I'm sorry, Ruth. He didn't tell you?"

It all rushed out. "This can't be true. He goes to work every day. He travels regularly. He's always busy."

Rob walked to the bar with its tiny sink and took a glass from the cabinet. He opened a bottle of sparkling water and poured it into the glass.

"Here," he said. "Take a sip."

My heart was racing. My brain was numb. I closed my

eyes and drank. Then I pressed the glass, still cool from the water, to my forehead.

Rob allowed me time to recover before he said, "I can't speak to what he's doing now because I don't know firsthand. We parted ways six months ago when we discovered he'd been working our clients on the side, apparently preparing to start his own firm. He was also meeting with other potential clients, again trying to gain them for his own endeavor. And he was mishandling confidential, proprietary information as part of that."

I shook my head. "I had no idea."

"I believe you. It's obvious you didn't know."

I leaned forward, setting my glass on his desk and pressing my fingers to my temples.

He continued, "Very few people here know the details. We handled it internally to avoid negative publicity, but it was especially difficult for me, both personally and business-wise. As you know, Justin and I go way back. He and I had a problem years ago, but I believed he'd changed. Instead I found that he's still impulsive, easily bored, and never satisfied for long. That's as much as I can say—and our attorneys would probably be very unhappy with me for having said this much—but given our experience with him, and your connection with him, you can see why I can't offer you a role here at Simmons and Baker."

I stood.

"One more thing, Ruth. You were always a valuable employee here, and I'd like to offer you some advice on that basis. Business is business, and I won't begrudge someone the effort to build their own business, but there are ethics to be considered, and Justin isn't always respectful of those.

152

Talk to Justin about this, of course, but in all things, think first about what is best for Ruth."

~~~~

I sat in my car in the parking lot and cried. I tried to think of justifications and explanations that would prove Rob wrong and cast a better light on whatever Justin had been doing, but each time it swung right back around to the fact that he'd allowed me to believe for the past six months that he was still employed at Simmons and Baker—that all of the late nights and plane rides were due to that job.

He'd lied to me for at least six months, and even before that he'd been trying to steal clients from his employer. Ugly plus ugly equaled ugly. Every time.

Chapter Twelve

I couldn't confront him immediately because he wasn't home. Long after our usual bedtime, he crawled into bed next to me, but carefully, so carefully that he hardly disturbed the blankets. He was so very considerate that if I hadn't already been awake, I might've slept right through him settling in on his side of the bed. I let him think I was sleeping.

As I lay next to him, I considered that perhaps people understood love only in retrospect. It was only after the fire had consumed the passion that they could see what they truly possessed. Or what had possessed them. And what they'd given up or settled for in order to obtain a temporary comfort.

~~~~

Sleep was long in coming, and when I woke late the next morning, Justin was already gone. I rose, feeling brittle and on edge. I teetered back and forth between rage and despair. Fruitless, that's how I felt. Everything I'd built had turned foul. My husband had lied for at least six months about his job and business activities. What else had he lied about? It didn't matter. That kind of sustained deception had ended any hope for us.

I would confront him today. And then somehow, some way, I'd have to figure out how to start my life again.

All. Over. Again. One more time.

I broke down in the shower and cried again. The hot water continued pouring over me until I pulled myself together and turned the handle to shut it off. The mirror, after the fog cleared, showed the truth of my dreadful night. I donned my slacks and blouse and went barefoot down to the kitchen to make coffee. I made extra, knowing it wouldn't help my nerves, but I needed courage. Lots of it. And I needed to think clearly. I carried my cup out to the patio.

A magazine was lying on the table. I must've left it there days ago. The cover showed a couple, no wrinkles, no bags beneath their eyes from sleepless nights, and no red rims from crying in the shower. This picture showed a happy, successful couple.

They are models. Not a real couple.

True. Not an actual couple, but there were real-life happy couples in the world. Unfortunately, Justin and I weren't one of them.

Like mother, like daughter?

Maybe I was destined for disappointment in love—just like Mama. But suppose Justin had an explanation? Suppose I'd been too quick to accept Rob's explanation for Justin's actions? I still had to confront him, but suppose the confrontation turned out to be the means to fix . . .

Stop, Jayne. Stop.

A breeze slipped past, touching my hair and flipping a few pages. I caught one word on the page—one among many—*detritus.*

D-e-t-r-i-t-u-s. My brain stumbled over the word, and I fumbled the magazine. As I grabbed for it, I felt a light touch on my arm. A dragonfly.

I froze. It's tiny feet lightly tickled my skin. As a child

I'd been afraid of them. Terrified, actually. I thought of Ruth Berry.

Her presence rushed at me. The heavy dark hair that curled down and around her ample shoulders, her long, thick lashes, and the glittery light in her dark eyes. I saw her so clearly—she might have been sitting opposite me at that very moment.

She'd told me once . . . In fact, she'd told me many things on many occasions, but on one summer afternoon when I was almost twelve, she'd told me never to let anyone treat me like trash, even if I believed that's what I was.

The dragonfly flicked its wings and took off.

I cried again, but this time quietly. The tears ran gently down my cheeks.

For a while, I held the magazine to my chest and let the tears have their way, and when I was done, I forced myself to take stock of my situation.

I was almost thirty-six. I had few personal assets other than my savings account. I'd spent a fair amount of my savings—not lightly, but without much worry because I'd thought we'd be together forever. I'd signed the prenup with the same trusting assumption. This house and the beach house and most of our other assets were in Justin's name, not mine. Most had been acquired prior to our marriage, anyway.

But not all. We'd picked up many of the vases and other objects on our trips. Justin had given me jewelry. It was stored in the safe. I didn't have the combination to the safe, but the jewelry was mine, and I would ask for it.

How would he react when I did?

Humph. I should ask for it *before* confronting him.

Thinking in practical terms helped me move in an active

direction. The biggest step, and most difficult, was to consult an attorney. As I expected, he said the prenup was solid. He advised me to give thought to what was acquired during the marriage.

I said, "Knickknacks and trinkets. Some jewelry. The beach house, but when we bought it, I never saw the paperwork. Justin said I didn't need to be on the mortgage papers. It's only in his name." I shook my head. "He doesn't discuss finances with me. I have no insight into. . ." My words faded away. I dragged in a breath and found a few more. "I know it sounds crazy that I let him shut me out. The accounting was complicated, he said so and I believed him. He was always meeting with the accountant and his financial manager."

The attorney sat back in his chair and scanned the bookcase and pictures on the wall to his right, then turned to me. "I can look into a few things. Find out about his credit, accounts, assets." He stared at me. "Are you sure he doesn't keep any of that information at the house? Might he keep financial documents in his home office?"

"He has a safe. I can't get into it." I added in a much smaller voice, "He keeps his home office locked."

He made a face and shook his head. "If you'd like me to investigate, give me what information you can. Name of accountant. Where he banks. That kind of thing. But I warn you that if he's that careful, it will be difficult to get a full picture. Plus, it could be expensive to pursue this, and we may find he has nothing more than an expensive lifestyle and debt. Be prepared for all eventualities."

He meant it kindly. I knew that. When his office contacted me a week later asking me to come in, I was apprehensive.

This time he not only stood when I entered his office, but he came around from behind the desk and took my hand. "Thank you for coming back in, Ruth."

For a moment, I was encouraged. He had good news.

"I'm sorry, but from what we were able to determine, the assets are fully leveraged. There's some cash, and we might be able to parse out what might be in scope for assets acquired during the marriage, but it could be a long, involved, expensive process with no guarantee of return."

"What about the beach house?"

"Only his name is on the title, and it's fully mortgaged. As is the Tennessee cabin."

"A cabin? What cabin? In Tennessee?"

"And the family home."

The conversation went downhill from there. He offered to continue looking but didn't recommend it. He advised me to give thought to the movable assets that I believed were mine or had been acquired during the marriage, and to do this while Justin was absent or at least predisposed to be agreeable.

"Ruth. I'm giving you my best advice. If the assets are as leveraged as they appear to be, and the debt—which may have been incurred during the marriage—is as deep as I suspect, then count yourself fortunate to escape without being caught up in that unhappy balance sheet."

With what dignity I could manage, I walked away.

I reached my car, and then I sat in the parking lot. There were no tears left. I was numb. I'd given my power away so very easily. The reality of having to accept failure and meekly move out was unbelievably painful.

If it came to me leaving, what could I justify taking? The items we'd bought on trips together, our wedding gifts, personal gifts from Justin to me—those all went on the list I was building in my head.

Justin would notice the missing items, so for now, I needed to work these things out in my mind—my divided mind that pitiably still thought Justin might wake up and realize what he was destroying. That he would have explanations. That my trust in him would be justified.

I had to stop clinging to phantom hopes and confront him.

As soon as he returned from his current trip, I would.

~~~~

He did return. I discovered he was home when I saw his car out front. His office door was closed, as usual. He was bound to be in there.

I was lurking nearby, getting up the nerve to force the confrontation, when I heard his office door open. I peeked around the corner. Justin was so intent on where he was going, he didn't notice me. I stepped into his office for a quick look, and through his windows I saw a shiny car outside. Justin's daughter, Sylvan. She was sixteen. Close to seventeen. I smiled and almost followed him out there as if we were the happy family I'd hoped we'd be—reality versus mindset with me caught in the middle—when I noticed that in his haste to speak to Sylvan, he'd left the safe open.

There were several envelopes in there, and in the middle of them was a jeweler's case that I recognized. It contained a sapphire necklace and earrings set Justin had given me on our first anniversary. Back when he loved me. *Shake it off,*

Jaynie. I grabbed the case, and in my haste, I got a few envelopes too. Several thick envelopes were bumped. They slid over the edge and fell to the floor. Panicked, I grabbed them, but I was out of time. There was so much in the safe that he might not notice the missing envelopes—if I got out quickly. I could worry about returning them later.

The sound of Sylvan's car door shutting warned me. I was out of the office and around the corner before Justin's footfalls sounded in the foyer.

Pressed against the wall, I held my breath. Would he notice things out of place in the safe? Nausea rose as I expected him to come looking for me, yelling and demanding to know what I was doing in his office, in his safe. When I heard the office door close and didn't hear him walking into the foyer, I dashed up the stairs. I shoved the envelopes and jeweler's case into a box in my clothes closet.

Ashamed and yet embarrassed to be ashamed, I collapsed on a nearby love seat. I sat there listening, anticipating his footfalls like a nervous sheep, desperate for someone, anyone, to show me which way to go.

I hadn't always been this way, had I? No, I'd stood up to my mother, to the kids in school. I'd left home straight out of high school and had made a good life for myself.

That's what you deserve for giving away your power. You earned this disaster, Jaynie.

Eventually, I had to come back downstairs. I practiced showing surprise at seeing he was home, mentioning what we might have for supper . . . that kind of thing. When we were in the right frame of mind, I'd bring up our recent problems and ask him why he'd been less than honest. I'd give him a chance to explain.

I arranged my expression appropriately and knocked on his office door.

No answer.

I looked out through the sidelights. His car wasn't out front.

His car wasn't in the garage either. He'd already left again, and without a word of greeting.

With little appetite, I kept my supper light.

That evening, I sat in my closet, my back against the closed door and the light on overhead, and opened the jeweler's case. I touched the shiny gemstones and platinum settings, wondering if these beauties were even real. Everything about my marriage seemed unreal or a fraud.

The envelopes were next. Not mine, but by now I didn't care. I opened the envelopes. There was cash in each one. Bills rubber-banded together in groups of fifty each, like I'd always seen with one-dollar bills. One banded pack was in each envelope. I thumbed through each group. All one-hundred-dollar bills.

Seriously? Who kept thirty thousand dollars in their home?

The same kind of person who kept their office and safe locked, even from their spouse?

And obviously, someone I didn't know and never really had.

~~~~

Over the next two days, I began to implement my plan. I brought my suitcases down from the attic. I hid the envelopes in the suitcase, wrapping them up in my clothing. I added other personal items of value and stashed the suitcases in my closet behind the hanging clothing. Next, I purchased some boxes at the local truck rental and stored them in the empty closet of a spare bedroom. Ashamed or not, if it took being sneaky, so be it. When the time to leave arrived, I wouldn't go empty-handed.

~~~~

On a night when Justin called to say he'd be staying in town so not to wait up, I packed another box with some of the kitchen cutlery and dishes and pans. It felt like some weird compulsive act and reminded me of how I'd fretted over saving my money for my getaway from Hope Road. I closed the flaps on the box and leaned against it, dropping my face to my arms.

I couldn't continue this way. I could feel myself falling apart, piece by pathetic piece.

Two days later, Justin came looking for me. I held my breath when I heard him calling my name, certain that he'd discovered I'd been in his safe or that I had spoken to an attorney. But no. In his world, I seemed to have become nothing more than a stray cat he no longer wanted to deal with, and it was time to put me out.

He stood in the doorway of our bedroom. "I'm sorry, Ruth. We can't go on this way." He frowned, almost looking puzzled. "Are you ill?"

"What happened, Justin?" I had retreated to the love seat. My legs felt woozy.

"What do you mean?"

"Did you ever love me?"

"Of course I did." He shrugged. "Ruth, there's no bad guys here. We fell in love. It was good for a while, but it didn't last." He moved toward me as if he might join me on the small sofa, but then stopped. "I'm not evil, Ruth. And no one here has failed. We fell in love. We fell out. It's just how life works."

"We? Why didn't you tell me when things began to change for you? You owed me that, Justin."

"Sometimes changes just creep up on us. I thought I'd seen someone in you, but that woman never . . . It doesn't matter now. You are miserable, and so am I. It's time to move on. We both deserve happiness, or as close to it as we can get."

I wanted to ask him about being fired, about working to steal his employer's clients . . . But I held back, asking, "Is there someone else? Are you cheating?" I drew in a deep breath, then added, "Have you been lying to me?"

He looked at me with something like pity. "No, Ruth." He sighed and came over to where I sat. "We had a great run. I wish it had lasted between us, but it didn't."

"Justin, can you tell me why? What happened? Whatever went wrong, we could've worked it out."

"It's no one's fault. It's just how life goes. I give you credit for persistence. But now I'm doing the kindest thing and making the decision to end it for both of us."

I said, "No, this isn't kind. This is despicable. It's as if you planned this . . . this . . ."

He interrupted. "You should take your personal items, your clothing, of course, and incidentals."

"What are you talking about?"

"You'll need to move out." He walked away. "I'll be gone this weekend, so this would be a good time."

I heard his footfalls move from the hallway to the

curving staircase.

Every variation of this devastating conversation had already played out in my head a hundred or more times over recent weeks, but actually hearing it from him caused something in me to snap, as if I was finally receiving that which had been too long delayed but was now being delivered with a fire hose.

Get out?

I ran after him. I grabbed the silky-smooth handrail and flew down the stairs. I had no sense of my feet touching the steps, but I caught up to Justin as he entered the foyer.

"Wait," I demanded. "We have things to discuss."

He turned toward me. His sleekly styled leather shoes looked so understated that they screamed *expensive*. His slacks, his carefully tucked-in, bloused-out shirt that only perfect tailoring made look good—his misleading appearance of prosperity and stability—it affronted me.

"What do we have to discuss?"

I saw in his eyes that this whole debacle had been rehearsed. Planned. He'd worked on this speech for a long time before finally giving up on the more passive-aggressive sabotage and delivering his speech to me in person.

"You've worked hard and long to justify your lies and faithlessness to yourself, haven't you?"

His blue eyes had turned icy, and his face was expressionless. He said, "This isn't easy for either of us. Let's not make it harder. Thankfully, the prenup resolves any questions."

"Marital assets, Justin. Money, other assets acquired during the marriage—"

He cut me off. "No. The market downturn a couple of

years ago wiped out early gains. I had to cover losses. We have expenses." He waved his arms at our surroundings. "Even this house is mortgaged to the hilt. Leveraged. Every asset."

"I don't believe you."

"Your belief or disbelief changes nothing. I'm going to have to restructure everything if I have any hope of avoiding bankruptcy. Go now before you have to worry about being saddled with the marital debt, Ruth. Take your clothing and personal items." He paused for one last bit of advice: "Six months of living separately and then we can move on. Start fresh. If you have any other questions, contact my attorney."

~~~~

He left for his weekend, and I sat on the stairs. My legs weak. My whole body feeling shaky. Weirdly, though, along with the shock came gratitude—that I'd given some thought to my next steps ahead of time. Because while I might be naïve and sometimes inflexible, I wasn't stupid.

Fear was there too, amid the shock and gratitude. It was all well for him to say I wouldn't be saddled with his debt. I couldn't trust him, and I had no insight into how much or who was owed. What would prevent creditors from coming after me if Justin managed to scoot out? I shook my head. I'd have to deal with that later. For now, I would focus on implementing my plan.

I finished packing and carried it all out to my SUV alone because I didn't know who I could trust—not the man who cared for our lawn and not the maid service. They were Justin's people. They'd been with him before I arrived and would continue receiving a paycheck from him after I left. I carried suitcases full of clothing and boxes of knickknacks and jewelry out to the SUV and loaded them into the open bed, back seat, and floorboards, thinking that I might be able to sell some of it. Justin hadn't given me permission to take our SUV, but it was one of the few assets in both our names, so I loaded everything I could fit into it and left.

There were no goodbyes. Not with Justin, not with our mutual friends, and not with his children, now four years older than when we'd first met—and except for a few visits from Sylvan, they were still relative strangers. I'd been erased from his circle.

My personal, pre-Justin friends were long gone. I wouldn't have wanted to face them anyway. I spent a few days in a hotel room licking my wounds before coming to terms with reality.

My reality? Everything I'd done, every choice I'd made since walking out of that high school stadium had been an exercise in hiding my truth, in sprucing up the veneer I chose to show to the world. I had some money, but no income. I had a car, but no home. I needed more money for a fresh start. And that meant going home to that place I'd put behind me so long ago.

Justin's money that I'd taken from his safe . . . I wasn't sure what to do about it. I felt justified in taking it and keeping it, considering how we'd split, but I didn't know where it came from or what might come from spending it, so for now, I didn't count it as spendable funds.

Legally, I was still Jayne Hale and would be for a while. I was born Jaynie Highsmith. That girl, Jaynie, who'd grown up on a dirt road in a disordered home with disorderly people—I'd left her, and my whole past, including my given name, behind when I went to Fairfax. I'd told people to call me Ruth. That it was a nickname. And they had. Over time, I'd become a new person. Even when I'd returned to Cub Creek for Mama's funeral, Mitch and I had visited at a restaurant. I hadn't gone anywhere near that old dirt road nor that house.

And it just about killed me to be returning there now.

I felt like Jaynie again, the kid with dirty feet and tangled hair and a mother who thrived on drama.

It was proof that no matter how hard you tried, no matter how far you lifted yourself up, or how long you wore that fresh new skin, you could never really shake the stink of where you started.

But this was temporary, I reassured myself. No more than that.

~~~~

I hesitated on the main road, slowing but staying on the asphalt, not quite turning onto the dirt road as I saw the row of battered mailboxes arrayed on their wooden rack—and nearly got rear-ended by a large truck coming up fast from behind. The driver leaned on his horn and swerved, blasting past me. My own vehicle, a large high-end SUV, pretty substantial in its own right, shimmied in the wake of the passing truck. The near miss startled me badly enough to make the turn.

The dirt road was still dirt, and a smattering of gravel had managed to dig deeply enough into the surface to defy time and usage. The small road sign I remembered had been replaced with a little larger, more substantial one. Hope Road. That name was fraught with more irony than I could ever begin to appreciate. And the mailboxes.... Some looked different. What was even scarier than the speeding truck was that most of the boxes looked the same, as if time hadn't passed. Or had passed more slowly here than elsewhere. Ruth Berry's mailbox had been first in the rack, and though the faded numbers had been replaced, that box otherwise looked about the same. A newer mailbox was in place of the one that had belonged to my uncle, long gone. Mama's mailbox was next—the third box. Or not Mom's, of course, but Mitch's. I put my hand on the door handle, almost stepping out to check it, then snatched my hand back.

We'd been her only kids and only heirs. We'd agreed on the disposition of the house and land when Mama died. Now I needed to change those arrangements.

Truly, with all my heart, I hoped Mitch would be home, because I didn't know where else to look for him. I hoped selling the old place wouldn't inconvenience him too badly. He wasn't returning my calls, so . . . he must still be living there. Must be.

The turnoff to the Berry house was on my left. Who lived there now? Ruth's daughter had rented it out right after her mother's death, but then she'd lived there for a while herself, or so I'd heard from Mitch when we caught up at the funeral. Too many tall pines and spreading hardwoods obscured the view for me to see the short distance down that side road to the house, and I had no reason or desire to drive down that way out of curiosity. My memories, both good and bad, were what I had. I cherished the good ones and tried to ignore the rest. No point in upsetting the balance. Deal with the present.

I passed my Uncle Lou's old house and pasture on the

left. The house looked neat and trim. Someone had done a lot of work on it, and the improvements looked recent. The yard around the house had been mowed. The pasture behind the house was overgrown and empty, and the old barn rose out of the tall meadow grasses like a ghost. I saw no cows or livestock in the brief glimpse I had as I drove by, and then the view vanished behind the house and the trees.

Soon my mother's house would come into view. I didn't realize I was biting my lip until I tasted blood. I braked, pulled my hands from their death grip on the steering wheel. I shook them to restore feeling. My palms were damp with nerves. I grabbed my water bottle and drank deeply. The nerves would pass. After I knew what I had to deal with and could work this out with my brother—when I had next steps nailed down and knew Mitch was okay with it—I'd feel much better.

I'd sell this house and get out of town. The world was out there, and this time I was going farther afield. That was it, and that was all.

Live in the present. Never look back, Ruth Berry had told me when I was young. Now I understood. Don't look back because you might just find the past—the slippery, too fluid past—was about to catch up with you and try to reclaim you—to drag you right back into the mud and chaos from which you'd escaped.

CHAPTER THIRTEEN

Ruth's treasure of silver dollars had totaled about two hundred coins. The coins were old and had been in good condition, so they might be worth more to a collector, but Ms. Ruth was long gone—and she'd been the true treasure.

Years ago, she'd cautioned me about losing my light. I hadn't understood I had a "light" until it was gone, and then I'd understood what she meant. After all these years, I still felt the lack. A fresh start would fill a lot of that emptiness.

Security and stability—that's what I needed. Once I had that, I could relax and breathe again. Maybe someday I'd be ready to chase happiness again.

The bench was filthy. The porch railing felt rickety.

I put my face near the glass of the picture window and shaded my view with cupped hands. The living room had no furniture that I could see. There was a quality to the daylight filtering in through the kitchen windows that seemed unimpeded by curtains or other objects. It spoke of emptiness.

If he'd abandoned the house, surely he would've called me.

In fairness, I never called him either. Until two days ago, when I needed to tell him about the change in plans. In a way, it served me right that he'd inconvenienced me this way. On the other hand, if he had moved out, then it would make it so much easier for me to proceed with the sale immediately.

It wasn't through lack of caring that we'd lost contact so easily. For me, it was part of keeping the past out of my present. When Mama had died and Mitch had needed me, I'd come. But since? We hadn't spoken.

When I was eleven . . . I had memories from my childhood before that age, but they seemed to belong to a different person. A child. A person whom I hardly understood looking back.

It seemed to me as if the year I was eleven going on twelve was the beginning of the disintegration of the already uneasy Highsmith household, but I hadn't seen it then. By the time I was twelve, it should've been obvious, but I wasn't paying attention because Wyatt arrived in my life—and had been in and out of my life for the next five years.

I'd escaped Hope Road when I was eighteen, but somewhere along the way, in the years I'd spent in the city, I'd lost my survival instinct. I'd confused "I'm not like my mother" with "I don't want to be alone." And Justin had found me.

I held my breath as I turned the key and opened the door. The air was musty. It smelled as empty as it looked. Old empty. Empty of furniture. Empty even of memories. The last was fine by me.

I picked up my purse from the bench and stepped inside the house, but left the door open just in case. I walked room to room checking the rooms and closets. All was empty, except for a small table and chairs pushed into a corner of the kitchen.

Opening the back door, I saw unkempt grounds—but not too long neglected because the overgrowth looked recent.

I could just catch glimpses of the fence on the far side of my uncle's old property through the trees, bushes, and weeds between this house and his.

Where was my brother? I turned away and faced the kitchen. Clearly, he wasn't living here now. No one was. There wasn't even a refrigerator or a stove.

I flipped the wall switch. There was electricity. I checked the sink. The water was on.

What next? Until Mitch returned my calls, his whereabouts would remain a mystery. So, it seemed the best course was to drive into Mineral and find a real estate agent and lodging for the night. There hadn't been a motel in Mineral when I was growing up here, but surely one or two had popped up during the intervening years.

As I was walking back into the living room, I heard a knock. The front door was nearly closed. I'd left it open. Maybe the breeze . . . The knock sounded again, and I jumped as the door swung wide. A tall man—backlit by the sun outside—stood in the doorway, his hand having just pushed the door open again.

"Ma'am?"

"Hello?" In reflex, I asked, "Who are you?"

"A neighbor. Sorry I startled you. I saw the car and came to check. Is there a problem?"

"What kind of problem?"

"Are you lost? Do you need a phone or a tow?"

Familiarity pricked at me, and then I realized. "Is that you, Wyatt?"

His relaxed stance changed. His new posture was guarded. "Jaynie?"

I offered a small but friendly laugh and moved toward

him with my arms partly extended, but suddenly, hearing Mama's distant voice, saying, *It was good I didn't tell you about Wyatt, about his mama and your father* . . . I pulled my arms back.

Wyatt hadn't moved. His hand was still on the doorknob. He said, "Feels like a lifetime since I've seen you."

"Likewise."

He cleared his throat. "Are you still living in Fairfax?"

"Sort of. Do you know where Mitch is?"

"He's not here right now, but he'll be back."

"Do you know where to find him?"

There was a long pause, and then Wyatt spoke slowly, choosing his words carefully. "Not at this precise moment, but he'll be back."

"When?" I was puzzled. What was Wyatt's problem?

"Not sure."

"What does that mean? Has he gone out for lunch or for a world cruise?" *Wow.* I cringed inwardly at my snarky tone.

"He wasn't expecting you?"

"No, he isn't answering his phone. His voice mail is full. If there's a new number, I don't have it. This place is empty. What's up, Wyatt? Why are you acting like Mitch has gone into the witness protection program?"

"It's good to see you are well, Jaynie." He looked annoyed, maybe disappointed, and as his stance shifted, I sensed he was about to walk out the door.

"Wyatt."

He shook his head. "Why are you here, Jaynie? Why now? If I'm reading this right, you don't know anything about his life, yet suddenly you're here and acting inconvenienced."

Frustrated, I said, "I haven't seen him since Mama died
. . . life got in the way. But I need to talk to him now. Do you
have a good phone number for him?" I waved my arms.
"Look at this place. It's empty. If he isn't living here, he's
living somewhere, and if you know where, please tell me,
because otherwise I'll have to file a missing person report."

"Leave your number with me. When I hear from Mitch,
I'll tell him you need to talk to him."

"That won't work. I'm here now. I want to see my
brother. Now."

"Good luck with that, Jaynie." He stepped out to the
porch and on down to the yard. He paused and threw back,
"Do him and yourself a favor. Don't contact the authorities.
He won't thank you for it, I promise."

I'd followed him to the doorway. I watched him walk
away, before turning away and, in a fit of anger, slamming
the door shut. Now what? What was I supposed to do?
Maybe I should go to the police . . .

I leaned back against the door. Wyatt. How unexpected
to see him here. And how weird that he seemed so protective
of Mitch. Was *protective* the right word? Or was he being
evasive? Why?

Wyatt . . . he looked good.

In fact . . . what about Wyatt? What was he doing here?

I pushed away from the door as a thought occurred to
me. Was he staying in his grandmother's house? *Living* in
his grandmother's house?

Life must've gone way wrong for him. He'd disliked
this place even more than I had.

And what about me?

My fingers itched to defy Wyatt's warning and call the sheriff's office.

Mitch wouldn't thank me for that? Wyatt had said that or something like it. What did that even mean?

I locked the front door behind me and went to my SUV, still loaded with suitcases, boxes, and bags. I'd find a hotel and hope the nearest was in Richmond or Charlottesville.

As I shifted into reverse, something hit my window. I jumped. The vehicle jolted back before I got it under control. My heart was still thumping, even after I saw Wyatt motioning at me to roll down the window.

Now what? I pressed the button, and the window came partway down.

"Sorry, Jaynie. Didn't mean to startle you."

"Yet you did."

He grimaced. "We should talk."

"Didn't do us much good before."

"I was surprised before. You were too. Let's try this again."

"Okay," I said. "All right."

He stepped back. I opened the door and climbed out. He seemed taller than I remembered. I felt at a disadvantage. Outside, here in the daylight, I saw he'd aged. Well, so had I. Time had been kind to him. I hoped I could say the same.

I said, "Tell me what's going on with Mitch."

"Let's talk inside." He turned without waiting, went up to the porch, and pulled keys from his pocket, with which he unlocked the door.

He had keys to the house. That felt wrong. But I kept it to myself for now. I needed to know what he knew. We faced each other across the kitchen table.

Wyatt said, "Mitch wanted to update the house."

I couldn't help a dismissive look at the stained walls and the vinyl floor tiles, several of which were broken or missing altogether. "Why?"

"He wanted to give it a facelift to make it more livable."

"He? You keep saying *he*, but he isn't here." I shrugged. "So he isn't working on it."

"Mitch had barely gotten started when he . . . was interrupted. He won't be back for a while. He asked me to get things in motion for him in the meanwhile."

"Where is he?"

"He wouldn't want me to tell you."

"Is he sick?"

"No." Wyatt shook his head but kept his eyes on mine. "Okay, you win. He's in jail. Incarcerated."

I leaned forward. "What? What happened?"

"I'm not going to say any more than that. It's up to him to tell you."

"I'll go see him."

He shook his head. "You can't. I told you so that you won't go to the sheriff's office." Wyatt tapped his fingers on the table. "You'll humiliate your brother. If you really want to know what happened, then wait. Give him the chance to tell you in person."

"That's ridiculous. Where is the jail? Or is it prison? When is he being released?"

"A few months."

"Months?" I shook my head. "No, that won't work."

"Won't work? For whom?"

"Me. I came home to sell this place."

Wyatt spoke as if carefully choosing his words. "Mitch

didn't know you were planning to do that."

"No, he didn't. It's a recent . . . thing. That's why I was trying to call him. When he didn't answer, I came in person." I stood up abruptly. I needed to move. I walked briskly across the kitchen and back again. "I need to talk to him."

"Did you hear me? Anything I said?"

"Of course I heard. Mitch is in jail for some reason that you won't share with me. He won't be released for *a few months*, whatever that means. But I need to sell this house now."

Wyatt's voice was very soft and low. "You can't do that to him, Jaynie."

I put my hands on the back of the chair, grasping the top of it so hard that my knuckles whitened. "I didn't. He did this to himself. I don't want to hurt him. But I'm not responsible for him—including actions that land him in jail—and he's not responsible for me."

"You don't mean that." Wyatt stood. He looked so very different from the teenage boy I'd known. He still had those coal-dark eyes.

In a softer voice, I said, "Let's start again. Tell me about yourself, Wyatt."

"Tell you what?" He sounded wary.

"Let's introduce ourselves again. It's been . . . how many years? Eighteen? Nineteen?"

Mama's voice was suddenly there in my head, almost like she was here in the room with us. But I couldn't ask about the thing Mama had told me. If Wyatt didn't already know, then there was no need for him to hear it from me because it wouldn't matter anyway. I wasn't planning on hanging around.

I took a deep breath to clear my head. "Well, let's start with what you're doing these days. How is it that you and Mitch are such good friends? Why would you be looking out for this house? Not only looking out for it, but apparently working on its renovation."

His expression grew hard. Stern.

I sat down again and put my arms on the table, leaning forward and pressing the question. "You left here with big plans. Where'd they lead you, Wyatt?"

"Long story. I've had a few different jobs over the years. Came back a couple of years ago. Ended up here on Hope Road shortly after your mom passed."

"Why?"

He ignored that question and said, "What about you? I heard you got married."

"I did." Didn't want to talk about that. "Things change."

He leaned toward me and spoke in a low, soft voice. "Go back to the city, Jayne. I promise I'll have Mitch contact you as soon as he returns. It's obvious you don't want to be here."

"I remember when you didn't either. When you hated it and couldn't wait to get out."

"True," he said. But he kept his voice low, not responding in kind to my escalation.

I sat back and drew in a deep breath before continuing. "I'm here for a reason, Wyatt. I'm not just hanging out for old times' sake."

He nodded. "I'll let you know as soon as Mitch comes home. You can talk to him then."

"I need to sell this place now."

"*Need?* That's a big word."

"It's time. Time to let it go and move on."

"What about Mitch?"

I shrugged. "What about him? He's lived here since Mama died, right? It's time he got on with his life too."

Wyatt pushed away from the counter. "Give it some thought. A few days at least." Finally, he looked away, and when he brought his gaze back to me, he said, "Have a heart, Jayne."

I stood. "Not fair."

"Probably not. But your brother needs a lucky break."

So do I, I thought. I asked, "From what? What did he do? What happened?"

Wyatt paused on his way through the living room. He didn't answer my questions. He said, "Fairfax isn't all that far from here. If that's where you and your husband still live, you should drive back to your home in the city where you can give the need to sell this place serious thought in more comfort."

I'd pushed hard. If he wasn't going to tell me more about Mitch, then so be it. "Thanks for telling me the truth. An abridged version of it, anyway."

"And that's it?"

"For now. What else is there?" I tightened my jaw.

"Jaynie . . ."

"Not really your business, Wyatt."

"Mitch already made a down payment on the work he wants done here."

I frowned. "You took it knowing he was going away?"

"*Because* he was going away. I told you. He's a guy who needs a break. Something to look forward to."

I lost it. "I don't believe for a minute that my brother thinks living here is so very desirable. Not in this armpit in the middle of an even bigger armpit of a place."

Wyatt stared. I couldn't read his expression. I was horrified by the ugly words that had come from my mouth. I was also justified.

"I'll leave you to your thoughts." He walked out and across the grass.

Armpit of a place? Had I really said that, and aloud? Wyatt had returned, and it appeared he'd returned by choice. *Crap.* I hadn't meant to offend. Shades of Bella? Maybe. I closed the door and leaned against it.

Now what?

Have a heart, he'd said.

He didn't understand that Mitch had sold his part of the house to me. I'd raided my savings and 401(k), and I'd let him continue living here. Justin had still loved me then. Maybe I would've made a different decision if I'd had my eyes open and had seen the future—the likely outcome of trusting a man who had already put aside wives. Plural. But I hadn't. I'd only wanted to see the good parts. The good possibilities.

I couldn't blame Mitch. He'd assumed the situation would continue indefinitely . . . and why not? I'd made it clear back then that I hadn't cared what happened to this place. In retrospect, I could see that I should have insisted we sell the house then and split the profit, leaving no awkward ties. As Justin had advised. *Ouch.*

With a groan, I pushed away from the door. It didn't matter why or why not. The decision I'd made had seemed appropriate to the situation at the time, so regret was pointless. But times had changed. And having a heart, as Wyatt had advised, didn't seem to figure into it now.

CHAPTER FOURTEEN

I'd driven into Mineral to find a real estate agent, food, and a place to stay. Plus, I wanted Wyatt to know I'd left. I was just fine on my own.

The Realtor's office was closed. I wrote down the phone number on the glass door. I found a diner for food, but there was no hotel or motel. There was a bed and breakfast, but it wasn't open for business yet.

I could've kept driving, but it felt like backtracking. I was only moving forward from here on out. No backsliding. No meekly accepting defeat.

A pillow and blanket were buried somewhere in the back of my SUV. I knew where there was electricity and running water . . . and hey, I owned the place. It would be like camping out but with utilities. I could even layer clothing under the blanket for a makeshift mattress.

Why not? I wasn't a wimp. I'd sleep on the problem tonight and figure it out in the morning, but I was definitely going to the police station to track down Mitch. I'd call that Realtor's office too. One thing was for sure, if Mitch wasn't here, he certainly didn't need the house.

I drove up the gravel road slowly, hoping to escape Wyatt's notice in the twilight.

But reality hit me when I walked back inside. Maybe there were too many ghosts here. And this floor was hard.

The house was stuffy.

No way.

Instead, I cleared the back seat of my car, piling its contents into the two front seats. I used the bathroom to wash up and brush my teeth, though it was a little freaky seeing myself in that mirror. I was happy enough to switch off the light and leave again. Stretching out on the back seat was not an option, so I curled up on my side. I did sleep, if not particularly well. Toward morning my foot cramped, and then my back and neck ached, and I remembered my age. And felt much older.

Dawn bloomed in shades of lilac and rose. I saw it through the side window while lying on my back with my knees drawn up. Mind over matter, I told myself. Focus on the goal, and the aches will go away. My eyes felt heavy. I was sure to have gained a few creases around them overnight.

This wouldn't work for a second night.

After I talked to the real estate agent and the sheriff, I'd have to find a room or short-term rental, however far away.

I eased myself out of the car and did some gentle stretching exercises. Luckily there wasn't a soul in sight. No one would know about my stupidity. I was pressing my palms flat against the side of the SUV, breathing deeply and stretching my back and legs slowly, when a voice behind me asked, "Still here?"

I looked up from my stretch.

"Where'd you stay last night?" Wyatt asked.

Pushing the hair out of my face and standing taller, I said, "I slept in the car, and I don't want to talk about it."

There was a long moment of silence. I gave him credit

for not responding to what I'd just said. When he did speak, he asked, "What did you decide to do about Mitch?"

I shook my head. "I'm sorry. I wish I could wait, but I can't."

"Give it two months, Jaynie."

"You're talking months before even beginning the discussion with him. I'd have to wait still longer before putting the house on the market." Frustrated, I asked, "When he does come home, how's that supposed to work? Do I just say, 'Welcome home, Mitch, don't bother unpacking or settling in because you need to find somewhere else to live'? No. It's better to tell him now. Give him time to adjust and think through his options so he'll be ready when he's free again."

"What's the urgency? You don't want to discuss your problems, and it's none of my business anyway, but ... Yesterday, I wasn't really thinking, only reacting. I was surprised. Today I can see you're in trouble. How bad?"

"Trouble? Me?" I sighed. "Yes, some, but nothing that selling the house and a little time and healing won't help. It will give me a chance to get back on my feet."

"Want to talk about it?"

"No."

"Want breakfast? Bacon and eggs, or are you vegan now?"

When your world has been coming apart and was continuing to devolve into absolute failure and humiliation, your stomach shouldn't growl at the mention of eggs and bacon. But mine did. And it was loud.

"Not vegan," I said.

He extended his hand. "Come with me, Jaynie."

"I don't want to talk about it."

"Agreed. Up to you. We're just talking food."

"I am hungry. I admit it. Where are we going?"

He laughed and pointed at the trees. Through that copse of trees was Uncle Lou's house and beyond that the Berry house.

"Follow me."

I grabbed my purse from the car and walked with Wyatt toward the trees.

~~~~

He worked in the kitchen comfortably and efficiently like a short-order cook, but more relaxed, as if he was having fun. I watched him, still trying to re-sort my reality. We were here in Uncle Lou's kitchen. It didn't look like I remembered, and the man who was cooking at the stove didn't belong in this house.

"How did you end up here? I mean, as opposed to your grandmother's house? I'm having trouble wrapping my head around you being here. The place looks good, though."

He cracked the eggs into the hot pan and then moved the bacon from where it was sizzling in the other pan onto a plate where a paper towel would soak up the excess grease.

"When I came back to town, I saw this property was for sale. I liked the idea of fixing up my grandmother's house and selling it. I was tired of dealing with renters. And so I bought this one, to live in one while fixing up the other."

He put our plates on the table. "Juice?"

"Yes, please."

"So you and Mitch have been neighbors for a while?"

He nodded. "Yes."

When we were both seated and sharing the meal, I asked, "So you have the two houses done now?"

"I do."

"What's next?"

"I plan to put them on the market soon."

"As far as I can see, you've done good work here, but modern houses are so big and fancy. How can these compete for buyers?"

"Not everyone wants huge. Plus, I've been able to keep the renovation expenses low, so these two houses are an excellent opportunity for someone looking for a small, easy-to-manage home, maybe a starter home or a retirement cottage. Each one has land around it—that's a plus, or a negative, depending on what the buyer is looking for. These three houses . . . private area . . . When Mitch asked about me fixing up his house, it made sense."

I still couldn't see his point. "Do you mean financially?"

"No. It just felt right."

Was he thinking of buying our house too? I didn't ask. I wasn't sure how I felt about it. It might solve a problem, though, if he could work out a rental arrangement or such with Mitch.

He asked, "You can't go home and wait?"

I choked and coughed. Wyatt moved like a shot. He put his hand on my back, realized I'd just swallowed wrong, and then handed me the juice glass.

"Need water?"

I shook my head and drank some juice. It burned a little in my throat.

"I'm okay," I said and coughed a little more, but the worst was past.

"Jayne. I have to ask. What happened? Do you need help?"

"A lucky break, that's all I need. Like Mitch, I guess. I need a turn of fortune and some time to get back on my feet."

"Why don't you stay at the Berry house while you're waiting for Mitch or deciding what to do? I moved the furnishings out of Mitch's so I could work in there. It doesn't make sense to move it back in before the work is finished when you can stay over at my grandmother's house." He stacked the plates. "I'm not ready to put the two houses on the market yet, so why not? You can be comfortable and safe there." He paused, then added, "And maybe pausing for a break, a rest, will give luck a chance to catch up with you."

I smiled. "Clever. That sounds like it came from a fortune cookie."

"Ah, perhaps I missed a career opportunity." He stared at me. "I see by your face that you're not sold on the idea."

"I don't know. It seems odd to think of being in Ruth's home without her."

"With the memories?"

I nodded. That billowing sheet might be a little too close for comfort.

"Take a look." He ran soapy water in the sink. "Face that fear because I can tell you, it's pointless. Find that out for yourself, then decide. If Grandma were here to offer an opinion, I can promise you she'd be happy to offer you shelter."

I joined him at the sink and picked up the dish towel. He handed me the first washed plate, and I did my part.

"Okay," I said. "Maybe." Mama's house had seemed very different, so maybe Ruth's house would too. If so, then it might answer my needs for a few days. The certainty of what I needed to do, which had driven me, seemed mired in a sudden fog. A few days to rest in solitude might be exactly what I needed.

After the kitchen cleanup was done, Wyatt said, "Do you remember anything about this house?"

"Very little. I was in the house once or twice as a kid, but he was long gone. My father and his uncle both died in that boating accident on the South Anna shortly before I was born." I'd wondered how my father's death might have contributed to Mama's decline. It was hard to believe that anyone would actually want to marry the woman as I'd known her. I shuddered. Terrible thing for a daughter to think concerning her own mother. But it was true. And that was a cold, unsatisfactory comfort.

"These last two houses were built about the same time. The first house, the one you grew up in, is the oldest by far, built by the first Mr. and Mrs. Highsmith. The other houses were built by family members, but the last house, the one my grandmother lived in, was sold out of the family first."

"Interesting that you know the history."

"All this land in here belonged to the Highsmith family a few generations back."

"I don't feel connected to them. Maybe because I wasn't in any real or practical way," I said as we walked into the small living room and stood at the front window.

The front room was almost square, and a large window overlooked the front yard. The room was painted a soft gray, and the trim was a neat white. Almost a minimalist effect, in my opinion. There was enough furniture to make it livable. The light surprised me. Mom's house had that same big window in front, but I always remembered her house as dark.

"Do you think houses absorb the emotional health of their occupants, or even strong events?"

"That's an odd question."

I confronted Wyatt's scoffing remark with a stern gaze. "Why not, really? Don't atoms move faster or slower according to temperature? Don't plants grow better or worse according to the nature of the light and the quality of the water? Wood can absorb scents and stains. Why not the other senses? The ones we can't see?" I waved my hand. "Look, I'm not saying houses have actual memories or even, what do they call it? Residual hauntings? But . . . Sorry, I'm not explaining it very well. Sorry I brought it up."

Wyatt moved closer to me, and we stood staring out of the front window together.

"No, I don't think houses can absorb emotions or events. Wood and fabric do take in stain and smells, and it might change their characteristics, but not their . . . essence. Their character. They don't have emotions. All that comes from the viewer."

He went back to the kitchen, and I followed him. He pulled a key ring from a drawer. "Here," he said. "Take the key and look at the house. I didn't change as much over there—mostly paints and fresh trim and new carpets—and when I moved furniture back in, I bought inexpensive. Just for use." He nodded at the room we were in. "You may have noticed I prefer a leaner style than vintage Ruth with doilies on the sofa and cherubs on the mantel."

Instead of protesting against the key he was offering, I smiled, disarmed by his turn of phrase. *Vintage Ruth.*

I'd loved vintage Ruth.

"Here, Jayne." He touched my hand. "Go see for yourself. No ghosts there. Not even many memories. And if any memories linger in there somewhere, I hope they'll be good ones."

Kind. Wyatt was a kind man. I'd always seen it in him, but that softer side had been hidden by his teenage intensity. His eyes were still as dark as his grandmother's, but there was a smoothed edge to his countenance. Maybe it was age. Maybe maturity. Or maybe refining.

And he'd called me Jayne instead of Jaynie.

I wanted to know more about where Wyatt had been over the past decades. What had he done and what had brought him back here? He'd said a little. If I hung around for a few days, I was pretty sure he'd tell me more.

~~~~

At the far end of the field—I'd thought of it as a meadow when I'd been younger—Uncle Lou's barn still towered with its long uninterrupted walls and roof. It looked better than I remembered. Perhaps Wyatt was working on it too. Above the tall grasses I saw a ladder leaning upright against the walls near the wide doors. I walked through a gap in the fence instead of climbing over or jumping it as I had years before, and then I crossed the dirt road to Ruth's yard.

Not Ruth's yard. She'd been gone a long time. The burn barrel was gone, as was the old shed. A small but newer storage building was near to where the old one had been situated. Ruth's flower spots were gone too, but they'd been gone before I'd left years ago, because Ruth had died two years before I graduated. Otherwise, from the exterior, the house looked much the same. The siding had been updated, and the roof was new. On closer look, the windows were new too. Ruth would've liked that. She'd often complained how hard it was to open those old wooden, oft-painted windows—and once having opened them, how hard it was to close them again. Ruth would've approved of all the exterior changes, except perhaps the loss of the barrel and the memory of the hours we'd shared around it.

I walked around front. Ruth's azaleas were still planted around the foundation of the house, and her big rhododendrons anchored the front corners of the yard, with two massive oaks and a smattering of tall pines filling in the rest of the yard. Same as I remembered. But the yard knickknacks were gone. Of course. And I hadn't given them a single thought until I noticed their absence. Her porch, unlike Mama's, was concrete. The porch was freshly painted in basement floor gray, and new black iron railings had been installed. Ruth's climbing rose was already working its way back up.

Same, but different.

Before fitting the key in the lock, I took a quick look around and then knocked. It felt wrong not to.

No one answered, of course.

I put my face close to the door and whispered, "Verisimilitude," like a talisman. The key fit smoothly into the lock and turned easily. "Sentence," I said more loudly. "This moment may reek of verisimilitude, but going home again is no more than an illusion. A trap."

Ruth's living room. Again, same, but different. I breathed, not realizing I'd been holding my breath.

Could I stay here until Mitch was released?

Maybe. Ruth wouldn't mind. A part of me minded. It

felt wrong. But it also felt appropriate. I could give it a try for a few days.

I paused in the doorway of her bedroom. Nothing I recognized here. But still . . . I pulled the door closed, but gently, and checked out the second, smaller bedroom, and found it satisfactory. The closets were all empty. There were two windows in this room, one on the side and one on the back wall, which gave me a view of Ruth's updated backyard.

Returning to Wyatt, my answer was a simple, "Thank you."

"Keep the key, Jayne. Do you need help bringing things in from your car?"

My car was jam-packed. I was sure he'd already noticed that, but I didn't want him to see the reality of that humble-jumble up close and personal.

"No, thanks. I'm not sure how much I'll bring in, and I'll probably use the opportunity to repack it. You've already done enough."

"There are a few sheets and towels in the linen closet and some pots and dishes in the kitchen. But it's a limited assortment, so if you need something and don't see it, just let me know. I probably have it somewhere, between the two houses and the barn."

"Thanks, again."

I drove my car the short distance from Mama's house and turned onto the dirt road between Uncle Lou's and Ruth Berry's properties and pulled into her parking area. It wasn't a real driveway, but it was the obvious place to park. Ruth had parked here. It felt so strange to remember it and be here now. A quick shiver danced up my spine. There and then gone.

Fetching my suitcase from atop the items on the back seat, I toted it up the steps to the door.

~~~~

As Wyatt had promised, I found sheets, a small stack of towels, and some washcloths in the linen closet. I made sure the house was locked up tight, including the slide bolt on the kitchen door, then took a shower. It was a small bathroom, but warm water had never felt so luxurious. I left my long hair loose to air dry and made up the twin bed in the back bedroom, then went to take stock of what was in the kitchen cabinets. Wyatt was right about a very few cooking items, and other than the banana and a jar of peanut butter I'd bought in Mineral, there was no food in the kitchen. I would need more for even a short stay.

Was I wrong to allow myself to be lured into staying a few days? Would it turn into a few days more, and then a month, and perhaps another would pass? When I could just go and see Mitch and work this out with him?

He was my brother. My big brother. Family should count, as should our history. Was Wyatt right? Did I have the right to risk embarrassing my brother? Or should I wait and give him a chance to tell me on his own timing?

What had he done to be convicted and sent to jail? Had he followed Mama's example of substance abuse and impulsive temper tantrums? I hadn't seen that in him two years ago.

In that moment, I thought of Justin. Was he missing me? Did he think of me at all?

I shook it off. Justin wasn't worth a single second of my

time.

Ruth was gone, along with her flowers and the leaf-burning barrel, and even the pile of paint buckets I'd used as seats, but the memories were suddenly strong. The idea of Justin, as an occasional heart twinge and flash of anger, seemed cheap and flimsy in comparison.

Getting over everything wouldn't be so easy—I wasn't fooling myself about that—but get over it I would.

The afternoon was open to me and belonged only to me. The dirt road faded into a rutted track as it headed toward the creek and the woods.

A walk, I thought, was next. A visit to my forest and my rock—the place where long ago I'd stored the old childhood memories that couldn't be contained within the boundaries of my heart.

CHAPTER FIFTEEN

Here was the spot where I'd jumped the creek. The creek looked narrower and generally less impressive, but somehow more dangerous. I saw the mud that might slip beneath my shoes. The tangled, weedy grasses and clumps of dead leaves along the bank might disguise rocks and roots waiting to trip me up. My brain was still whispering, "Don't," as I took the leap.

There were no lady's slippers along the woodland path, but plenty of undergrowth and clawing branches. Every living thing was fighting for its share of the sunlight. Except for the creatures in the shadows that rustled through the undergrowth.

I almost missed the path to the rock. I pushed aside branches and found it. The rock looked smaller too. The trees on three sides of the rock had grown taller and seemed to crowd the open flat area of the rock. But the open side that overlooked the creek was unchanged, as was the creek. In this spot, and from this vantage point, Cub Creek looked exactly as I remembered it.

Where had I buried my childhood treasures? Low-hanging branches, moss, leaves—they'd grown, but otherwise the ground cover seemed undisturbed, as if I'd been the last person here. It had kept my secrets, had waited for me. I was content to let it all wait a while longer. The past already felt too close. I was feeling pressed into a vise between the past and the present. I wasn't sure I could handle more just now.

The rock was warm. I knelt and pressed my hands flat against the rough surface. It was a rock, nothing more. Small insects scurried across the rough, pitted surface. There were doubtless spiders in the bushes and possibly a snake or two. I wasn't afraid, though, because I knew they weren't interested in me. I was anonymous here.

I eased myself down, but carefully, hoping to avoid live critters and dirt. I stayed stiffly upright, my shoes flat against the rock and me hugging my knees.

Still, curiosity drew my eyes toward that area where I'd buried my treasures. After so long, they were more like time capsules. The toolbox was probably rusted through and the contents destroyed, thanks to time and weather and nature. But not Ms. Ruth's treasure because it was in a glass jar. Unless the lid had disintegrated or the glass had broken.

I didn't dig into nearly twenty years' worth of leaves and forest litter to find out. I told myself I'd bring a tool, but mostly I was protecting myself, my self-image, by continuing to conceal that which I'd stolen. By refusing to see it, I could pretend it belonged to another life. No more than a memory.

Not a thief, my heart protested. An accidental thief, perhaps. I could've returned the jar of coins, whether to the house or to Ruth's daughter or to Wyatt, at any time before I left Cub Creek. But I hadn't.

I wasn't ready to dig the past back up yet. Hadn't I

already done enough of that? I pressed my face against my arms.

All the fuss and bother about whether to wait for Mitch to be released and come home—and to then hit him with the reality that I was going to sell his home out from under him— was all a little too much. I squeezed my eyes tightly shut and tried to envision what my new life might look like. I had options. I also had baggage. It was my choice what to keep and what to leave behind.

~~~~

On my way back I jumped the creek again. I was still celebrating my successful landing when I saw Wyatt down the road standing by Lou's fence—rather, Wyatt's fence now—watching me. We met midway.

He asked, "Want to share supper with me this evening?"

"Sure. What time?"

"About six." He nodded. "I knocked on the door, but you weren't there. I wondered if you'd vanished again, but I saw your vehicle, so . . . It never occurred to me that you were hiking in the woods."

My cheeks grew warm as the image of the purloined silver dollars flashed in my mind. "I spent a lot of time in those woods when I was growing up."

"I believe it, but you don't seem . . . the type . . . now."

"Yeah? I'm not. But then I never saw house flipping in your future back in the when."

"In the when?"

"When we were young and all things seemed possible." I leaned against the fence. "What did you mean—vanished again?"

"Graduation." He spread his hand and waggled his

fingers like a magician. "Poof."

"You left right after."

"I mean yours."

"You were there?"

"No, but soon after. I came back for a few days and drove over. Mitch said you'd already gone to Fairfax to start your career."

"Which was, at most, a couple of hours up the road. You could've called or come to visit."

"I almost did. But then . . . Then I got to thinking that you'd made good on your promise to yourself—that you'd be out of here ASAP and wouldn't be looking back."

"A lot like what you did."

He leaned against the fence too. "I guess we were part of each other's back-when. We both needed fresh starts."

I told myself to relax and enjoy this brief reunion. There was no risk here. After so long, Wyatt and I could be friends, at least for the short time I'd be here. I leaned against the fence, and Wyatt did too.

"I went to Fairfax to do administrative work in a fancy building for a government contractor. How about you?"

He opened his hands wide again, but this time he stared at the palms. "I like building. I built houses; I built furniture. I drove nails and carved molding and was never happier. At least, for a while." Abruptly, he closed his hands and crossed his arms. "I stayed on the West Coast for a few years. When construction fell off, I left. Did a little here and there and then got involved with houses in this area."

"Did you lose your business?"

"Yes, but before that happened, I lost myself. When I found myself again, I left. I stopped different places along the way, but eventually I ended up back here."

"You're here by choice."

"I am. For now, anyway. I'll go where life leads me. But this feels like home."

"I'm sorry I called it an armpit."

He laughed.

I wanted to ask how he'd lost himself. And how he'd found himself again. I didn't ask because I didn't want personal questions about myself either.

"I'm sorry, too, that you had hardships."

"Why?" he asked.

I shrugged. "Why not? No one should have to go through hard times."

Wyatt gave a small laugh and uncrossed his arms. "Seriously?"

"Of course. Don't give me that nonsense about adversity making us stronger."

He shook his head, but he kept smiling. "It's true. Hard times aren't fun, but they are part of making us who we are."

"My whole childhood was one long series of hard times."

His face changed. The teasing quality vanished and was replaced with something more like surprise, like when you suddenly see an odd-looking insect for the first time and your eyes widen for a quick moment and then squint for a sharper look.

"Oh, stop," I said, waving my hand to dismiss his strange look. "You knew my mother. Not well, perhaps, but everyone knew what Bella Highsmith was all about." His expression didn't change. "Chaos. Crazy stuff." Now angry, I crossed my arms and looked away.

He spoke softly. "So I know that she and my mom went from being close friends in high school to enemies later. And I know that your mom had her crazy side, and she yelled a lot and could be intimidating. But everything has two sides."

I interrupted. "I hope you aren't suggesting that her behavior was in any way justified."

"Try listening, Jayne, instead of jumping ahead. What I'm saying is that everything has two sides—good and bad, strong and weak, logical and irrational. Your mom had a temper, but everyone knew that if they messed with you, they'd have Bella to deal with."

"Except . . . Never mind."

"Except what?"

"Seriously, never mind." I pushed some stray hairs out of my face. "She had a temper. She invoked it when she chose. Any value in that is obscure at best, and destructive absolutely. I left here to get away from that. I made a life worth living. A job. A safe, stable place to live. The respect of my coworkers."

"Then why are you here?"

Another silence, this pause so long and wide, I couldn't traverse the gulf. I pushed away from the fence, and without a word or sign, I walked away until I reached Ruth's back door, and then I vanished inside.

~~~~

When my temper passed, I drove to Mineral to buy groceries. I accepted that I would be staying. Not for long, but for a while. When I decided where next to go, I could come back when Mitch was released.

I'd known, when I woke up that morning after a good night's sleep and a peaceful roof over my head, that I wouldn't go to the sheriff. Nor could I sell the house out from under Mitch. For now, I needed rest and some food. I'd taken that first step last night, and I was headed to Mineral and to the nearest grocery store. It wasn't more than a ten-minute drive—with a heavy foot, as my Mama might say.

I kept it simple—just the basics except for a few treats—and unloaded the bags in one trip, carrying them into the house. And since I was staying awhile—even if a short while—I would also bring in some of the bags and boxes from my car and re-sort and go through them. I anticipated that would be stressful—and to that end, I had a chocolate silk pie ready and waiting in the fridge as a consolation.

A splurge wouldn't hurt. After all, I wasn't having to pay rent or motel charges. It was nice to have some breathing room.

A quick double knock sounded against the back door. I peeked around the curtain before I opened the door.

"Hey," I said.

"Groceries?"

"Mission accomplished."

Wyatt seemed uneasy. "Can we talk for a moment?"

I stepped back, opening the door wider. "Yes, please come in." He did, and I suggested, "Why don't you sit? I can actually offer you a cup of coffee or iced tea." I smiled. "Feeling pretty fancy around here. Amazing what basic groceries can do to lift a mood."

Wyatt stood beside the table but stopped short of taking a chair. "I don't want to dampen that mood, and I don't know if this is anything to be concerned about or whether it even has anything to do with you."

"What?"

"A man was here." He nodded toward the dirt road. "He was snooping around outside your mom's house, staring in the windows and such. He seemed very interested in the tire tracks. No one's driven or parked in that area since you did. Then he walked into the field and out to the barn. Trespassing, obviously, and not caring."

"And you think . . . what?"

"Not sure. He had a look to him. Maybe the kind of guy someone hires to look for someone or something?"

"He might have been looking for Mitch. You haven't told me what Mitch did that got him into trouble."

"Could be about Mitch, but I don't think he was local." He shrugged. "A local guy wouldn't make himself at home on someone else's private property and definitely wouldn't be messing with the barn doors and pulling on the padlock. So I walked out there. He didn't seem bothered that someone had been watching him. He remarked on your mother's house looking empty. Vacant. Asked if anyone had been at the house recently. I told him he was trespassing."

"Oh. And then what?"

"He said he'd heard the property might be for sale—if not now, then soon—and he was trying to get a jump on anyone else who might be interested."

"What did he look like?"

"Dark hair. Beefy through the shoulders."

"Not Justin."

"Your husband? Sorry, I don't know anything about him."

"My soon-to-be ex. Justin has sandy hair and a nice build, but the kind you get from an elliptical, not from weight lifting."

Wyatt seemed to consider that. "Maybe he was looking for you or maybe for the SUV."

"Why?"

"It's an expensive vehicle. Could Justin have reported it missing or stolen? Is he making the payments?"

I shook my head. "Are you suggesting a repo man? Well, that's just silly. The guy didn't come with a tow truck, did he?"

"Or a hired detective. He was driving a car. A sedan. Whether he's looking for you or the vehicle, that SUV will give you away. No way to hide it parked out here." He shrugged. "Not that I'm suggesting you're hiding or anything."

"No, I'm not hiding. On the other hand, it feels very creepy to think that some strange man was here snooping and might come back." I went to the front window and looked out. "It's not like I have a choice. There's no garage. I could maybe move the SUV around back, but who would that fool? It's too visible."

Wyatt had followed me. "You could put the vehicle in the barn."

"Seriously?"

"Sure. Why not?"

"Hey, I didn't rob a bank or anything." I was joking, but not entirely. After all, I did have thirty grand stashed among my odds and ends. I laughed and tried to make it sound genuine, but I detected a tiny shake in my voice. My confidence had deteriorated over my time with Justin. It needed a good laugh and a boost.

"Honestly, I can't imagine why anyone would be looking for me. Justin told me to . . ." He'd told me to leave, and I didn't want to say that aloud for Wyatt to hear. "The SUV is in both our names. I'm sure he wouldn't object to me taking it." After all, I added silently, how else did he expect me to get myself and my junk out of his life?

"On the other hand, I did want to rearrange some of the gear I have stowed in it. If there's room in the barn, that might be a good place for it. You know, being out of the weather and away from the wild pigs and coyotes and such."

His face did that funny blank-to-amused transition. "By all means, let's avoid the wild pigs. There's plenty of room in there. And to make sure your stuff stays safe, I'll give you a key to the padlock. Will that work?"

He said it with a quirk to his smile. I smiled back, but I wasn't really feeling it inside. Why would anyone be looking for me? Justin had never been here, but since I'd grown up here, it wouldn't have been difficult to find me—if someone was looking and thought I might have come back to where I'd grown up. But why would Justin think that?

"Headache?"

"What?"

"You're rubbing your temples."

"Oh. Yes. A small one." I shrugged. "Joking aside, Wyatt, I don't know why anyone would be looking for me. I haven't done anything wrong, and I have no enemies that I'm aware of. It's probably some sort of weird coincidence. But—and I mean this—I don't want to bring any trouble to you."

"No trouble, Jaynie." He gave me a funny look. "Do you still call yourself Jaynie? Sometimes you get an odd look when I say your name. Are you going by Jayne now?"

"Jayne or Jaynie is fine. Maybe it's just a bit of the past

breezing by when you say it that I'm reacting to. Your voice
. . . we age, but our voices stay much the same. Have you
noticed?"

"I think you're redirecting the conversation, but it's
okay. You tell me what you want to tell me when you want
to. For now, why don't I drive your SUV to the barn and you
take the broom out of the closet and give the tread marks
beside the house a light once-over?"

I stared. I opened my mouth to protest, but then closed
it. It was pretty crazy speculation, but it could be connected
to Justin. Justin had lied to me many times. His employment,
his business practices . . . I suspected he'd lied about other
things too.

"Here are the keys." I pulled them from my purse and
handed them to him. "I'm sure you must know this, but the
fob will unlock the door automatically when you stand next
to it."

"No worries, Jayne. I can handle it."

I shook my head. "No worries."

He reached forward and touched my shoulder, gently
and briefly. "Jayne?"

"Yes, Wyatt?"

"Remember supper is at six o'clock."

"Do you think he'll be back?"

"Maybe. Yes. Since I don't really know why he was
here I'm going out on a limb here, but I do think he'll come
for another look. He won't see anything or anyone that
interests him this time either, and he'll move on."

"How do you know?"

"I don't. But if I was hired to find someone and it was
only a hunch that they were here, that's what I'd do. Not

much else to hang around for.'"

"That's true enough."

"And, Jayne, you haven't really said anything about your situation, but do you feel safe? What about the jerk you left behind?"

"How do you know he's a jerk?"

"You left him, didn't you?"

"I had no choice."

"Then I'm all the more certain he's a jerk. Tell me about him."

"Not now. Maybe sometime." No time, I added silently. I needed to maintain some shred of dignity.

"If you don't feel safe enough staying alone over at the Berry house . . ."

"No, Wyatt. I'll be fine. He won't be coming for me. He—" I didn't intend to say it aloud, but the words fell out of my mouth anyway. "He doesn't want me anymore."

So much for dignity.

I walked away to get the broom, adding silently, No, he won't be coming after me. . . that is, unless he wants his money back.

~~~~

When I was done, I left the broom leaning against the back porch. I walked through the field where the growth had been mown short to allow vehicle access.

Wyatt believed the man had been particularly interested in my tread marks from when I'd arrived two days ago. I'd been parked at Ruth's house since yesterday. Now, in the barn. How crazy this seemed.

The barn doors were open. I stood on the threshold, allowing my eyes to adjust to the cavernous interior. Light filtered in between the boards, enough for me to make out most of what was stored inside. First and foremost—my car. It looked huge parked inside, but in a way it looked smaller in here than when it was parked next to the small houses. Equipment was stored at the far end of the barn. Against the wall opposite me, boxes and furniture were neatly stacked. Mama's furniture?

Maybe some of her possessions were packed in those boxes.

The eaves disappeared into shadows, deep and dark enough that they suggested infinity. But no, it was just a big old barn. It smelled musty but otherwise fine. I touched the wood, and it felt strong yet. Good bones.

I jumped, startled, when Wyatt said, "When Mitch contacted me about fixing the place up, he asked me to clear it out. I didn't keep the sofa and chair or mattresses. They were old anyway and would've been too tempting for rodents."

"You startled me."

"You were busy admiring the barn."

"True. How is it still in such good shape?"

"One of the last tenants before I bought the house had plans to use the field for grazing and the barn for the stock. He put a lot of time into repairing it, and after I purchased the property, I kept on with what he'd started. The structure is still sound."

"No one ever stayed at Uncle Lou's house for long. Some came with plans and some just needed a temporary place to live, but they never had children. I know because I was always on the lookout for other kids to play with. And they never stayed. The house was empty more than it was lived in."

"Your uncle drowned with your dad, right?"

"Yeah. Dad's uncle. I never knew him. Either of them, actually."

"Sad."

"I've wondered how it might have been different for Mama. For all of us, really. But I think my mother was destined for dissatisfaction anyway. She was never happy. Mama had problems."

Wyatt and I stood silently for a long moment. Then he gestured to the large empty area in front of us. "We can unload your vehicle in here and you can sort through the contents at your own pace." He put his hands out. "Not trying to tell you what to do. It's just a suggestion."

I did need to go through and repack. My departure had been swift. Working in here would save me from having to spread it across the front yard or carry it all into the house. On the other hand, Wyatt was here. Even in the barn, it felt like I'd be exposing my jumble of possessions. They looked more like garage sale bounty than the belongings of a woman who had her act together. But Wyatt didn't know the circumstances of my departure. He only knew that my marriage had failed. Marriages fell apart every day.

"I appreciate the offer, Wyatt. I'll take you up on it. I won't be here all that long anyway."

His face was mostly shadowed, but his voice was soft as he said, "No need to rush off. Might as well wait for Mitch here as anywhere else."

"Thank you for the offer, and I appreciate your help, but I need to get my life back on track." I'd hung on to my marriage and Justin too long—way beyond good sense.

Why? I shivered. I was a wimp, apparently. Or too hopeful for my own good, maybe? Fooling myself into thinking I could make things good again?

It didn't matter. We were done now. I wasn't inclined to look back. I'd remade myself and my life before. In fact, I was feeling a change in my heart now. I wanted to run with it. Mitch was the stumbling block, and that wouldn't be forever. I could occupy myself with planning and preparations while I waited.

Wyatt said, "Mind if I open the back?"

"Oh, sure." I pressed the tailgate button and stepped back. "Just the bigger items. I'll handle the rest."

He went for the suitcases first, but to get to them he had to unload some of those smaller items. I turned away and opened the side door to unload what I'd stored on the seat and in the floorboards.

"By the way," Wyatt said, "you might notice some guys working around your mom's house. The painter is there now. Over the next few days, they'll be checking out the plumbing and other things before we start repairs. The structure is actually pretty sound."

"Painter? Shouldn't someone . . . shouldn't I be approving colors or something?"

"Mitch told me what he wanted before we started." He added, "It's neutral colors."

"Why, Wyatt?" I pushed away from the SUV, annoyed. "Why spend time, money, and effort fixing up that house?"

"Why not?"

"Who would want to live there?"

"Mitch?"

I said, "Besides Mitch."

"People need homes."

"Not that one. There are new subdivisions everywhere. I see all the trees being cleared—I assume they're selling the timber. And the new-subdivision-coming signs are popping up all along Route 522. Why mess with that old house?"

"Believe it or not, assuming the plumbing and wiring is good, it's mostly cosmetic work. Houses like these"—he nodded as if to indicate all three houses—"are affordable. Not only do people ask me when they'll be going on the market, but one local developer approached me about buying the houses plus the acreage to subdivide it and build even more small homes in here to appeal to retirees who don't want to pay for square footage they'd have to spend their golden years maintaining and dusting and all that."

"Subdivide it? You mean the field, the woods?" I was thinking of my memories. But I hadn't wanted those memories, had I?

"Yep. From the main road to the creek. He wants to build it with the barn as a focal point. Create storage units inside that are keyed to the individual properties to ease living space in the houses. Maybe garden plots beside the barn."

"How could he get enough houses in here to make that worthwhile?"

"There wouldn't be much green space between them. The houses would be packed in pretty close." He shrugged. "These three existing houses would be taken down altogether if they go with a high-density plan."

"But . . ."

"What's wrong, Jayne?"

"I don't know. I can't even imagine it." I walked to the

open barn door and stared out across the butterfly field—the meadow of my childhood. And the barn. The image of its hulk sitting as a backdrop to the meadow and the forest a backdrop to the barn was permanently in my memory, it would seem. It all fit together in my head like integral puzzle pieces, along the fence, the dirt road, and the creek.

Wyatt said, "But that's all on hold right now, though the developer is doing a lot of planning. He'll go with this acreage or he'll take his project elsewhere, but he understands that for now, I won't do anything or make any commitments until Mitch is back."

"Mitch?"

"This developer started talking to me after Mitch was already gone. I don't want to agree to something this big without talking to Mitch face-to-face."

"Which is what you've asked me to do. Wait and talk to him when he returns." My voice trailed off. I wasn't really asking this as a question, just thinking out loud. Wyatt seemed to understand that. And then it hit me that Wyatt seemed to understand an awful lot about what was going on all around my childhood home and even about what was going on with my brother. Some irritation may have shown in my voice as I said, "So all of this property—from the main road to the creek, as you said—except for Mama's house and acreage, already belongs to you and you have a buyer who wants to develop it?"

"What's wrong, Jayne? I hear it in your voice. Say it now if you want to weigh in."

"I don't know, Wyatt. I don't know why I'd object. I just don't know."

He moved closer, and his voice went even softer. "It's

undecided. I have mixed feelings myself. But no one lives forever. I ask myself what will become of this little tucked-away corner of the world when I go or get old or leave—whatever. Should I do something with it that will benefit others? I can sell the houses individually and let the future take care of itself, or I can go for the big development. I don't know. The money is probably better selling it to the developer in its entirety. But this corner of the world would never be the same. I was here much less than you, and I wasn't that attached, but since coming back . . ." He shrugged. "One thing I've learned through my many mistakes and failures is that you have to come to terms with the past or you'll never be free of it—you'll never truly become who you're meant to be."

I turned away. I felt like he was giving me a lecture of sorts. But Ruth's authority to advise and guide me did not transfer over to her grandson.

"Why don't I go ahead and pull out the rest of the stuff?" he asked. "It's easy for me to reach. Long arms." He smiled. "I promise I won't be nosy."

"I'm not hiding anything."

"Didn't say you were."

"Mine isn't the first marriage to fail."

Humiliated. That's how I felt. Those words had simply burst out and were too honestly said to pretend I wasn't bothered by the truth of it.

He paused. After hesitating, he touched my arm gently. "I lost too. Failed? Sure. I made stupid choices. Not with marriage, but other things—my life—out in California . . . went drastically wrong."

He reached out to me, perhaps instinctively, and I pulled

back.

"I've got this, Wyatt. I appreciate your intention." I remembered Ruth's hands on me, calming me. But Wyatt wasn't Ruth. And I wasn't a child. And there were complications to be wary of.

Wyatt stepped back. "I don't want to preach or intrude. When you come over for supper, I'll give you the spare key to the padlock." He paused before exiting. "I'll pull the doors closed when I leave, just in case. You have your phone?"

"Yes."

"If I see any strangers, I'll give you a call. And now that I think of it, if you have your location enabled, you might turn that off. Unless you want to be found."

I gaped at him for a moment before saying, "No one is tracking my location. I'm not hiding. I have no reason to hide or avoid anyone."

He said, "See you at supper." He stopped in the doorway and added, "Drop the bar inside until you're ready to leave. After you're out, go ahead and close the padlock." And he left.

I stood alone inside the barn. Without Wyatt, and suddenly alone here, the guilty child feeling rushed over me. Mama had forbidden me to come anywhere near the building, much less be inside it. For safety's sake, to prevent hospital bills, or to avoid liability if someone saw us there and then it burned down and we were blamed. Suddenly, unbidden and out of my control, scenes rolled over me. Mitch angry because Wyatt and I had stolen a kiss in the night shadows cast by the barn. Him sending me home and staying for a chat with Wyatt...as if Mitch was my dad. I'd been so angry at him. And at Wyatt, too, for staying to talk to Mitch and not chasing after me as I stalked away.

Uncle Lou's barn had been a consistent landmark through the first eighteen years of my life. Standing still, my hands braced against the car door, I could almost believe Mama was going to come running in here any minute now, shouting at me. But there was no Mama. And no Jaynie either. Just me.

I hadn't been able to tell Mama goodbye. Despite our differences, if I'd known her time was short, I would've come back while she was alive. Coming for the funeral had really been for Mitch. I'd felt as if I'd been slapped in the face by the inability to tell her goodbye. Almost as if her unplanned, abrupt, and premature departure had been designed to give her the last word.

She hadn't been what most would call a good mother. I wouldn't call her that either. On the other hand, she'd kept a roof over my head and hadn't beaten me.

But she'd always had bad habits, like a temper and a weakness for pills and alcohol. It was small surprise that she'd died as she had—plowing her car into a tree.

And no goodbyes.

She'd been young. Only sixty.

Should I have done more? Tried harder to be in her life? There was no one here to say yes or no. Besides, I could do any judging just fine on my own.

I hadn't liked her much, but I'd loved her anyway. In her own way, I knew she'd loved me. In between all the other stuff—her personal devils.

Had Justin loved me?

CHAPTER SIXTEEN

As Wyatt suggested, I dropped the bar into place after closing the barn doors to ensure no one waltzed in uninvited. He didn't want to lock it from the outside, effectively trapping me inside, just in case something went wrong. For myself, I didn't want to be locked in here or anywhere else by anyone.

I picked through the suitcases for clothing I'd need over the next week or so, along with my jewelry and other personal items, including the cash. Ultimately, I packed all of that into one suitcase and zipped it around. This was all I'd take into the house for now.

I sat on an upended crate next to the cardboard boxes to pick through them. It sort of reminded me of perching on Ms. Ruth's white paint buckets. Within the boxes were an odd assortment of knickknacks, small statues, and vases. It had only been days since I'd gathered these items that could reasonably be justified as mine and acquired during the marriage. Yet as I held them, I wondered at what I'd chosen. A few were sentimental trinkets. A couple were actually valuable. Most were gifts that Justin had purchased during those first two years when he loved me.

He *had* loved me, hadn't he?

After a long pause, I realized I was staring at the sunlight streaming in through the high window. The lofts had been clear of hay for many, many years, but dust was ever present, and the light filtered through the dust motes in streams. Almost church-like. Heaven-like.

It was no more than ordinary daylight and dust, but it comforted me. It seemed odd that between then and now, despite the triumphs and losses of the people who'd lived along Hope Road, the barn still stood.

I held a porcelain figurine. I remembered the day Justin and I had seen it in a shop window in southern France. I'd admired the figurine, and before I knew it was happening, the shop owner was wrapping it and Justin was saying we'd put it on the mantel in the morning room as a memory of our trip.

He *had* loved me. At least as much as he could love. I suspected Justin had loved the shininess of a new conquest. But in the end, he'd only been interested in the *shiny*.

Had I loved Justin? Truly?

Yes, I thought so. Those first two or so had been good.

Maybe over time he'd grown less shiny in my eyes too, and there hadn't been enough love between us to overcome that.

I turned the figurine in my hands.

How much might I get for it? I didn't have the purchase papers verifying authenticity, but it was stamped with a seal on its base.

Yes, it had value, but what struck me most was the pettiness of it in my car and now in my hands. Dissatisfaction simmered inside me at how I'd handled the whole thing. I should've overruled my instincts and confronted Justin early on. And later, after consulting the attorney, I could've chosen to fight Justin. I should've refused to leave and made him force me out.

Where was the dignity and the self-respect in any of that? Was it in fighting for assets I was entitled to? Perhaps spending years of my life in courts paying lawyers and accountants a fortune to untangle Justin's finances? No one had made me sign that prenup. I'd believed in Justin. In us. Now I didn't and I wanted to be done from him.

Detritus. This stuff in my car and littering the floor of the barn was just so much trash. Some of it might be valuable, but it was too sad if this was all I had left to remember my marriage by.

Whose life had I been living? Mine?

Or someone who'd tried to clothe her life in the persona of someone she'd loved and respected? *Call me Ruth.*

I set the figurine aside.

Along the back wall were stacks of boxes and odds and ends of furniture. As I stared, shadows shifted, and I recognized the profile of bedposts with distinctive finials sticking up above the rest.

Leaving my perch on the tailgate, I wandered over into the past.

Wyatt said he'd emptied the house at Mitch's request so he could proceed with some minor renovations. He'd also said he'd tossed certain things like the old mattresses and some seriously broken junk.

I rested my hand on the nearest bedpost. The boxes were neatly stacked and labeled. Kitchen. Bedroom. Bathroom. And so on. An odd stick was protruding between the bedframe and the boxes. Seeing it, it materialized into an easel. A wooden easel. Mine.

From a lifetime ago.

Wow. Blast from the past. I reached toward it, but it was just beyond my fingers. I rested my arm along the top of the headboard.

That easel had been a Christmas present. When I was ten or eleven, maybe? Santa had brought it. Funny how even though I knew Santa wasn't exactly as billed by the time I was eight or so, still I didn't connect Mama with the gift of the easel—not mentally or emotionally. Which was ludicrous. In fact, I now recalled a new sketchbook and pencils had also been under the tree that morning.

Mama. The ugly stuff seemed to survive with more vividness than the kinder moments.

In fact, remembering the kinder moments almost made it worse. It was easier to condemn or dismiss the person who never did right.

She'd had a turkey baking in the oven that day. Suddenly the aroma surrounded me. I heard her voice calling out as if she were just behind me, *Jaynie, get the potatoes mashed. I'll do the gravy.*

Yes, Mama.

Had I said it aloud? I shuddered.

Yes, Mama had cooked when I was younger. Not every day, and usually not very well because she didn't pay attention. Couldn't keep the focus. But she tried. The attempts had disintegrated over time. My taking over the cooking had grown over time as she had less control over her emotions, her rages. But it hadn't always been that way. At least not all the time. Not every day.

She could've done better. It pissed me off that she hadn't.

Did she understand that she'd let us down? Both Mitch

217

and me?

I thought she probably had.

Had she cared?

Yeah, probably. But not enough to be able to do it better.

Maybe she really couldn't. Couldn't get out of her own way to a better life. Without wanting to cast more stones at her, I accepted that my mother had thrived in chaos . . . until it killed her. Which made my anger and resentment seem all the more pointless.

I shook my head. I bypassed the odds and ends I'd taken with me from my life with Justin, slowing only to grab the handle of my roller suitcase, and I left the barn.

~~~~

Shortly before six o'clock, I left Ruth's house, crossed the dirt road, and walked through the opening in the fence and across to the back door of Uncle Lou's house. Rather, Wyatt's house. At least until he sold it. Whether he decided to sell it along with his grandmother's house and land to a developer, or just to sell the houses along with their property to individual buyers, he'd made it obvious he was selling. He wanted to move on too, just as I did.

When I knocked and he yelled, "Come in," I did.

As I surveyed the pots and pans on the counter and stove and the half-set table, I said, "This is nice of you, but not necessary."

"Too late now," he responded. "The mess has already been made. Can you sort out the plates and flatware?"

I found the utensils and arranged them. "I don't recognize these dishes." Not Ruth's or Mama's.

"A tenant left them behind. Maybe a few tenants. I've

got quite an assortment in the cupboards."

"I remember a few of the renters, but none of them stayed long. Mostly they kept to themselves or came and went quickly. In between, it seemed like the house stayed empty."

Wyatt laughed as he pulled rolls from the oven.

"Can you blame them? It can't have been comfortable living in the no-man's land between Bella Highsmith and Ruth Berry." He laughed as he dropped the rolls into a basket for the table. "People worry about EMF and all that. I imagine the human-generated negative energy pulsing between those two probably made anyone in this house uncomfortable."

I paused, holding the utensils mid-placement, my mouth gaping. "What are you talking about? I know they weren't close, and may not have liked each other, but I never heard them utter a single cross word to the other."

Wyatt gave me an odd look as he put the basket on the table and set the butter dish next to it. "Seriously?" he asked. He handed me a glass. "Sodas and juice and bottled water are in the fridge. I'll let you make your own choice. No alcohol. Sorry. I don't keep it around. Not good for me."

His remark distracted me all over again. I went silent and chose a soda from the fridge. I could only interpret his words to mean that at least part of his troubles in California were connected to alcoholism or addiction or something like that. I straightened the paper napkins and reset the forks, which had somehow gone a little crooked.

A bowl of tossed salad was on the table, and Wyatt was back again, this time with a casserole dish. "Smothered pork chops. I hope you like them?"

"No doubt I will, if the aroma is any indication."

"Have a seat, and I'll be right back."

I did. Still bemused. Still quiet. I fidgeted, touching the paper napkin and utensils. Wyatt returned and set a small box on the table next to my plate. I just looked at him.

He said, "A welcome home gift." He pushed it closer to me. "Nothing fancy, I promise."

He was waiting. What else could I do?

"Thank you, Wyatt. Dinner looks wonderful. I wasn't expecting a gift."

"No need to be polite. Trust me, I enjoy cooking. It's nice to have someone to share it with. It's been quiet in this . . . not really a neighborhood, is it? Our little hollow, I guess. That's as good as any other word. It's nice to have company."

The box was in my hand. A small white gift box. The box felt . . . energetic? Almost weightless, but still heavy. The heaviness wasn't physical weight, but I felt pulled down by the past, like quicksand fighting for attention. But Wyatt was waiting. I lifted the lid.

He said, "It was Ruth's. I thought you'd like to have it as a keepsake."

I took it from the box and let the brooch rest in the palm of my hand. Bright glass stones twinkled in the overhead kitchen light . . . colorful flower petals, a daisy, a buttercup, and a tiny butterfly. That feeling of heaviness was gone. As if . . . as if it had been freed. My eyes stung. No. No crying. No tears allowed. I smiled at Wyatt. "Thank you. I do remember it. She wore this brooch with a scarf." I gestured around my neck and shoulders.

He added, "And there's something else. I won't call it a

gift because I know it already belonged to you. I was surprised to find it packed away with my grandmother's things." He unwrapped a small brown bag and pulled out the dragonfly pendant.

Speechless, I looked at him and then back at the dragonfly.

Desperate to speak, I forced words out. "I lost it. I never knew where it went."

"Mystery solved. Grandma must've found it and didn't get to return it before she passed. Mom didn't know it was yours, or she would've given it back to you."

My hand hurt. I was clutching the dragonfly too tightly, and the metal bit into my palm. I relaxed my fingers and opened them slowly. The dragonfly pendant. As bright and silver as the day she'd given it to me. I'd wanted to reject the gift that day. I'd always been afraid of dragonflies. But why? The pendant, while not expensive, was still beautiful. One day, I hadn't been able to find it. Not wanting Ruth to think I'd been careless with her gift—which I had—I never said anything. Had she wondered why I never asked her if she'd found it?

"How did you know it was mine?"

"I remember seeing you wear it back in those days when we first met." Wyatt cleared his throat and with sudden gusto said, "Ready to eat?"

Grateful for the break from the intense emotion, I said, "Yes, please do. It smells wonderful." I moved to return the brooch to the box, and I replaced the cotton insert. The dragonfly necklace settled around my neck, and the pendant, though seeming so light, lay especially heavy against my chest. I put my hand over the pendant and smiled. "Thank you."

For a moment I thought he might be blushing, but the hint of red in his cheeks passed quickly, and I wasn't sure.

"My pleasure," he said.

In an involuntary movement, I patted the pendant again. Still there. And my face felt warm.

I laughed. "These pork chops are steaming hot, aren't they?" I waved my hand at my face. "But they smell wonderful."

"Hopefully they taste good too."

I went to work with my knife and fork. The salad was lovely, the rolls were hot and fresh, and the pork chops were smothered in gravy and onions and absolute goodness.

"I'm going to be busy working off these calories."

"You and calories don't have any problem. You look wonderful, Jayne."

"Thank you, Wyatt. You look good yourself, but then you seem to be busy all the time. I guess that's how you stay in shape?" I took a long sip of soda. "I have to go back to something you said before. I knew about the tension between Mama and Ms. Ruth, though neither talked about it. You also said something before about problems between Mama and your mother."

"Sure. They were friends in high school, but also rivals."

"How so?" I kept my voice even, interested, but testing. Did he know? Would he say?

He shook his head, smiling. "I shouldn't smile. I'm sure it was all very dramatic and intense back then. To hear Mom tell it, for the people around them it was considered an almost epic rivalry. Even in later years when Mom spoke of it, her fists would clench and her eyes would get all squinty, as if ready to go at it all over again. Bella and Dee. Dee and Bella." He set his fork down and leaned back in his chair. "When teenage friends go to war with each other, it can be particularly ugly."

"Rivals over what?"

"I'm getting there." He gestured toward my glass. "Need a refill?"

"Over what, Wyatt? What were they rivals for?"

He grinned. "It started with the junior varsity cheer squad and who was going to be team captain. Bella with her red hair and aggressive energy versus Dee, whose dark hair and outwardly calmer demeanor hid the temper inside. They settled for cocaptains. It all seemed okay for a while, though I think a lot of people fueled the rivalry with remarks. Two pretty—no, per Mom, two gorgeous teenage girls who each wanted to rule their world.

"Mom said that over time they each did things—she doesn't excuse herself—to provoke or sabotage the other. By the time they were juniors, they were fighting over boyfriends." His tone changed as he said, "Mom said one of her big regrets—and she was pretty sure it was Bella's regret too—was that instead of competing to get into college, they were chasing after and fighting over boys. She said that, looking back, she doesn't even think it was about the boys or having boyfriends, but the competition. They were so focused on the war between them that they lost sight of their personal goals, their future."

I asked, "So who won?"

He shrugged. "No one. Or maybe you, Mitch, and I are the ultimate winners, since we exist."

Did he know? Was he about to admit it? "What do you

mean?"

He grinned again. "By their senior year, Bella had zeroed in on George Highsmith. My mom had had a crush on George. They both grew up here, you know. But George was head over heels for Bella, so Mom set her sights on Tyson Harper. Both won. Or lost. Depending on how one looks at it. Tyson eventually took off. Apparently, marriage and fatherhood weren't what he was expecting."

"You were young when he left."

"Soon after I was born."

I was thinking of Mama telling the new father that his wife and George had had an affair and that the paternity might be in question. I was sure that Mama hadn't said it quite that politely. "I'm sorry. It must've been hurtful and confusing."

"Yes."

I digested that for a moment. "Again, I'm sorry."

He gave me an odd look. "Don't be. It's not your fault." He went on to say, "Mom said Bella and George's wedding was held the day after graduation, but no one was happy about it, least of all Bella, because Mitch was already on the way. Mom said it marked the beginning of a sad downhill slide for Bella. Her father died of a heart attack within a year, and Bella was stuck with a husband she may or may not have loved, an infant, and a mother who was nearly destroyed by grief."

"Not what she'd envisioned for herself." But different thoughts were running through my head. He didn't know. Wyatt wasn't so devious that he would've omitted that while talking about Dee and Bella and George.

"When the other kids began to peel off after graduation,

either going away to college or taking off on other adventures, Mom and Bella were following the paths they'd set, and they were not very happy about it."

We sat in silence for a moment. I knew a little about how it felt when your dreams were taken, or when you found out that what had seemed so wonderful showed itself to be empty. A waste. Mama's world must've change beyond all recognition.

I said, "I remember Dad's grandmother. She lived with us until she died. I vaguely remember meeting my father's parents. Mama didn't get along with them. She said they came over after Dad drowned wanting to sell the house and property and weren't too happy that Granny Highsmith had given it to my daddy which meant it was now Mama's. Mama said they had some idea they could force her out, but they had another think coming when it came to pushing her around. At some point they moved away. Judging by remarks Mama made when she was having a mood, they had other children and grandchildren they stayed closer to, but honestly, my memory of them was cold and unpleasant, so. . . I have a few memories of my mother's mother. Grandma. Not much. But she died when I was very young."

Wyatt had started gathering up the utensils and plates.

I sighed. "I see people with lots of family. Grandparents, maybe even great-grands, cousins, siblings, nephews, nieces, and so on. Even friends who are as close as family. They have cookouts and reunions and a hundred people come. Holiday dinners require additional tables and borrowed seating. Everyone is noisy and laughing, and there's lots of hugging. I know that exists. But not for me. What about you? Do you have grandparents you're in touch with? Cousins?"

He set the small stack of plates back down on the table. "Mom and Bill live in Indiana now. He was unemployed for a while, and when he found a new job, that's where it was. We talk on the phone. My father may or may not be still living out there in the big, wide world. I went looking for him, but no success. You know about Ruth, of course."

"But not about your grandfather. Ruth's husband. Mr. Berry. Your mother's father. Ruth never spoke of him. I took that to mean she didn't want to. I never saw a picture of him or anything else."

"Berry was her family name. Ruth never married."

I frowned. "What?"

Wyatt shrugged. "Ruth never married, and she never spoke of him. Was it due to heartbreak or anger or because she didn't want people gossiping? Who knows?" He stood and picked up the plates again. He set the dirty dishes on the counter, then turned back to face me. "As to your other question, I think it's fractured families. Fractured lives. Some families, some people, overcome it and maintain those close relationships, but many don't. Those are the people who spend holidays alone. Who have to manage their lives alone."

A sadness so deep that it felt like a thick wool blanket settled around my shoulders. Not *my* sadness but a sadness I felt in sympathy with those who were alone, but not by choice.

I stood in silence beside Wyatt as he washed the dishes and I dried.

He asked softly, "You okay?"

I nodded. "I never . . . I mean, I should've known a lot of that already, right? Mama never spoke about any of it. She didn't like me asking questions either. Ruth never did. I knew there was something unhappy between them. They wouldn't talk about each other, in a deliberate sort of way." I shrugged, feeling rather like a failure again, not only as a friend to Ruth but also as a daughter.

"They did that for you, I'm sure. Neither of them bad-mouthed or told tales about the other, right?"

"True. Actually, they said very little about any specific differences or the cause." And they'd done that for me. They'd put me ahead of their history and feelings. Ruth . . . I would've expected that of her. Mama . . . not so much. "Mama didn't encourage me to hang out with Ms. Ruth, but she didn't try very hard to prevent it either." I shrugged and paused with the dish towel and the last plate in my hands. "I didn't think Mama knew how much I hung out over there. But of course, she must've."

Wyatt took the plate and towel from me and set them on the counter. "Kids have their own way of seeing and interpreting. I'd like to show you something. Come with me?"

Now what?

He led me to the living room. I'd been in here the day before. But this time he took me into the short hallway to the bedrooms. We stopped in front of a small, framed drawing on the wall. I didn't recognize it. It was as if I'd never seen it before this minute—until Wyatt snapped the overhead light on. I stared as the lines and curves, the rough textures and awkward shading, found memories in my brain, and I could almost feel it rewiring, reincorporating this old memory. This event.

I felt light-headed. Oxygen deprived.

I'd drawn Ms. Ruth. A portrait. I remembered doing it, and my fingers twitched.

She'd framed it? This drawing was by a middle schooler—probably when I was thirteen or fourteen. It was imperfectly done, but it also showed promise. *I'd* shown promise.

And Ms. Ruth had framed it.

Wyatt said, "I always thought you'd be an artist. Maybe even have a gallery to show your drawing and paintings. You used to talk about that."

"Did I?" Yes, I supposed I had. "It was a child's pie-in-the-sky dream."

Ms. Ruth had framed it, and Wyatt had kept it. And had hung it here where he must see it multiple times a day.

Wyatt said, "Enough of memory lane. Let's get some fresh air."

Numb, I went along. But when we got to the back door, I saw the daylight was fading fast.

"Are you sure? It's almost dark."

He shrugged. "Hey, we know the territory well. And who's going to complain? Between us, we own all of the property around here."

After a light, but ragged laugh, I said, "I guess we own the world of my childhood."

He offered his hand. "What do you say we go out and enjoy it this evening?"

.

CHAPTER SEVENTEEN

As we walked in the fading light, I could almost imagine I was back, not only in the *place* of my childhood, but also in the *time* of my childhood. It was that quicksand effect. Blink, the ether shifts, and now you're there. The same grains of dirt from long ago were still beneath my feet, merely shuffled and rearranged. These were the same houses and the same barn, all cloaked in the growing dusk and seeming unchanged by time, age, or improvements. The trees were the same too, though taller and fuller. As if, instead of the trees growing taller, I was the one who'd returned to the size of a child.

Despite being taller and with a thinner, more angular face and jaw, the dark-haired man walking beside me was unmistakably Wyatt.

If I reached out and took his hand, I imagined I could almost span the distance between eighteen and thirty-six. I couldn't. And I wouldn't. It was enough to be walking down the dirt road and through the neighborhood of my early years—with him. I was happy inside. Grateful for the trip, if not the impetus for it.

We turned the corner and passed Ruth's house on the left. Ahead of us, where the creek met the forest, the shadows were inky black already. Around us, the fireflies lit up here and there, rising from the grasses and flitting among the treetops. Wyatt was leading me somewhere. I was lost in this strange medley of past and present, content to follow. As we approached the barn area on our right, he veered toward the fence. When we reached it, he offered his hand.

I'd thought of taking his hand before. Now I balked. "The fence?"

"You aren't too old to climb up, are you?" With an easy shift to a more formal tone, he bowed slightly and said, "If you need a step up, it will be my pleasure to assist you."

"I've got this." But I tested the boards. It was a patched fence. I'd never given a thought to falling or picking up a splinter in my younger years. I was acting like a senior citizen. I stepped on the bottom board, then swung a little sideways to plant my bottom on the top rail. I held my breath, listening for a creak that didn't come.

"You all set?"

"I am." I laughed. "It's been a while. Aren't you going to join me?"

He grinned.

"Chicken?"

"I think that, for both our sakes, I won't add more weight to the rail." He stood close to the fence, and to me, and leaned against it, nearly brushing my thigh. "I'll be here, ready to catch you, if the worst happens."

I wanted to laugh, and I wanted to smack him, but not too hard. "Then maybe I'd better get down."

"No," he said. "Stay right there. Watch with me." He pointed skyward.

I stared and shook my head. "Watch what? It's dark."

"Precisely."

Annoyed, I asked, "What am I supposed to be seeing?"

"See that star? The bright one?"

I looked in the direction he indicated, and I did see a bright point of light shining. Others were beginning to be visible. But this one was bright and larger than the others.

"Yes."

"It's not a star. That's Jupiter. It's about as close to Earth as it will get."

"Jupiter."

He continued staring straight ahead. "And if I stare hard enough and squint a little, I can almost imagine I see its rust-colored streaks. I know that's not possible, but a few months ago, Mars was close. You could definitely make out the red tint, even with the naked eye."

We watched the stars emerge one by one and then in clusters, surrounded by the silence of a peaceful night given over only to insects and the occasional sound of a night bird calling.

"Now," Wyatt said, and I jumped a little. He took my hand and pointed it toward a tree that rose above the general dark shapes of the forest horizon. "See that star hanging just over the top of that tulip poplar?"

He'd kept my hand in his. I was content to leave it there.

"Yes."

"Do you know whose star that is?"

"I bet I do."

"It's part of the constellation Scorpius. Ruth claimed that star. On one of those nights when she and I were sitting at the fire in the backyard, she told me." He squeezed my fingers gently, then released my hand.

My fingers felt orphaned. I clasped my other hand around them and whispered, "Antares."

"Yes," he said. "That's right."

"Did she tell you about the ether and swirls?"

He groaned. "She talked about lots of things. She was full of theories and philosophies."

"And kindness."

He shifted. I felt his hand on the rail near to my thigh.

"She was. A kind soul. A gentle person to both people and plants." He laughed a little. His voice was low and warm. "As long as you didn't make her angry. Then she had a temper to end all tempers."

"I never saw that aspect of her. She did tell me she'd had a checkered past."

"She probably meant her hippie years. Mom said Grandma attended Woodstock back in the day. Shocked the whole family, I understand. Free-spirited and independent-minded."

"And yet she ended up back here?"

"No need to sound sad about it. Sometimes it takes people a while to figure out where they should be. Besides, she didn't end up back here—it's where she came to after. She was a young woman then and soon to be a mother. Her father bought her this house—the house you knew as her home. She said she thought he chose this out-of-the-way spot because he wanted to hide her from everyone they knew—unmarried, pregnant, and prone to dressing like a hippie."

"But here . . ."

"She settled in and was mostly content, I think. Her parents made sure she'd have an income before they died. She could've left, but she didn't. In fact, I hope I'm not telling secrets, but I think Ruth and Uncle Lou had something going on for a while."

"Seriously?"

"Seriously."

"I had no idea." I shook my head. "What about you? You left. You went away just as you'd always dreamed. And now you're back. Too." I left it open-ended.

"The world is a smaller but more crowded place. Anyone who wants excitement can travel and find it. These days I'm okay with the kind of excitement I'm finding around here."

I hardly heard those last words. They were spoken so softly that they faded into nothingness. I let them go. I didn't have answers either.

"You sighed."

"I did."

Wyatt said, "Back when I was in high school, I believed my future was waiting for me out there." He waved his hand generally at the world. "I thought that by the time I hit my thirties I'd have found what I wanted to do with my life, and I'd be well established in whatever business I'd settled on. I'd be living in a city—a big city, not a place like Richmond or Charlottesville—and certainly not this in-between place. No, it would be a big, busy place where the sun always shined and people had important things to do and knew how to play big too."

"Did you find what you were looking for?"

"I think that was part of the problem. I didn't know what I was looking for. No specific goals. Goals can change along the way, but at least they help you focus on a starting point versus a scattershot approach. Each step along the way, I thought I knew exactly the right thing to do, and never once did it work out. Eventually I settled in construction and found

I enjoyed it, but even then I fouled it up."

"How so?" I asked because I sensed he wanted me to. He wanted to tell me what was on his heart.

"Spent money unwisely. Worked hard to recover. Made bad choices about business partners. Harder to recover from. What I learned was to never put control of any aspect of your life into the hands of another human being. They are flawed at best. Cruel, callous at worst."

"That's why you're here now?"

"I hear it in your voice. You're asking if I'm hiding here. If I am, it's by choice. I'll only take on what I want, when I want. I'll live on my terms. For right now, that's here."

"Okay, then. Sounds like you've got it worked out. What about the alcohol remark you made earlier? Was that part of the problem?" I raised my hand. "If you don't want to talk about it, that's okay."

"I don't mind, though I'd appreciate it if you kept it between us. No, I'm not an alcoholic and I'm not an addict. But when I was doing those things . . . those ill-advised choices . . . they always seemed to lead to other things. As if some part of my brain was turned on . . . activated, and then became interested in other risky behaviors. My business suffered. I was never happy. As if that didn't even matter. As if it was about the pursuit and the experience—that happiness was something you settled for in old age when you were out of energy to keep trying for more."

"What changed your mind?"

"After many months of living too fast, of parties and ignoring serious trouble, I got sick. Really sick. Hospital sick. My heart came close to calling it quits."

"Heart attack?"

"No. It stopped. I was lucky that it chose to stop near the manpower and equipment that knew how to do something to start it again."

"Oh. Wyatt. I can't imagine."

"I was in good shape before I started the downhill slide—which is what living in that fast lane actually is. Once they cleared my system—I mean of everything—I recovered pretty well, but it took a while. By the time I was well enough to tackle life and work again, I discovered that my partner had cleaned me out too. Business was belly-up, and creditors were howling."

"Oh," I said again. I couldn't think of what to say. "I'm so sorry. But how fortunate you are."

"Exactly. Exactly times a thousand. When I was in the hospital and they were checking me out and putting heaven knows what into me, and clearing who knows what out of me, I saw this fence. This place. When I was sitting in that awful pink vinyl chair and looking out of the hospital window at the roof of the next building—at the gravel-and-tar roof and the air-handling systems—I was seeing my grandmother's house, her yard. This fence. I was seeing the fireflies. And mostly I was seeing her point at that star. She could find it, regardless of season, as long as it was shining over our piece of the world. I'd see that star."

Starlight. Ruth and light. Whether in us or outside of us
. . .

"Pardon?"

"Oh, sorry. Just thinking about what you were saying. So then what happened?"

"When I was released and went looking for my business partner, who'd come by early in my hospital stay and hadn't come back, I found disaster. And I wasn't unhappy. It was like someone had snipped the tie that had bound me to that course, that path. I'd been so busy trying to stick to the course and numbing myself to the pain of it that I almost killed myself.

"I cleaned up what I could of the business. Tied up as many legal ends as I could. Tracked down my partner and we resolved most of the debt. And then I came home. These houses . . . at least two of the three . . . could've been flipped and me out of here and on to other things long ago. The possibility of a bigger development deal gave me a reason not to rush. Or maybe I'm that old guy now and in no big hurry to chase after more."

"But eventually, Wyatt . . . sooner or later, you'll move on, right?"

He shrugged. "Probably."

"If Mitch is agreeable to the sale?"

"That's up to you and him. A potential deal isn't necessarily going to be dependent on all three properties." He smiled. "There was something else my grandmother used to say. She said not to borrow trouble. Just focus on today and your part in it. So I guess that's what I'm doing right now."

"You grandmother, my dear Ms. Ruth, told me not to get upset or angry when things didn't go the way you'd planned because your frustration would just contribute to the chaos in the ether."

Wyatt said, "I don't know about contributing to the ether or anything else, but for sanity's sake? Focusing on my own life and being in touch with that? Yeah, I know about that." He offered his hand. "May I walk you home, Jayne?"

I accepted his hand and stepped down from the fence.

He said, "I hope you enjoyed this evening's entertainment."

He meant the night sky, of course, but I said, "I am a little overwhelmed that you shared so much of your life and troubles with me. I'm honored, Wyatt."

He nodded. "Takes one to know one."

"As in?"

"One person who has endured troubles recognizes that in someone else."

"True enough. I just switched out Mama for other troubles."

"You still hold her failings against her?"

"Yes. No. I don't know. I think I became the sheet in the wind."

"What?"

"Another Ruth-ism. I thought I'd flown free when I left here, but all I did was switch out Mama for other things, or people, that weren't really good for me. I think I may finally be able to let go of some of that."

"Because you're home."

I ignored that and kept walking toward the house.

Mindful of the man Wyatt had seen snooping around earlier, I'd locked the back door when I left the house. I pulled the keys from my pocket, and he waited as I opened the door and flipped the kitchen light on.

"Are you okay? Comfortable?" he asked.

"Yes, thank you. And dinner was wonderful."

He nodded. "Good. Any worries, you call. Anyone knocks on the door, don't answer. Not until we're sure about that guy. Anyone knocks, you call me, and I'll take a look out and see who it is. Call me."

"I will. Truly. I'll be fine. I don't know who that guy you saw is, or why he was here, but no one cares where I've gone. I don't say that to be seeking pity. It's just the simple truth. No one will come looking for me."

~~~~

That night, as I pulled my pajamas and toiletries from my suitcase, I also retrieved a photograph—the one of Ruth and me together and smiling from a lifetime ago. I'd kept it with me over the years but had not displayed it after moving into Justin's house. Now I carried the framed photo to the built-in bookcase in the living room and returned it to its former spot.

Trying to sleep in a narrow twin bed that made me feel more than ever like a kid—albeit an overgrown one—my first thought was *I'm going to roll right off the side*, but there was also a certain comfort to it. To being relieved of any expectation of adulting or serious considerations. No one can feel like a serious adult squashed into a twin bed. Didn't everyone need at least a queen these days?

I smiled and plumped the pillow behind my head and pulled the blanket over me and up under my chin. I had to crook my legs at the knees; otherwise, my feet were too near the area at the foot of the bed where the bedding was tucked in and constrained my foot movement too much. I rolled over on my side and pulled my legs up a little more. That was better. The pillow was some sort of fiberfill, but new, so it wasn't lumpy. The sheets were cotton, and not the thread count I was accustomed to, but on the other hand, I wasn't sharing it with a man who no longer wanted me and feeling that hurt. There was no TV or music playing or even filtering in from another room or another user. The room suddenly felt even darker and more suffocating. I rolled over and tugged the sheet along with me, thinking how strange it was that Wyatt was here, that he'd fed me and had—totally unplanned for—provided a haven for me to stay in. I'd never been in this room as a child, and had never slept in Ruth's house, but Wyatt had done a good job of removing personal items—a.k.a. memory triggers—while still leaving the essence of the house from the years she'd lived here. So, I wasn't worried about dreaming of her. I was more worried about other memories—memories of summer evenings and autumn afternoons. Of spring and Ruth's flowers. Of the woods, of the creek, of my rock. Of perhaps Ruth digging in the closet and finding a dress.

I rolled over onto my other side and tugged the sheet and blanket along with me again.

I was thinking of tomorrow—of emptying the rest of my junk from my vehicle. I had plenty of room in the barn and could even give the car a good cleaning inside. I thought I might ask Wyatt if he had a handheld vacuum and . . .

CHAPTER EIGHTEEN

Up early the next morning, feeling rested and surprisingly light and cheery, I showered and dressed in shorts and a cotton shirt, found my sandals, and went to greet the day. As I walked over to Wyatt's house and stepped up to his back porch, I heard men's voices and general work noises coming from down the road, from my mother's house. Instead of knocking, I went to see what was going on.

Apparently, I wasn't up all that early after all. A white van was parked out front. It had a plumbing logo on the side. A pickup truck was beside it, with equipment jumbled in the truck bed. I was speculating about whether to walk into the house when I heard my name called.

Wyatt was crossing the yard, coming from his house.

"Morning, Jayne."

"Morning, Wyatt."

He was holding two cups of coffee. He offered one to me.

"You psychic or what?" I asked.

"Nope. Just saw you at my back door, and then you were gone. I can add two plus two pretty well."

I took a sip. "It's good."

"A friend sent me some packages from Hawaii. Kona coffee."

"Hawaii. I've never been."

"Easily fixed. It's just a plane ride away. For now, just enjoy the coffee. Would you like to see what's up? The plumbing is in pretty good shape, as it turns out. Matt is tweaking it, and he'll install a new hot water heater. A small one, and not expensive."

"How is Mitch funding this?"

"No worries. He'll pay me when he can." His gaze swung away, then came back to me again. "Truth be known, Mitch helped me out a time or two over the last couple of years. I don't mind extending a hand back."

Suddenly I felt a little odd. They'd become more than neighbors? Also friends. Wyatt had always been my friend, not Mitch's. Mitch was five years or so older than Wyatt. In fact, they were almost . . . brotherly. I shuddered.

"You okay?"

"I'm fine. This coffee's great. Need any help with the repairs?"

Wyatt gave me a quick frowning smile. "Seriously?"

"Seriously."

He shook his head and shrugged. "Well, I dunno. You have any skills? You don't look all that handy to me."

I frowned right back at him. "I'm plenty handy. What'd you have in mind?"

He grinned. "For starters, let's go check on Matt, and we'll see where that leads us."

~~~~~

Matt was in the utility closet connecting the hot water heater. "Wyatt?" he asked.

"Yes. And Jayne. Mitch's sister is here too."

A head popped out, with light-brown hair and a

congenial expression. "Hey, Jayne. Nice to meet you."

"Hi, Matt."

He was back at work before I could finish my wave. Mitch's sister, Wyatt had said. He and I exchanged glances.

Matt's voice came again. "Better shape overall than I expected." He backed out of the closet and dropped some tools into a heavy-duty bag. He wiped his hands on his shirt. "Mitch had some other work done on the pipes recently. Some might've been done by him or friends. No worries. I sorted it out."

"Thanks, Matt."

"Hello?"

Wyatt and I turned. A young man was standing in the open front doorway.

"Come in, Kenny. Matt's just finishing up."

The young man set a bucket of sheet flooring paste down in the living room and joined us in the kitchen.

Wyatt said, "Jayne, this is Kenny. Kenny, this is Jayne, Mitch's sister. He's the vinyl man. As soon as Matt's out of the way, Kenny's going to pull up this old floor and get a new one down."

"A new floor?" I was having trouble processing this.

Wyatt shrugged. "It's a small floor area. All we needed was the right size remnant."

"Please to meet you, Jayne."

I nodded and held out my hand. Kenny grabbed it and shook.

Lamely, I asked, "You know Mitch?"

Kenny grinned. "He's a good guy, Mitch is. Guess you know that, though." And he went back out to his car, apparently to retrieve his other supplies.

I tugged on Wyatt's sleeve and nodded toward the back door.

He said, "Be right back, Matt." He followed me out.

We stood on the back-porch steps. It was something of a jungle out here. No one had cleaned up much out here yet. Maybe someone who knew Mitch would show up to do the yard work too.

"What's going on, Wyatt? These men don't sound like they're just here to do a job."

"They're friends of Mitch."

"What? Friends of Mitch? Is it like some kind of club?" I cringed at the sharp, almost jealous tone in my voice.

"No. Just friends who are looking to give Mitch a helping hand with a fresh start."

"But—" I broke off. It was the tone in his voice—his calm, even response that stopped me. Even so, I had more to say. I grabbed his arm again and this time pulled him out into the weedy yard, farther from the house, because I could feel my temper rising, and I was sure my voice would too.

"You were talking about selling all of this to a developer, weren't you? You're doing this renovation for Mitch and at the same time looking to sell it? Isn't that a massive contradiction?"

Wyatt brushed at a small black bug climbing up his pants leg, before saying, "Keep in mind that I don't own this lot." He gestured toward the house and yard. "This belongs to you. So, if there's an opportunity that you and Mitch want to be part of, that's fine. But there's no deal yet, and this work needs doing now because Mitch will be coming home, and he has asked for our help."

"When?"

"When is he coming home?" He shook his head. "I don't want to get your hopes up and won't go into details, but it may be sooner than expected."

Just then, his phone rang. Wyatt pulled it from his pocket and checked the screen. "Sorry, I've got to take this."

"Go ahead. We'll talk later."

He strode away toward his own property. I was glad, really. That harsh cynicism that had washed through me had surprised me, and it had mostly passed now. But I had so much running through my brain. I needed to think.

I thought of the Highsmith family. My father's people. Who'd originally owned all this property and had sold off lots for the other two houses, first to Uncle Lou and then to someone else who later sold to Ruth Berry, or rather to her father. Now maybe we'd—I'd—be selling too. Maybe it was part of the greater scheme of how the world turned. In seasons. Life seasons.

Feeling calmer and definitely curious, I went back into the house.

Kenny was working on the kitchen floor, scraping up the ancient linoleum where the adhesive wasn't giving up easily. He said, "Matt's gone," without looking up. When he did raise his head and saw only me, he said, "Is Wyatt coming back?"

"Yes. He'll be right back."

"Good." Kenny never stopped. He continued working up the linoleum while trying not to gouge the underlayment.

I admired his patience, but the dedication mystified me. I'd figured out that there was some level of charity work going on here. Kenny probably wasn't getting paid for his time.

"Need any help?" I asked.

He threw me a quick, slightly amused, but kind look. "Thank you, ma'am, but I've got it."

"Not *ma'am*. Jayne."

"Jayne, then."

"So you know my brother?"

"Mitch? Yes, ma'am. I mean, Jayne."

"Did you work together, or . . . ?"

"With Mitch?" He paused his work to look up at me. "Not really, but most everyone knows Mitch. He's the kind of guy who's always there to lend a hand. When my sister had to move, he was there to help load the truck. When my car broke down, he came over to my house to work on it. He doesn't have much himself, but if you go by the soup kitchen, you'll probably see him in the serving line. Not meaning any offense, but I heard someone call him a bum once, and I corrected them—Mitch Highsmith is a giver. If all he has is the shirt on his back and you need it, he'll give it without pause. I heard somewhere that people were wolves or shepherds or sheep. Self-explanatory, I guess. But Mitch? Mitch is a shepherd."

"I see."

"But you already know all that."

"He and I haven't been close in recent years. But," I added, "he was always a good big brother to me. Always watched out for me as best he could."

"Yeah? Not surprised. Mitch is a good guy."

A good guy. A good guy, that's Mitch. The words ran through my head like a refrain.

"Thanks, Kenny."

"For what?"

"For helping. For telling me why."

He looked puzzled. "Happy to."

I wandered off, moving through the house again, this time seeing it less as a place of my childhood where the bad memories dominated. And not my home either. Regardless of ownership, this was Mitch's home.

Mama had depended on him to watch me. She'd used him for companionship. He'd been there for both of us to the best of his ability.

And *used* was the wrong word. Most of the time, Mitch and Mama had gotten along well—hence he'd taken the heat for me when Mama was ticked off. Plus, I don't think he minded watching TV with her. I'd always considered him lazy. But he'd been there, with fortunate timing, on that day when Boone and Mama had fought in the kitchen, and he'd made Mama kick Boone out. Mitch had done what he could. Almost six years older than me—he'd spent most of his childhood and teenage years watching out for me, his kid sister.

He'd never complained. I couldn't think of a time when he'd argued or refused or talked about stuff he'd rather be doing. Never blamed his circumstances for dropping out of school.

My lazy, unmotivated brother Mitch. I needed to think about this. Was there more to him than I'd understood? Was I so self-focused (*yes, Ruth, I hear you*) that I was actually judging him by my own understanding—or lack thereof— and continuing to think of him according to the assumptions of my much younger self? My own personal filters—not necessarily a true view of my brother.

"Jayne?"

I turned toward Wyatt. He was halfway hanging out the door.

"Sorry, startled you again, didn't I?" He grinned. "You okay?"

"I am. I'm good." But I had a lot to digest. "I'm heading out to work in the barn."

He nodded. "Probably no reason to worry, but please secure that door. You have the key for the padlock?"

I patted my pocket. "I do."

"Keep your phone handy. Call me if you need me."

I smiled. "I will. Thanks."

Thanks, I thought again. We owed him. Our whole family did. We also owed him the truth. And it seemed like maybe I was the only one who knew the truth.

I spent the rest of the morning in the barn unpacking everything and sorting and repacking. Some of the items I'd targeted and taken as valuable were, but really, any money I might get for them was limited, considering I couldn't show any kind of ownership papers. I'd felt empowered—and almost powerful—as I'd planned what to take in the days leading up to my departure, and then as I'd swept through the morning I left. Now I felt vaguely embarrassed. I felt absolutely entitled to this and more, but my hands felt somewhat stained by it.

The money was different. I should feel entitled to it, especially since I was walking away from the other assets, including the mortgaged property. But it gave me an uneasy feeling.

Still in the barn, I sat on the seat of the car and opened the center console. I'd kept moving the six envelopes around from the car, then to the suitcase, then back to the car. Last night, I'd stashed them under the mattress.

Crazy that Justin kept so much cash in the house. Maybe rich people did that . . . or people who liked to act like they were wealthy. Or people who were treading a fine line between legal and not legal? Had he really mortgaged everything and had we truly been living on the edge of disaster? Maybe.

Could the man Wyatt saw been sent to find the cash?

I was glad I was shielded from prying eyes here in the barn. I couldn't put the cash in the bank, not for a while anyway. Any account I opened would be immediately traceable to me, and Justin would find a way to get his hands on it.

I scanned the barn. It was too wide open, with no real hiding places. At my rock? Buried with my toolbox? No, that was fine for childhood treasures, but the countryside and the woods weren't as empty as they'd been twenty years ago.

So Ruth's house it was. I'd find a spot better than under the mattress. Time would help me figure out what to do with the money.

~~~~

I returned to Mama's house . . . Mitch's home. Wyatt wasn't around. No workers were there. I peeked inside. That vinyl looked super. A clean, simple pattern that didn't contribute to clutter in a small house. A remnant, per Wyatt. Nice piece. A job well done.

But the glue had left a bit of a stink, so I left the back door open and propped the storm door wide. As I descended the back steps, I noted the black iron railing was spotted with rust where the finish was peeling. I ran my finger lightly over the spots, some quite large. The railing itself was still firmly set in the concrete. Could it be sanded and repainted? The finish wouldn't be smooth, but it might stop the rust. I'd ask Wyatt about it.

When was I going to speak to Wyatt about trickier things?

A straggly weed had wrapped itself around the black metal. I gave it a yank and it yielded, pulling free. I grabbed the next and gave it a yank too.

Beyond the back steps and near the old fireplace was where I'd placed my lawn chair . . . *yard chair* as Ms. Ruth called outside seating. I snagged the weeds that were coming up between the patio blocks too. They came up in bits and clumps and occasionally in long runs of roots that disturbed tiny ants and set them to running. My hands were dirty, but the dirt would wash off. My nails might need more professional help, but I kept going. Perspiration prickled along my hairline, and I ignored it. I crouched, sometimes kneeling on the hard block, and worked my way across. I ignored the ache developing in my lower back. Something cold ran down my spine. My bra was sticking to me, and when I tugged at it, I left dirt and stains on my shirt. Heaven knew what I was leaving on my face as I pushed stray hairs away.

I lost track of time, feeling wonderful with the physical activity despite the grimy sweatiness—and maybe that felt good too, in a freeing way.

The truth shall set you free . . . I'd heard that one before.

Wyatt said, "What are you doing?"

I jumped up, startled. Or tried to. The world spun and lights flashed in my head and before my eyes.

"Whoa," he said. "Steady."

His hands were on my arms and shoulder, and I was back to kneeling on the ground. The corner of one of the patio blocks was biting into my shin.

"Stay right here."

He rushed off. I heard a door slam somewhere. My head was steadying, but the lights weren't quite gone, so I waited. He returned with a bottle of water and a wet cloth.

"You're dehydrated. It's not even that hot, Jayne." He uncapped the bottle and handed it to me. While I drank, he applied the wet cloth to my forehead. "I'm guessing you don't do much outside work." He flipped the cloth to the cooler side. "How long have you been out here anyway? You've mostly cleared this whole patio."

I took the wet cloth from him and pressed it to my face. My whole face. Finally, I dropped it lower so that I could look over it.

"Wow. I guess I did. Maybe overdid . . . I was fine, and then suddenly I wasn't."

"That's what happens when you ignore the early signs of dehydration and maybe heat stroke."

"I'm fine now." I looked at my arms, with bits of nature clinging to them, and saw my shirt and legs. "Wow, again."

"Can you stand now?"

"I'm sure I can."

He kept his hand on my arm while I rose and checked my steadiness.

"I'm fine."

"Good. Headache?"

"No, I'm fine. Truly. Just need a shower and fresh clothing." I smiled. "Thank you, Wyatt. I feel so odd."

He tightened his grip. "Dizzy?"

"Not that kind of odd. I feel . . . cleaner somehow. And we owe you, Wyatt. Both Mitch and I. Even Mama. We owe you big-time." I sounded a little drunk.

"Why don't I cook supper again this evening? Take a shower, cool off, and maybe lie down for a while, then come on over and we'll rustle up some supper."

"No, thank you. Truly." I patted his arm, then removed it from mine. "I'm okay now. I'm going to rest and think. I have a lot to think about."

He nodded. "If you change your mind, just let me know."

"Thank you again, Wyatt."

~~~

I showered in tepid water. I used soothing lotions and played some music softly in the background. Peace. I sought it. I was close enough to touch it. It wouldn't last, I knew that, but for now I felt more clearheaded than I had in a long time. Justin and my time with him had faded somehow—as if the time with him had actually belonged to someone else. Had faded as everything here became more real.

Wyatt and I must have an open and honest discussion. He needed to know what Mama had said. I did trial runs in my head of how to tell him, how to phrase it. There'd be hurt. Hurt that I'd known and hadn't told him? Maybe. Hurt that his mother had kept that part from him? Likely.

I stretched out on the sofa with my bed pillow. I needed to find the right words to discuss this with Wyatt. We had a future, I thought, one way or the other, but this could alter our ability to choose that future.

It didn't matter because Wyatt deserved the truth. And I knew I was right because I still felt peace despite, or perhaps because of, my decision.

That which Justin didn't have—the ability to be honest—I did have, though it had been partly buried for the last few years. I had it, I had the guts to do what needed to be done, and I could do this. For me, for Mitch, for Wyatt—for the good of all of us.

CHAPTER NINETEEN

I woke in the night and moved from the sofa to the bed with hardly a blip. In the morning, I felt better rested than I had in years.

Ruth had told me that sometimes we got lucky and escaped payment for wrongs done. Other times we got even luckier because we had to own up to them and clear them from our conscience. I didn't blame myself for what Wyatt had or hadn't been told. That hadn't been my responsibility. But I was an adult now, and even aside from knowing that I wouldn't be able to remain friends, but no more than friends, with Wyatt, required me to tell him.

Oddly, Justin and his children were also on my mind when I woke. I'd dreamed of them, and of their mother, Sharon, whom I'd never actually met. I regretted not meeting her. Perhaps connecting with her directly, person-to-person, might've made a difference. Or it might've tied me to Justin that much longer.

Regardless, it hadn't worked out. In part, because it took more than one person to make a team work. That was all old news anyway. So why had I dreamed of them?

As a warning, apparently. Because as I stood now at Ruth's front window with its view of the gravel road, I watched Wyatt and a young woman walk into view. I stared as if pulled by a magnet or maybe a talisman—and all thoughts of the open, honest discussion I'd intended to have with Wyatt flew away.

She walked with the grace of youth and beauty. Her white-blonde hair hung nearly to her waist but with perfection—that kind of cut that always kept its perfect form no matter how the wind blew. She walked with the smooth assurance that money and security bought. She'd grown up well, though, and had kept her sweet personality. Nearly seventeen now. Almost grown, but not of legal age for another year. Was she here with her parents? Justin? Surely not. With her mother? That made no sense.

Sylvan being here on Hope Road could only mean she was looking for me.

Ruth.

But why? How had she found me?

I gripped my hands so hard my fingers hurt. I couldn't hear the conversation happening between them, but I could guess at it. Sylvan would be asking Wyatt where her stepmother was. I imagined her soft voice asking, "Ruth Hale? Is she here? Medium height and build. Reddish hair. Do you know her?"

Wyatt would say, "I don't know a Ruth Hale," but he'd be wondering about the coincidence of the first name being the same as his grandmother's.

Sylvan would point toward Mama's house, saying, "But that's where she grew up." This conversation, or something very like it, would lead them to walk this way.

They turned toward the house and crossed the grass.

Wyatt was clearly confused. His body language told the story as his shoulders were back and his posture was rigid. He looked around like maybe someone was playing a joke on him. A cruel, tasteless joke. His grandmother had been gone for many years, but love and respect endured. He might even have suggested to Sylvan that they go ask Jaynie if she knew anything about a woman named Ruth. Sylvan would've said, "Jaynie who?"

I closed my eyes, then slowly reopened them, but I was frozen in place. I couldn't open the front door without a prompt, an impetus. I stood there until Wyatt knocked. And knocked again. Hard.

Sylvan, clearly uncertain herself and unsure of this strange man, had hung back as they approached the house, but when she saw me open the door, she ran up the porch steps.

"Ruth. He said you weren't here. I was sure you must be."

"Ruth?" Wyatt stared at me, his eyes growing darker as his frown grew. "Care to explain?"

"Sylvan? How are you here? Why?"

"I don't understand what's going on, Ruth."

I spoke directly to Sylvan. "It's okay, honey. I'll tell you about it."

"Please do," Wyatt said.

"I went to your house. This man was there"—she pointed at him as if he might dispute her account—"and he told me you weren't here, but then he said you were." She crossed her arms. "I don't understand."

She seemed truly distressed.

"Calm down, Sylvan. I'll explain, but let's do some introductions first." I slid an arm around her waist and stood with her arm to arm.

"Wyatt, this is my stepdaughter, Sylvan Hale. Her father

and I are separated and divorcing." I looked at Sylvan, saying, "I'm assuming you know that?"

"Yeah. Dad said."

"That's why I'm surprised to see you. As for the name— my given name is Jayne. When I left here, I wanted a fresh start, so I told everyone to call me Ruth. I never changed my name legally. I considered it a nickname in honor of a very dear friend from my childhood."

"Unbelievable," Wyatt said.

Sylvan had shifted her position, moving away from me, but seeming now to share Wyatt's disapproval.

"Wyatt, you may believe it or not as you choose. I suspect that after you give it some thought you won't be all that surprised." Probably an outrageous remark, but hopefully it would sidetrack him long enough to give me some time alone with Sylvan.

"So, Sylvan, my real name is Jayne, but I had a dear friend long ago whose name was Ruth. When I went off to the city to start my adult life, I asked people to call me Ruth. It was silly and sentimental, but she meant a lot to me, and I wanted to remember her."

She frowned. "Why are you here? I mean, this isn't the address of the house where you grew up. This is someone else's house."

I wanted Wyatt to leave before I got into the weeds of my marriage and its dissolution, yet he showed no signs of moving on.

"Come the rest of the way inside, Sylvan. We'll sit down and talk it through properly. For one thing, I'd like to know how you found me and why you went to the trouble to do so."

She walked into the room. Wyatt stayed by the door. He said, "I expect an explanation."

"I promise."

He cast a quick glance at Sylvan before adding in a low voice, "I mean it, Jayne."

I nodded. "Later."

He left. As he was crossing the lawn, I closed the door gently and turned to face my stepdaughter. Ex-stepdaughter? Maybe.

"Can I get you something to drink? Water or iced tea—that's all I have. Not too much in the way of groceries." I tacked on, "Yet."

"Iced tea, I guess."

She looked a little sullen. I recognized some of my own anger and frustration at that age.

I walked into the kitchen and poured us each a glass of tea. When I returned, I saw she'd taken a seat on the sofa but was perched on the edge of it, her backpack on the floor between her feet.

She took one sip of her tea, fastened her eyes on mine, and said, "Why did you leave?"

While I was trying to come up with an acceptable answer, she quickly added, "Dad said you were the one who left."

"I did, yes, but only because he insisted our marriage was over." I set my glass on the coaster. "What's this about?"

Her frown sagged along with her shoulders.

"I knew it. Mom saw him with another woman, and she warned me a change might be coming. I didn't want to believe it. I asked him, and he said you wanted out of the marriage."

"Did you tell him you were going to find me?"

"No. Mom either. She was going on a trip, so I told her I was going to be visiting a school friend for a few days."

"I see. Now how did you know where to find me?"

"When your mother died, you mentioned going home for the funeral."

I waited.

"Well, it was easy enough. I tried to find an actual obituary online—you know, where they list the family and such—but couldn't. I did find the death notice in the local newspaper, though." She smiled softly. "Bella Highsmith. I remembered the name from when you told me because it sounded like a literary character's name, or maybe the heroine in a romance novel. It's a name with . . . with . . ." She stopped. "That sounds stupid, but that's how I found you. While I was searching online for the obituary, the newspaper article about the accident came up."

"Seriously?"

"Sure. I even printed it out in case I needed any of the info to find you, but I didn't. It was easy."

"Wow. I had no idea."

"Where's your car? I expected to find Hope Road and then see your car—and then I'd know for sure I'd found you, but when I didn't, I had to speak with that man."

"His name is Wyatt. And the car is here. It's parked back in the barn."

"Oh? Cool. I saw that big barn. That one?"

I smiled at her sudden delight. "Yes, that one." I touched her hand again. "Is everything okay at home?"

"Yes, the usual."

"And yet you are here."

"I want you to come back. Come home."

"Come home?" I echoed.

"I promise I'll come over more often, no matter what Dad says."

"That doesn't make any sense, Sylvan. You know that." I shook my head. "Your father doesn't want to be married to me any longer, and I can tell you honestly, I feel the same."

She shrugged. "I like you. I don't want anyone new."

"I didn't have any choice about leaving. And if he's seeing someone new? You can understand that's impossible." But in my head the refrain beat, *Justin, you are a liar, liar, liar*.

"I know I sound like a stupid kid."

"No, sweetheart. You sound like a young person who's tired of dealing with new stepmoms." I shook my head. "I can't help you with that. If I could, I would. But your father and I are finished."

She burst out, sounding more like a five-year-old child, "But why? You both said you loved each other. What happened?"

"It was something else, though to be honest, being unfaithful could certainly be enough to end us. I didn't know about her, but in retrospect, I'm not surprised. Things had been going downhill for us for a while." This time, instead of touching her hand, I took it in mine and held it firmly. "Sometimes people feel emotions that seem like love but aren't really. It might be loneliness or a desire for security, or even physical attraction. In the end, when it starts falling apart, I suppose it comes down to whether both people believe it's worth fighting for. If neither party wants to fight to keep it, to protect it, then maybe it was never really truly love.

"If one good thing came out of our marriage, I would say that it was having the opportunity to know you. I don't need to be married to your father to be your friend."

Sylvan stared across the room, appearing deep in thought. Her eyes settled on the bookcase and then on the only photograph sitting on the shelf. She stood and walked over and picked it up. She looked at it and then at me. "Is this you?"

I nodded. "Jaynie Highsmith. The woman I'm laughing with is Ruth Berry."

Sylvan gave me a long look and then glanced at the photo again before saying, "I'd like to know more about her. She must've been very special for you to have adopted her name." She replaced the frame on the shelf. "What should I call you? Ruth or Jaynie?"

"Jayne will do. I'm finally Jayne, and surprisingly enough, after all these years, I find the name fits quite well."

"Can I use your restroom?"

"Certainly. And if you're hungry, help yourself in the kitchen, Sylvan. There are snacks in the cupboard. If you'll excuse me for a few minutes, I believe I owe Wyatt an explanation."

Her expression darkened. "Is he your boyfriend? Are you seeing someone too?"

I smiled. "No, he's not my boyfriend, and I'm not seeing anyone. I'll tell you about me and Wyatt and I were childhood friends, and he was Ruth's grandson."

"Okay." She seemed to accept my denial but pressed her hand to her forehead. "I have a headache."

"There's aspirin in the bathroom and water, tea, and

some other things in the kitchen. Make yourself at home."

~~~~

"Wyatt," I called out. He turned away from the man with whom he was talking and walked toward me. "I'm sorry. I never thought to tell you that I'd taken Ruth's name. I'm sure that came as a shock."

"It was confusing. And . . . unsettling." He looked more annoyed than angry. "You should've told me. You became Ruth Highsmith? And then Ruth Hale?"

"Not legally. I told people my friends called me Ruth. Every time someone said 'Ruth,' I felt . . . comfort."

"You can call yourself anything you like. Grandma didn't have exclusive dibs on the name. But why would you want to pretend you were someone else?"

"I wanted to be anyone and anywhere else for the first eighteen years of my life. I think that was obvious to everyone who knew me. Jaynie was never a happy person. She lived in chaos."

"I disagree."

"You don't have the right to disagree."

"But I do. Let me say it better. I remember hearing your laugh. In fact, the sound of your laughter comes back to me as clearly as the bird calls, as the sound of the wind rushing through those trees, of the creek itself washing over and around the rocks. I could never think of this place, no matter how far away I was, or how far down I went in my life, without remembering those crazy things you and Grams used to talk about, and hearing your laughter when something struck you as funny, and how your eyes flashed when you were angry—I swear, even your hair got redder the angrier you were. Don't you remember any of that? Because I do. I do."

Wyatt walked closer to me, his voice growing softer the nearer he came.

"Was your life perfect? No. Not by a long shot. Neither was mine. But we overcame. We did. But if you only remember the bad times and lose the good memories, then you never won at all and you might as well still be back there—right back in the place and time we wanted to escape from."

For the space of those moments when Wyatt was speaking, all noise around us ceased. His eyes, his low, earnest voice hypnotized me. He was wrong. Of course he was. Occasional laughter across the years of my childhood didn't negate the bad stuff. He was right that it was important to remember the good stuff too. But that's where my brain stopped. Was I guilty of leaving way too much of myself behind, whether on purpose or not? Throwing out the good with the bad?

As if reading my mind, Wyatt added, "It all works together, Jayne. If all you want is good, then you'll have to bide your time here on earth waiting for heaven. If you don't want to waste your time, your life on this earth—and that would truly be a shame—then you have to acknowledge and reconcile the bad along with the good."

I wanted to say something smart. Clever. A little cutting. Something that would show I already had the answers and didn't need them from him or anyone. Like Ruth.

Then Wyatt said, "We all have our blind spots. I knew you'd gotten married because Mitch told me." He laughed softly, his voice a little hoarse. "And despite knowing that, in my mind you were never anyone other than Jaynie Highsmith, the girl I knew growing up. If you or Mitch ever mentioned your married name, my brain refused to hear it." By now, he was almost whispering. "Maybe my own memories all these years later are a little suspect, but one thing I'll never forget—you, Jayne Highsmith, were always the brightest light in my world. You were the one I saw whenever I thought of home."

He was drawing me toward him, tightening his arms. And I was allowing it. I stopped him. I stopped us both. I put my hands on either side of his face and said, "We have to talk. But not now. Not yet."

"Jayne."

I pushed away from him, grateful to have an excuse. "Be patient, Wyatt. I have to deal with Sylvan first."

In case things weren't already crazy in my life, the meter had just hit a new height. I left Wyatt, who'd all but declared his feelings for me, because I had to run back to his grandmother's house to counsel my husband's daughter. Was this what it was like to have family?

Maybe. But sometimes doing right by loved ones could mean having difficult conversations.

But not with Wyatt. At least, not today. For now, I had Sylvan to deal with.

~~~~

Sylvan had emptied her backpack on the coffee table, creating a mess, but the untidy pile was relatively contained, so I wouldn't fuss. I went into the kitchen to rustle us up some food. We ate sandwiches at the kitchen table.

I asked, "What is your plan? I don't want to interfere

between you and your mother. Do you need a place to stay?"

"Do you have room? I can sleep on the sofa."

"No need. You can take the bed in the front bedroom."

"Are you sure?"

"If you're sure your Mom isn't worrying."

"Nope. She hasn't called. She's having a good time with her friends. As long as I'm home by Monday, no problems."

"Do you want to discuss your father and our divorce? I'll try, if you do."

"Not now. For now, my head feels full and it aches."

"Why don't you take a nap?"

She left, and during the short time it took me to clean the kitchen, Sylvan had wrapped herself in a blanket, curled around a sofa pillow, and had fallen soundly asleep.

~~~~

Being around a teenager took me back a few years. They were busy and awake and eating and then suddenly napping. Reminded me of toddlers but with more autonomy. Next time I looked at the sofa expecting to see her still asleep, she was gone. I saw her sitting in a lawn chair out in the shade of the oak.

I wanted to talk to Wyatt. I wanted to go through the remainder of my goods in the barn. But I wouldn't attempt either with Sylvan here. She might recognize or question or show pity. I didn't want her pity. Nor did I want her saying something to her father—inadvertent and unintended—but potentially complicating about either Wyatt or the household goods in the barn. She might even recognize some of them. Sooner or later, Justin was bound to discover I had the items from the safe. He might also decide I'd taken valuable items that he didn't consider mine. At some point, I expected to have to discuss all this with him again. Did I want that? Had I taken certain items in hopes he'd follow and find me?

No. I was done with Justin. That six months was seeming longer instead of shorter. But at least it would be a true end to my association with him.

"Sylvan?"

She looked up. "Yes?"

"Want to take a drive into town?"

Sylvan and I drove into Mineral to do some grocery shopping and had an early supper at a restaurant while there.

She was curious about everything from the wooded farmland to the old houses to the small shops. She insisted on getting out and walking around the old train station. She moved like a kid. I was a little wistful but also sad. We could've had fun together. We truly could have if we'd been allowed.

When we returned to the house, she helped carry our purchases inside. She set the grocery bags on the kitchen table. As I followed her in, she said, "What's that?"

She was standing at the kitchen window. I joined her there and saw the flames flickering.

"Fire," I said.

"I know, but why?"

Wyatt was moving around a firepit. One of those movable ones.

"What's he doing?" I asked.

"Exactly. What?"

I laughed. "Let's go find out." And I led the way out the back door.

As we approached him, he turned toward us and said,

"Surprise!"

I looked at him, silently questioning, but Sylvan ran over to look.

"It's a firepit, right?"

"Yes, ma'am. Store-bought, in fact."

"Why?" I asked.

"I couldn't produce a barrel from the old days, but this is pretty close." He grinned. "I'm not much into sentimentality, but after talking about Grandma yesterday, and hearing Sylvan call you Ruth"—he shrugged—"an evening spent sitting around a fire seemed the thing to do."

Sylvan said, "But it's hot. We don't need a campfire."

"Oh yeah we do," he said. "It's just exactly what we do need." He fastened his eyes on me but didn't smile. He didn't need to. I received it anyway.

"We do, Sylvan. You'll see."

Her expression made it clear that she thought we were crazy. She rolled her eyes and shrugged. "It's your thing. Who am I to point out that it makes no sense?"

"Precisely," I said. "Just go with it." I turned to Wyatt and added, "Sylvan and I did some grocery shopping. We'll go fetch some sodas."

Sylvan followed, saying, "Water for me. I don't drink soda."

"Good for you," I said to her, and laughed. "I don't either, except for when I do."

She rolled her eyes again.

I was amused. She had chosen to be here. I suspected there was more to her choice than she'd yet revealed.

By the time we returned, Wyatt had arranged the lawn chairs and added a tray table.

~~~~

The late-June evening was long. Dusk faded into twilight as we sat around the firepit. The burn was low because we truly didn't need the heat, but the occasional flame and spark blended with the emerging fireflies, and soon the conversation eased into companionable silence. When Wyatt excused himself to go inside for more ice, I turned to Sylvan and said, "Why did you follow me here?" I looked at her. "I'm not saying you aren't welcome, because you are, but why?"

"I told you."

"You told me a reason, but it didn't feel like the *whole* reason."

Sylvan stuck a long twig through a hole in the fire guard and poked it through until it fell into the small flames licking at the wood.

"You said you wanted to know me better."

"I did. I do. I tried."

"Did you still?" She added, "Dad said you didn't want to be bothered with us."

He'd told me almost the same thing in reverse.

"Sylvan, it wasn't like that. Could you have misunderstood?"

"No. Mom was sick for a while. One year, I asked Dad if I could come for Christmas, but he said you were already committed to spending the holiday with your family and there wasn't room for me. Mom told me Dad was a liar. I know she wanted to take those words back right away, but it doesn't work that way because I'd already heard them. I started paying closer attention. My dad is a liar, isn't he?"

I went to her and put my arms around her. She pressed

at her eyes and tried to laugh.

At that moment, Wyatt cleared his throat. He set a bag of chips on the table and said he'd be right back with other stuff.

"I'm sorry. So sorry. You must think I'm stupid. A stupid child."

"Not at all. People, even the ones we love, can be confusing and frustrating. Your dad isn't . . . perfect. Neither am I. Who is?" I ran out of comfort words. Fresh out of wisdom.

"He's a liar, isn't he?"

"Oh, Sylvan, I don't know. Liar . . ." My heart said yes, but aloud I said, "That's a hard word. We all lie sometimes. I do think he lies as needed. He may even think he's doing it for our benefit." It turned my stomach trying to sound balanced and even-handed, but this was my chance to prove to myself that I would've done the right thing, would've been a good influence if I'd had the chance to build a relationship with her.

"The girl he's seeing now—"

I interrupted. "Girl?"

"Well, she's a grown woman. She's my friend's older sister, and so I think of her more like one of us—not quite legal. But Kay is older. She's in her late twenties."

Like me, I thought.

"Their father is one of my dad's biggest clients in his new business. An important client, who isn't too happy with him right now because of Kay. And it's wrecking my friendships too. Not just with Ann, but with friends of friends."

I didn't know what to say to her. This was his daughter.

How could I cut him down in her eyes? She seemed to be struggling for reassurance, even looking to me to provide it. I was touched that she seemed concerned that I was okay, in addition to her relationships with her friends.

We heard the distant slamming of the storm door from across the dirt road. Wyatt was on his way back. Sylvan looked at me by firelight, pressed her lips together, and didn't say anything more. Frankly, I was relieved. I wanted to say very different things about Justin. And yet, his daughter—knowing she *had* wanted to know me better—and seeing Wyatt bringing sodas and marshmallows to the rescue, warmed my heart.

"Sylvan, my childhood wasn't great. My mother . . . well, she was an unhappy woman who looked for happiness in all the places she was least likely to find it." I shrugged. "So I understand, at least in part, why they do foolish things. Don't worry about sounding stupid or anything else. I get it. If not for Ruth, Wyatt's grandmother, things would've been much harder for me. Everyone needs a friendly ear."

I continued, "She lived here. Her house and her backyard. I spent a lot of time right here in this yard with her. She was the smartest person I ever knew. She knew everything about everything."

Wyatt made a noise. My glance at him was sharper this time.

He shrugged. "Sorry. She was my grandmother and I loved her, but mostly she just loved to talk and you were a willing listener."

"Why would you say that?"

"I don't mean that you weren't important to her, but, Jayne, my grandmother . . . she liked to discuss things. I couldn't quite get on board with the crazier stuff."

"Crazy stuff?"

"She talked a lot about ether and the cosmos and stuff that sounded like she was referencing karma and Zen and existentialism and essentialism and all the -isms, but putting them in a blender and coming out with her own version of the universe according to Ruth Berry."

"Of how to live. That's what she came up with." I wanted to be calm, but this was Ruth we were discussing. "Her point was that none of them had it all right. People spend so much time debating theories and philosophies and getting all worked up over stuff that they can't control or influence anyway and neglect their own lives and the lives that depend on them. Ruth's point was that we should live. Each day. Each moment. Not create chaos to feed the insanity."

Wyatt frowned, but Sylvan said, "I like that, actually."

"Mom never had much patience with Grandma's . . . philosophies either."

"Maybe that influenced how you heard it." I added, "I guess we all have our filters."

I saw the change in his expression. He wasn't going to debate this, and I was glad. I didn't want Sylvan to hear any negatives about Ruth or even to be exposed to Wyatt's and my jaded opinions about human nature. She already knew a lot. I wouldn't dim her light, whether it was hope or faith or just learning her own reason for being, for anything on earth.

"In short, what Ruth Berry taught me was to listen to what was going on around me, to be aware, but to listen most closely to my heart because that's where I'll find the truth. I'll know it when I hear it." I touched my chest. "In here. And that I'm responsible for my own understanding and my own choices."

Sylvan nodded solemnly, her gaze forward and fixed on the sparks and flamelets in the pit. "I'm going to remember that," she said. Then she added, "I'm not going to worry about the new baby and that it's going to screw up my friendships as well as my family. I'm just going to move forward and do the best I can, and as soon as I can, I'm getting out. I'm going away."

CHAPTER TWENTY

"I'm getting out. I'm going away."

Not the goal I'd meant to inspire, but I couldn't focus on restating what I'd said because I'd been knocked sideways by what Sylvan had said just before that. Not only a new girlfriend but a baby? Really?

So apparently the reversal procedure had worked? I found it hard to believe that he'd changed his mind about wanting another child, so I presumed his years of ignoring birth control measures had led him to be careless—and to be caught by an irate father.

How dare he? What a lowlife, dirty dog he was, as my Mama would likely have said. Not only lying about leaving Simmons and Baker and doing them wrong, but also cheating on me.

I heard his voice. *"I'm not evil, Ruth. We fell in love. We fell out. It's the luck of the draw, or maybe it's just how life works."*

I rubbed my temples, trying to put Sylvan and Wyatt and Justin, too, out of my mind. It was just too much for one day. Tomorrow would be a fresh day. I'd spend time with Sylvan and encourage her to find ways to make her *todays* better and not bet everything on some future she wouldn't want by the time it arrived. I'd tell her not to compromise her current self in hopes of reaching a better future state. I'd tell her to keep her light shining every single day.

~~~~~

The next morning, I cooked up a real breakfast for Sylvan and told her we were taking a tour.

"Where of?"

"A tour of the land of my childhood."

A light frown crossed her face, and then she brightened. "We're taking a walk in the woods?"

"Yes, ma'am, and generally around. It's a beautiful day, but it will be hot this afternoon, so we'll get out and about early."

"Excellent."

We toured the meadow and the barn as I told her stories, mostly sanitized for her benefit, and then walked the dirt road to the woods. We jumped the creek.

On the far side, I said to her, "You were so graceful. Like a ballerina leaping."

She blushed. "Years of practice, whether I wanted to or not."

I led her to where the lady's slippers grew. There were none, but they continued to exist in place in my memory. I said, "Take off your shoes."

She looked at me doubtfully but did as requested. We stood facing each other, our feet bare against the earth. I put my finger to my lips to hush her when she started to speak.

I whispered, "Do you feel it?"

She looked down at her feet and stared. She looked back up at me. "I believe I do. Is the earth . . . humming?"

"It does for me too. I'm sure there's a logical explanation. Maybe a quartz seam or a subterranean stream forcing its way through broken rock like an underground waterfall to feed Cub Creek. But none of that matters. What matters is its voice."

"Like an underground waterfall?"

"Well, maybe not. The point is that we feel it right up through the soles of our feet."

Her face lit up. "I do. We do."

"It follows mostly along this path, but it's strongest here. When I was a child, I danced here."

Sylvan nodded, her eyes wistful. "I can imagine it. What a magical childhood you had. So much freedom."

"At times," I said, but stopped there. I held up my hand. "I'll steady you while you brush your feet off and put your shoes back on."

"I don't mind being barefoot."

"You will when we leave the path. There are twigs and acorns and sticker bushes. You haven't led a barefoot life. You are tenderfooted. And I've been away from it so long, I've become tenderfooted too, so we'll be glad of our shoes."

"Okay."

I led her to the rock. We sat on its smooth-rough surface, warmed by the sun but cooled by the shade of the encroaching trees. And we were lulled into silence by the sound of the creek flowing past.

A bird launched into song, and somewhere farther along another bird answered.

She spoke softly. "This was your special place?"

"When I was a child, yes."

She nodded. "I have a place like this too, but not as away from everything. I go out to the gazebo. No one else uses it now. Mom is busy with stuff, and Edward is never home and really hasn't been for years. Dad is gone, of course. I could have almost any spot in the house to myself. But I like to go out to the gazebo. You wouldn't know, but there's a bunch of huge rhododendrons around it. Leta keeps the bird feeder filled so that I can listen to the songs. I go out there to read or sometimes just to think. Sometimes my brain feels . . . feels sad and sometimes feels like it's on fire."

"I'm glad you have your own place too. Actually, I also wanted to correct something I told you."

"What?"

"Well, this is the thing. Last evening you said you were focused on leaving, on getting away. I want to tell you that it's fine to plan for the future, but don't forget to live each day, Sylvan. Don't let the idea of a better future take away your joy in living each moment, each day. If you take care of today and feed it with the right ingredients—love, respect, and gratitude—the future will take care of itself."

"And hope?"

"Always hope, Sylvan. Even when it seems scarce, nurture hope in the present to have what you need for a future worth living in."

~~~~

After we'd returned and Sylvan had gone to nap, I was in the mood to do little things. The small, contained activities that didn't tax anyone's brain cells. I gathered up the debris from Sylvan's backpack that was still littering the coffee table. Not so much, really. A pen, a small package of hard candies, a few receipts, and a letter-size paper that was slightly crumpled. The printing on it caught my eye. She'd mentioned printing out the account of the accident.

Mitch and I hadn't discussed the details. Alcohol and a tree. Really, I didn't want more of a picture than that in my head. Didn't even really want to think on that too much because regrets tried to surface. Last words, last moments, perhaps a late-in-life reconciliation between us. Even though I had a more positive image of Mama in my heart after the last couple of days, we'd lost our chance for a meeting of the minds. A talk that would help us to bridge the disorder between us. But I couldn't help myself.

It was a short news article about a single-car accident that had occurred on Cross Country Road involving two county residents, Bella Highsmith and Boone Lewis.

My breath stopped. Boone.

What?

I read it again, certain I'd misunderstood something.

Bella Highsmith of Hope Road, the driver, suffered fatal injuries. Both Ms. Highsmith and her passenger were ejected when the car rolled down the embankment prior to striking the tree, but Mr. Lewis is expected to recover.

No. My heart raced. My blood pressure must've hit new heights as it pounded in my ears. A loud ringing surrounded me, and my vision blurred. I closed my eyes and willed myself to calm down. Somewhere during all that I sat, because when I opened my eyes, I was on the sofa with my knees pressed against the coffee table and that paper still clutched in my hands.

I went to find Sylvan, but she was in Ruth's room, curled up in a blanket on the bed. I backed out of the room. There was no reason to disturb her. She knew nothing about Boone and what he'd meant to me. Apparently still meant. Because

I was angry, and I hadn't felt this kind of ugliness snapping around me since the last time Mama and I had gone at each other over something. Instantly I was that kid again, wanting to blow sky-high and keeping it in . . . holding it inside but simmering at a dangerous pitch.

Mitch had known that day at the funeral home. And even when he'd called me to tell me she'd died. He'd known. Had Wyatt known? He must've. The two of them had kept it from me. Mitch then. Wyatt now.

How dare they?

I flew out of the house. I needed to blow up somehow, somewhere and I went looking for Wyatt. He was walking up the road with another man. They were moving slowly and talking. I stopped, staring at him. He looked up, saw me, and then looked again. He said something to the other man, who went back toward the house, and then Wyatt came my way.

I waited.

"Jayne? Is something wrong?"

The words hung up somewhere in my brain. I tried to be calm. "Did you know?"

"Know what?"

"When did you know?"

"About what, Jayne? What's going on?"

"About Boone."

This time he didn't respond so quickly. He paused. I saw him doing some quick thinking.

He said, "About Boone . . ."

I nodded. I grimaced in a mocking, painful version of a smile. It hurt my face.

"Why didn't you tell me?"

"Jayne, it was in the paper. It wasn't a secret.

Remember, I came back soon after the accident. Mitch told me you didn't know. He had some crazy idea of protecting you."

"You knew Boone was involved, and you knew I didn't know." I shook my head. My body felt all jittery.

"There's more to it, Jayne."

"Boone was in the car with my mother. How drunk were they? Or was it drugs?"

"Jayne—" He took my arm, and I yanked it free.

"Never mind. I'm going to that jail. It's the regional facility, right? Time to stop protecting Mitch's feelings. He sure didn't give a crap about mine, leaving me to find out this way."

Wyatt grabbed my arm again. "Stop it. Stop now. Mitch knew that the mention of Boone would only make things worse in your eyes and solve nothing."

"No excuse. I had the right to know."

"Did you?"

That stunned me. I stood silent for a long moment.

"Where's Sylvan?" he asked.

"Napping."

"Can you leave her a note letting her know you'll be back soon?"

"I suppose."

"Then I'll take you."

"To the jail? It's a longer drive there and back than a quick trip."

"Trust me, Jayne."

I laughed, ugly. "Justin used to say that too."

"Did he? Well, he'd made vows. I haven't." His grip was firm, but his voice was gentle. "When I say trust me,

Jayne, know that I have no underlying motives. I'm a friend."

"A friend? Maybe a sometime friend?" I said it harshly and meant it, but as he released my arm, I knew I was wrong and wished I could erase that moment. Instead, I looked away and said, "I'll be right back."

By the time I'd scribbled the note to Sylvan and left it on the coffee table next to a glass of water and a cookie—so I'd be sure she'd see it—Wyatt had pulled his truck up in front of the house.

I grabbed my purse and went out, feeling like I was about to do battle.

CHAPTER TWENTY-ONE

We didn't speak. I was too full of words, and Wyatt was probably offended by my "sometime friend" remark and maybe annoyed that he was having to do this—take this field trip. What else to call it?

What would I say to Mitch? I wanted to rehearse it, but how could I? I'd have to go on instinct. Or simplicity. Just simple truth. Which is what he should've shared with me.

Out of the silence, Wyatt said, "We're almost there."

We hadn't even reached Mineral yet. Wyatt slowed down for a turn onto a paved road that led to a retirement home. It was like several brick ranch-style homes adjoining. Agnes's Home for Adults.

"Not Mitch. Not the jail," I said.

"No."

He parked in front of the building near the long wooden handicapped ramps.

"Wait here," he said. "Stay here and watch."

Wyatt strode up the ramp, and with a quick knock on the door, he went inside.

I waited as instructed. I was already annoyed, had been apprehensive, and now I was growing impatient. The door opened, and I saw Wyatt stepping outside. His arm was reaching back inside, and soon I saw him assisting a man with a cane across the threshold. Wyatt and the old man . . .

I heard Ruth's voice spell out *g-e-r-i-a-t-r-i-c*, and I remembered to be patient.

The two men went to plastic chairs arranged on the porch, and each took a seat. As I stared, I heard *Boone* whispered in my head.

Twenty years had passed since I'd last seen him. It had been on the day Ruth died. Cold washed over me, followed quickly by heat.

He moved slowly and with a pronounced limp. He'd been older than Mama. He was probably seventy or so now. He'd lived a life that was physically damaging and had survived an accident, one that was fatal for my mother. An ugly voice in my head asked, *Why don't you just walk up there and ask him if he's satisfied with his disgusting life? With the damage he did to so many people—including my mother?* And a softer voice added, *He's old. And he didn't make those choices alone. If you condemn one, then you must condemn both. All.*

Who was I to condemn anyone?

Wyatt leaned closer, as if to better hear what the old man was saying. Then he stood, but the man remained seated. They talked for a few minutes longer, and then Wyatt left him there. By the time Wyatt had reached the truck, a woman in a uniform had emerged and was putting a blanket over the old man's legs.

Wyatt said, "Seen enough? Do you need to see more here? Or want to confront anyone?"

I closed my eyes and reopened them slowly. "No."

"He was injured in the accident. Can't live on his own anymore. I understand he was going downhill pretty fast even before the accident, but the injuries kind of finished him off."

"Oh, how sad for him," I said sarcastically. "He was bad news for my mother, and he brought ugliness into my life. He was disgusting and made everything worse."

Wyatt gave me a funny look.

I waved my hands, my body shaking, as I said, "I don't want to talk about it."

"He made it worse. I don't doubt it. Disgusting at best, right? Creepy. And you felt threatened at times."

"You bet."

"I'm not suggesting you pretend like it was nothing. If he actually laid hands on you . . . if he hurt you or tried to . . . If so, you let me know and I'll confront him myself. If you want someone to go to the police with you, I'll do that too." He looked at me sideways. "I'm not a sometime friend, Jayne."

I turned away and stared out of the window. After a minute, he turned the ignition but we didn't go far before he pulled off the road again. No buildings. Just woods.

"There's more you don't know. I wanted to let Mitch tell you. But since you have your mother's temper—though you control it better—I'd better tell you now."

He settled back. He spoke dispassionately.

"Mitch said he didn't tell you Boone was involved because you'd be angry, and a lot of old stuff would be resurrected. He wanted to spare you. He said he knew how you'd react because he couldn't let it go either.

"Mitch went a little crazy. That was about the time I arrived back in Cub Creek. I watched him disintegrate as if anger was eating him alive. He became convinced that it was all Boone's fault and went to confront Boone yet again, and when Boone wouldn't answer the door, Mitch broke in. Boone called the police, and Mitch was given a warning. Boone got a protective order. One day Mitch saw him at a mutual friend's house. Lots of drinking was going on all around. There was a fight. Given the prior warning and protective order, and Boone being old and injured already, Mitch was arrested. In fact, once he sobered up, he confessed that it was his fault and he deserved punishment. He pled guilty."

With my elbow on the armrest, I put one hand across my face and leaned my forehead against the glass. Poor Mitch. Of all of us—Mama, me, even Boone—Mitch was the least at fault.

"About a month into his sentence, Mitch called me. He'd gotten word from Boone's lawyer that Boone had gone to the police and confessed that he was responsible for the violation of the protective order, and that he'd started the fight, throwing the first punch and even striking Mitch with his cane."

Wyatt shook his head. "Boone asked his lawyer to draw up whatever documents were needed to petition the court for Mitch's release since he, Boone, was responsible."

My hand dropped to my lap. "Really?"

"Wait 'til you hear the rest." He glanced at me, and I nodded. "So, Mitch said no, that wasn't his recollection, and while he appreciated Boone's effort to make amends, he thought he should serve out his sentence. Which statement apparently made Boone more determined. He insisted that Mitch didn't remember what had happened because he was drunk. Which statement echoed what Mitch had said before the court."

Wyatt shook his head. "Look, I don't pretend to understand how all that worked within the legal system, but legal doings went forward. After about a month of squabbling between Mitch and Boone, the legal powers agreed that based on new witness evidence, Mitch would be released early. That came down just before you arrived. Any day now, Jayne, I expect to get a call from Mitch telling me he needs a ride home."

"That's why you and those other guys have been working so hard on his house."

"Exactly. We want to be ready."

"Then we need to start moving the furniture back in too. Sylvan and I can stock the cabinets. He'll need a new mattress. I have enough cash to cover that."

"Where do you stand now with selling the house?"

After a long pause, I said, "That may yet happen. For instance, if that development offer comes to fruition and we all agree . . . but not too soon. I'm thinking we'll wait at least six months, just to make sure."

"Sure of what?"

"Well, to give Mitch time to recover. Also, to be sure that everything pertaining to my divorce and any marital assets or debt is properly spelled out and official. Justin himself told me how important it was to be clear about such things."

~~~~

Sylvan ran out of the house as soon as we drove up. She opened the door, and before I slid out, she reached the truck.

"Ruth . . . Jayne, a man came by asking about you. Wanted to know if you were here. Before I thought about it,

I told him you were. That you'd gone off on an errand but would be back soon."

I looked at Wyatt, then asked Sylvan, "Was he dark-haired and stocky?"

"Stocky? I don't know. He was wide and had big shoulders. He did have dark hair. Did I do wrong? Should I have told him no?"

I cast a quick glance at Wyatt, then turned back to Sylvan. "No worries. You did right. It's about time we find out what that man has on his mind."

But the man didn't come back. Instead, it was the man he worked for who drove up in his shiny car, and as the dust he'd stirred up settled back on the meticulous fenders and hood, Justin climbed out of his new car and walked up to Ruth Berry's door, where I was waiting for him.

CHAPTER TWENTY-TWO

Whatever Justin might have intended to say when he first saw me, seeing Sylvan standing beside me changed it up.

"Sylvan, what are you doing here?" His face flushed. "Ruth, tell my daughter to go get her things. She'll be leaving as soon as we're done with our conversation."

Ruth—being called Ruth—had sounded perfect until recently. Now hearing it from Justin ... the effect was jarring.

About a week ago, Justin told me that we'd fallen in love, had fallen out, and were now moving on. *It's just how life works.*

Sylvan moved closer to me. "I'm almost seventeen. You can't tell me where to go."

"You won't be seventeen for six months yet, and that's not eighteen, much less twenty-one, so get your belongings. As soon as Ruth and I have a chat, we'll be going. Put your things in your car."

"I'm staying here until my visit is over."

"I'm your father and legal guardian."

"Mom is my legal guardian too. And my custodial guardian." Sylvan set her lips and crossed her arms.

"I control your allowance."

Sylvan made a rude noise.

He turned to me. "Tell her, Ruth."

In that moment I understood I could hurt Justin through his child. His daughter, whether he wanted her devotion or her trust fund—she was his weak point. The soft spot in his lying heart. I didn't care about him, but I didn't want to hurt her.

I said, "I agree with Sylvan."

"It's none of your business, Ruth."

"You brought your business into my life." I shrugged.

Sylvan screamed, "Stop calling her Ruth. That's not even her name." She turned to me. "Tell him to call you Jayne. And tell him it's not right to keep replacing one woman with another." She scratched at her face as if she might remove the skin.

Pulling her hands away gently, I held them in mine. There was only one small scratch on her cheek. I pressed my finger to it gently. "Sylvan, listen to me. Who your parent is . . . it isn't you. It doesn't predict anything about you—unless you let it."

Justin was simmering, and it didn't seem that my words of wisdom were helping the situation. "Ruth. Jayne. Whoever you are. May I speak with you privately?"

I gave Sylvan a long look. She met my eyes. My heart hurt to see the pain in them.

"Do you mind?"

She shook her head, but with short, aggravated, abrupt movements. I touched her cheek again. "Would you fix me a cup of tea, sweetie? I could go for a hot cup of that honey hibiscus lemon."

Sylvan looked almost hypnotized. "Yes, I'll fix it."

"Your father and I will be right back."

"Okay."

I gave her a gentle push toward the kitchen. Once she was in motion, I gestured to Justin to follow me out the front door.

He was already talking as we descended the steps. I kept walking until we reached the dirt road.

"If you didn't come for Sylvan—and you didn't—then why did you? You'd better not be here after my vehicle. That SUV is mine, and you need to pay it off if you haven't already done so."

"You know why I'm here."

"Did you want the figurines and vases back? Because I think those are considered marital assets. I left some for you and took some for me."

"Shut up, Ruth. You know what I want."

"A quick divorce, right? I hear you're in a hurry to get married again, huh?"

"Again—not your business."

"Because you got lucky again? Fall in, fall out—love happens and then evaporates? But lucky for you it came right back around again."

"I'm not going to talk about that."

"Sensitive subject? Maybe it's the baby on the way? Maybe there is a mommy and daddy and grandparents to be who aren't too happy with you?" I paused. "In fact, for now I suggest you forget about the divorce. I think we may need to revisit that. The first attorney I consulted encouraged me to walk away, but I have another who thinks differently." I didn't, but I could.

His face went a vivid red, and his blue eyes turned icy with a mean, dangerous look. "You wanted me to reverse the vasectomy. It's your fault, Ruth—Jayne—whatever your name is—that she's pregnant."

"Out of the habit, are you? With using protection, I mean. Were you ever in the habit of truth or fidelity?" I started to cross my arms, but instead put them squarely on my hips and faced him head-on. "Watch yourself, Justin. You are a cheat and a liar whose own daughter is having doubts about him."

"And you are a thief."

"I only took what was mine. And left behind much more that was also mine."

Justin shook his head and leaned in closer. "I want the cash you took. I need it, Ruth. Badly. And I want my daughter."

"I thought you said that was none of my business, at least as regards Sylvan."

"What do you want?"

"Actually, I'm inclined to be cooperative for the right incentive."

"What does that mean?"

"If your attorney offers the right contract language."

"We already have a marriage contract. More than that, I am serious about my assets being heavily leveraged."

"We need very precise language that no debts acquired during the marriage will fall to me. That you indemnify me against anyone attempting to hold me liable for any of those debts, including yourself and your heirs and the debt holders. You keep the assets. The houses. The property within those houses. I keep what's currently in my possession, with your blessing and agreement . . . not including your daughter, of course. However, that said, she is always welcome to spend time with me. She's a lovely young woman. I think she must take after her mother. One of these days I'm going to go visit Sharon and find out for myself. Maybe soon."

"That's ridiculous."

"It just depends on how badly you want that divorce. As for me, I'm in no particular hurry. I don't have a due date or unhappy potential in-laws . . . who might also be business . . ." I let the words fall away since I wasn't totally sure of the business part.

His face was a deep red, and his expression looked threatening. I refused to step away.

"Our attorneys can talk details, Justin."

We'd continued walking up the dirt road as we spoke, and we were near the mailboxes. Justin needed to vent and struck out at the rack of mailboxes—I'm sure imagining my face right there among them. The rack shivered but held, and Justin was now cradling his fist with a pained look on his face.

I laughed again but this time with serious intent. I said, "As for Sylvan, you can't buy her. She's not for sale. What she does is up to her."

We both heard the truck barreling up the asphalt of the main road. I remembered that first day when my SUV had almost been hit, and in that same moment, I stumbled as gravel shifted beneath my shoes, and Justin grabbed my arm. He shoved and I flew several feet, but *away* from the road. I landed hard, with the loud blare of the truck's air horn before and after. In the near-miss moment, everything had ceased— no horn, no rumble of the huge tires on the road or the noise of the motor—a fraction of a split second—a moment in time between before and after—and I was still breathing at the end of it.

Because of Justin.

I sat up. Gravel had scored my knees and my palms. Justin stared, and then he was there beside me.

"Are you okay, Ruth?"

"You pushed me."

His face had drained of all color.

I added, "Out of danger."

"Of course I did." He knelt beside me and offered his hand. "I have my flaws—big ones, maybe—but I'm not a murderer."

He brushed the gravel from my palms and dislodged the pieces that were stuck more solidly. I watched, mystified.

"Did you ever truly love me, Justin?"

After a very long pause, he said, "I did, Ruth. I loved you with all my heart. Those things just never last."

"Jayne. My name is Jayne."

He shook his head. "Ruth or Jayne or whoever you are." He stared me hard in the eyes. "I did love you. When we married, I hoped it would be different for me this time. But it wasn't." He lifted me to my feet. "On the other hand, my Ruth would never have challenged me for my assets and my daughter on a dirt and gravel road in the middle of nowhere. I find this new Ruth interesting." He continued holding my hand. "Pleased to meet you, Jayne. Maybe I'll have the opportunity to get to know you better one day."

I reclaimed my hand from my charming Justin. He made everything seem perfectly right and reasonable when he focused his attention on you and the need suited his intention. There was a huge gaping gulf between a smooth persona and what a person might truly be capable of. What seemed all fine and polished like the fanciest marble was sometimes just a rock. And not even a nice rock.

"Thank you, Justin. I'll have my attorney contact yours."

He sighed. "If you must. I'd like my cash back. And my daughter."

"Why don't you let your daughter spend the rest of the weekend here? She told me she has to be home by Monday. As for the cash? The attorneys can talk. I'm unemployed, remember? And my husband kicked me out." I shrugged. "But I'm open to reasonable discussion. Just remember the contract terms when you speak to your attorney. It's important to get them right."

I turned and walked away. Head high, shoulders down and back, like a model's stride. Easy and confident. Just little old me taking my life back. *Take that and stuff it, Justin.*

Chapter Twenty-Three

"Jaynie?"

I recognized his voice, older and rougher, but still my big brother. I turned from putting pillows on the new sofa in Mama's living room. Mitch was standing in front of the picture window. He seemed like a stranger.

"Jayne. I don't go by Jaynie anymore."

"Sure."

With the light from the window behind him, I could almost believe he was that young man still—tall and slim— but then I saw his shoulders were rounded, and as he turned toward the light, it was clear that what had seemed to be laugh lines were true, deeply carved wrinkles. He seemed at a loss for where to go or what to say next. I was too.

"I'm sorry for your troubles, Mitch. Wyatt only told me some of it. At first, just enough to keep me from storming the jail. I hope I did right by waiting for you to come home."

He nodded. "You've come home too. I'm glad you did. When you left the last time, I didn't expect to ever see you again."

My heart . . . there were no words in me to counter his last remark. I cleared my throat and struggled to continue. "Wyatt told me you wanted to fix the house up to live in."

After a tiny indrawn breath, Mitch said, "If that's okay with you."

"Sure. In fact, we've been working on it." I gestured toward the new furnishings. "I added a few things to make it livable."

"Good. Thank you."

It was obvious in his posture and expression that he had nowhere else to go. This wasn't much, but home was home.

"Wyatt picked you up?"

"Yes. He was there waiting when they released me. He's a good man, Jaynie. I mean, Jayne."

"He is." I forced myself to ask, "Is there anything you want to tell me?

"Not really."

"Wyatt told me about Boone . . . because, you know . . . so I wouldn't go after him."

"No excuses from me. I owed that jail time for what I did. You understand that? I always tried to do good things with my life. To help people in whatever way I could. But when Mom died like that, it seemed like I fell apart. Every step of the way after that day, with each choice . . ."

He shook his head. "But I took those steps anyway." After a long pause, he added, "I would've saved Mom if I could've."

"No, that wasn't on you. Nor on me. Bella Highsmith chose her own road. Ultimately, she paid for her choices. Make better choices, Mitch. In the last couple of days, all I've heard is how wonderful you are from people you've helped, or from people who know others you've helped. That's more good than most can claim to have done. More than me, for sure."

I nodded, adding, "And now you've earned some rest."

"I am tired," he said.

"If you're good with it, I'll be back later to fix us supper."

"Like the old days?"

"No, I'm never going back to the old days. We have better times ahead of us, Mitch." I stepped out the door, but in only seconds I heard my name called.

"Jayne."

I turned back to him. "Yes, Mitch?"

"I don't want to talk about it, but if it's important to you to know, then I will."

"You don't have to tell me anything."

He frowned. "It's embarrassing."

I stayed silent. I could've said that Wyatt had already told me the details, but maybe Mitch needed to tell me himself. And I needed to let him, to help him come all the way home again.

"I haven't always done the right thing, Jaynie . . . Jayne."

"Neither have I."

He smiled. "You always had Mom's temper."

"Me? I have a temper, yes, but it's nothing like Mama's."

Was he grinning? If so, it vanished quickly.

He said, "The day Mom died . . . Afterward, I couldn't let go of it. I blamed Boone. When we ran into each other around town, that anger rolled up and over me. I said things, deliberately provoked him."

I wanted to cry, but I reeled my emotions back in for my brother. "Oh, but Mitch, they were in it together. Mama chose that path as surely as she ever chose anything."

"She'd been doing better, Jayne. Not drinking. Doing

well. I don't know what happened to upset that."

He slapped his hands, then twisted them together. "I couldn't let it go. I don't know why. Seeing him around town living his life while . . . I confronted him at his house. He got a court order to keep me away, but one day, some weeks later, we got into it again. I could've walked away and I didn't. I could've killed him, Jayne. I was wrong and knew it. I pled guilty and was glad to have it behind me. I welcomed the punishment and the end to it."

He shrugged and shook his head. "Soon after I was sentenced Boone hired a lawyer and they went to the district attorney and told him that Boone had started it. That he'd thrown the first punches and I was defending myself."

"He lied to help you."

"To make amends, I guess. Because of him . . ."

"Because of him you went to jail."

"No. I went to jail because of my anger and my own temper, my choices. I've made some bad ones in my life. I got out of jail because Boone came forward."

"Boone doesn't deserve any credit."

"And I didn't deserve to be released early. I was guilty as charged."

"Boone was . . . unspeakable. Always."

"Maybe, but like us, maybe he gets to overcome his flaws and become a better person too. I've forgiven him, Jayne, and you should do the same. He's old and sick. Your anger is wasted there."

After a long moment of silence, he added, "But I should've been a better son. A better brother. I have a few memories of our father. Like snippets. I remember he was a nice man. A kind man who laughed a lot. At some point in her life, Mom was happy too. I have memories of her laughing. Real laughter. Her eyes would light up. I remember. But she lost her joy. I always hoped she'd find it again, but she never did."

I'd lost mine too. Ruth had warned me not to bury it. And I'd done exactly that. But I was finding it again.

"Wyatt stored the salvageable furnishings in the barn. We moved some things back in for you. When you're ready to choose what else, let me know and we'll give you a hand."

"One more thing," Mitch said. "On the way home, Wyatt told me you were here. He said that stuff might've gone wrong for you too."

"Yeah. It did. Pretty far wrong. Turned out the man I married wasn't a good guy after all."

"I see. Well, you look great. Maybe even better than when you were here for Mom's service. Kind of . . . happy."

"Oh? Thanks, I guess."

"I just mean that if something went wrong in your life, maybe it was actually a good thing. Maybe it suits you."

"Maybe so, Mitch. Maybe we both got lucky when things went wrong."

~~~~~

Wyatt had gone. His truck was parked at his house. I walked along the gravel road—our Hope Road—to Ruth's house. I made a quick detour into the shed in the backyard and was rewarded with finding a garden trowel. Not as good as a shovel, but probably more suitable to the job. I stood there holding it and wondering. Different shed, but same garden trowel? Maybe.

The dirt that clung to the metal was so old that it seemed

more like cement. The wooden handle was worn smooth as silk. Wyatt must've moved whatever was salvageable from the old shed to the new.

Pansies, I thought. And when I did, I remembered that Ruth had said I should also think of her and our talk about letting our light shine.

I followed the dirt road toward the woods, but instead of crossing the creek, I stopped and sat on the bank for no good reason and examined the trowel .

Maybe *procrastination* could be my word of the day?

The water flowed by, hitting a rock or stick here and there, swirling and then getting back into the flow again. I thought about the past days. Sylvan's surprise visit, Justin wanting his daughter and his money back.

I laughed silently thinking of that money. It didn't feel like mine to spend, but I could use it as leverage in discussions with Justin. I was going to do exactly as I'd told him—let our lawyers work it out. And I wouldn't blindly accept what they told me I deserved. I wasn't my Mama, but I could use some of her toughness, her willingness to speak up even if the words and delivery sounded rude beyond belief.

Mama—I remembered times when I was sick, and she'd held my head while I vomited in the trash can or toilet. I remembered the soft, cool cloths on my forehead. I remembered the warm soup she'd heat up or the ginger ale she'd bring to me. Even though she was mostly a mess, if she could do even a little good, then surely I could do so much more. I could knock back my pride and the importance I put on my own need.

Not so fast, kiddo, I heard Ms. Ruth say as I stood and

brushed the earth from the seat of my shorts. *You can't fix what's broke with just a snap of the fingers. But you* can *fix it. The tools are all inside you. You can find them if you try.*

Picking up the trowel, I jumped the creek and entered the woods.

It seemed to me that a person could spend a moment, or a lifetime, reveling in good memories or good times or regret and never move forward. Meanwhile, the present was speeding along with or without you—sweeping up and taking love, laughter, and light with it. Leaving you in the dust of yesterday. As for me, Jayne, I was now about the present and welcoming of tomorrows.

At my rock, with the trowel beside me, and my battered, rusted red toolbox at my feet, I closed my eyes and rested my face on my arms. I had tried to advise Sylvan, and Mitch too. What more could I say to them? What would Ruth say? I visualized turning to Sylvan and saying, *Keep your light shining and you won't get lost. Be true to yourself and you'll be true in life and to everyone around you.* Then I would look Mitch in the face and tell him, *Surround yourself with good things, however small they seem. Fill your life with the good so that there's no room for the destructive. Build the person you want to be. I can't do it for you, but I will help.*

Then I envisioned repeating each of those things to myself—those same messages.

"Jayne?"

Wyatt. *Well, of course.*

I smiled. "Welcome to my rock."

"Your rock?"

"One of the few secrets I haven't yet shared with you."

Confused, he extended a hand as if offering me

assistance. He said, "Are you okay? I saw you walking past, and you looked upset. You were carrying something. A tool, maybe? Do you need help?"

"No, I'm good. Good enough, anyway." I smiled. "Thanks for bringing Mitch home. He seems very tired. I hope he'll be okay."

"He will, given time and support." He added, "Mind if I join you?"

I patted the rock. "Please do. Have a seat."

He was tall. It was a long way down for him as he settled next to me on the hard rock. He asked, "How are you feeling about Boone?"

"Boone? I detest him—the long-ago him. I left this place seventeen years ago and pretty much erased him from my mind. I tried to do that with Mama too, but it was harder. At any rate, the wrongs I held against Boone are old news. Time will take care of what's left of him on its own. He doesn't have any place in my life. Done."

"I'm glad."

"Wyatt, I owe you a confession, an explanation, and an apology."

"You don't owe—"

I raised my hand to stop him. "No. This debt is real, actual, and sincere. And seriously past due. Difficult, too, so bear with me."

For the short distance to the hiding place near the back side of the rock, I crawled, careful on the rough rock not to scratch up my knees even more that they were.

"Jayne, what are you doing?"

"Hush, please. Just wait."

Pushing the bushes and low growth aside, I worked the

earth with the garden trowel. Soon Wyatt was there beside me, squeezing in to see what I was doing.

"Can I help, Jayne?"

Handing him the trowel, I said, "See if you can cut through that last root? Be careful, though, there's glass buried in there that I'd rather wasn't broken."

I held the greenery back out of the way, and when he'd snapped that last natural barrier, I pushed his hands aside and reached in. Dirt and bits of moss clung to my hands and the jar as I lifted it. It was heavy. I remembered how Ruth had carried it, and how it was clearly heavy to her too, as she'd set it on the kitchen table.

Now her grandson crawled backward, and I did the same, but awkwardly, keeping my arms around the jar. Soon we were again sitting on the rock side by side, our childhoods long in the past as we contemplated the same jar of coins.

I tried to read his face. It was bemused. Confused. Curious too, maybe.

No excuses, Jayne. I patted the rusting metal jar lid and brushed at the dirt. The silver dollars were tarnished again. They needed cleaning and polishing.

"These belong to you," I said.

"I don't understand."

He must have recognized them as his grandmother's. The only thing he wouldn't understand was why they were in my possession.

"That day when your grandmother died . . . when I found her . . . Rather, before I found her because I didn't know she was home and she didn't answer the door, so I let myself in. The jar was on the kitchen counter. I was just . . . I don't know . . . I didn't intend to take them. To steal them."

There, it was said. Intended or not, I *had* stolen them.

I added, "I put the jar in my backpack."

My hands were still tightly gripping the lid and the glass body of the jar. The weight of it against my legs, the feel of it against my hands, took me back to that real place in the past when I'd been almost sixteen.

"When I found her, I forgot about the jar. Then the sheriff and everyone else arrived, and I didn't remember the jar until it was too late. If they'd seen me pulling it out of my backpack, they would've ... They wouldn't have understood. I planned to return it to the house after everyone left, and no one would ever know I'd taken it."

I shrugged. "But I didn't return it. I don't know why I didn't. I just didn't."

Brushing my hands over it one last time, I lifted it and passed it to Wyatt.

Wyatt made handling it look light and easy. He turned the jar in his hands, examining it, as if it were one of those carnival games where you guess how many gumballs are inside for a prize. As he moved it, the coins knocked and clunked together, making their own music. And now he was frowning.

The prize was his. I felt lighter now. It was almost the last secret.

He hugged the jar with one arm, wedging it between his arm and thigh while he twisted at the lid.

Why open it? It felt wrong. Like rubbing the genie's lamp when you'd already gotten your wishes. I found myself alarmed—overwhelmed—at what? It was his. I had to let go. But I couldn't help myself. I grabbed his hands. "What are you doing?"

"My turn, Jayne. Be patient."

I released him and watched as he struggled with the lid. Finally, despite the dirt and rust that had worked their way between the metal and glass over the course of twenty years, he twisted it off. That's when I saw the bit of paper among the coins.

Wyatt had seen it too and he put his fingers into the jar. He turned the jar to shift the coins until the slip of paper was within reach.

"The paper must've been on top but shifted down as the jar traveled." He opened the folded paper and read the words, then he read them aloud, his eyes half on my face. "These belong to Jayne Highsmith."

"What? But . . ."

"They were yours all along. Ruth wanted you to have them."

"You don't look surprised."

"I'm surprised to see them here and now, but not that Ruth intended them for you. She'd already told me that. When we didn't find them after she died, I assumed she'd already given them to you."

He shook his head. "Even so, it never, not in a million years, would've entered my mind that you might have stolen something from my grandmother." He handed me the slip of paper.

She'd written more. "These belong to Jayne Highsmith. For her trip to France or wherever else the light leads her." I gasped, feeling the words run all the way through me. "I had no idea. None."

"Will you stay, Jayne?"

I sighed. "Here?"

"Why not?"

"For a while, certainly. I'd like to spend some time getting to know Mitch again."

"And me?"

"You too, Wyatt. I'll hang around for a few months probably." I looked away. "When I was young, Ruth told me that I had a light—that everyone does but that they lose it if they don't live it—if they try to hide it to fit in better. I gave up everything about who I was to fit in. To be respectable. To have people look at me with approval. But losing my true self made me vulnerable to poor choices, and to someone like Justin.

"I squandered it—all that light—in chasing happiness, or what I thought would bring me happiness. Instead, it was always in me." I hit my chest. "In me. All I had to do was to let it shine. Let it be my truth and ignore those who didn't appreciate it, instead of trying to find my truth in the eyes of others." I shook my head. "Am I making any sense at all?"

"Yes. And I know what you're saying is true because I tried to be successful—to be what I thought that meant. And it went sideways. Badly."

"Can healing truly be as easy as returning home and deciding I've forgiven Mama? Understanding what I owe Mitch and living up to it? Do I now jump for joy and yell, 'All's well, and happiness is achieved'?"

"Is a happy ending so impossible?"

"No. But . . . I think expecting one happy ending is. Each moment we live is another opportunity to be squandered or embraced. Maybe we live a series of happy endings. Are we supposed to chase them over and over?"

"Sounds exhausting."

"Exactly. If we're so busy chasing happiness, how are we ever supposed to live it?"

"I think you can only live your happiness by being yourself and finding your joy there. And sharing it. You don't receive joy. Joy is for sharing."

This was the time. The moment.

"Wyatt. I have something else to discuss with you." I took his hand and held it tightly for a second before releasing it. "I'm sorry to bring this up after all these years, but . . ." I shook my head. "Your mom and my dad . . . I'm sorry. I don't know how to say this."

"Maybe you don't need to." He shifted a little closer to me. "Are you talking about Demaris and George? Their . . . indiscretion?"

Shocked, I said, "You knew?"

"Not until my senior year. Mom had been telling me for a while that I should stay away from you. She'd said things like that before but without giving a good reason—only that she wanted our family, and me in particular, to stay away from anything to do with Bella Highsmith and her family."

"But she agreed that you could take me to the dance? That doesn't make sense."

"In that instance, I guess I steamrolled her. I told her we were going together regardless. She tried the usual excuses and I wasn't buying it, so she pretended to give in, but she was stalling for time, hoping something else, like maybe your mama, would interfere and solve the problem. When that didn't happen, she started an argument. Poor Bill, who didn't know anything about it, started having chest pains, and off we went to the hospital."

He sighed. "I think Mom believed that she could keep

us apart well enough to prevent any . . . feelings. When it became apparent that wasn't doing the job, we moved. That's why I spent my senior year in a different school. I was one very unhappy guy. Finally, she had to tell me about the parentage question was behind it all."

"But you didn't tell me."

"I wanted to. And I didn't want to. I was going to anyway because it felt like the right thing. I thought I would tell you the truth that day on my way out of town. In my head, I thought that was the best way. Tell you and then leave, so we wouldn't have to relive it over and over. But when I saw you . . . I found I couldn't. All I could say was goodbye."

He shrugged. "I figured, in its own, perhaps unsatisfactory way, that solved the problem. How did you find out?"

"Mama told me just before graduation, practically on my way out the door."

"Ouch." He reached out for my hand.

I looked away.

"But, Jayne, it isn't true."

"What?"

"When those DNA tests became so readily available, I tried to find my father. I wanted him and I to take the test and find out the truth, but I failed. I never found him. When I moved back here, though, and Mitch was here, I realized testing could tell us if we shared a parent."

"Mitch did the testing with you?"

Wyatt smiled. "He did. And we are not related."

"We aren't."

"No."

"So, if we had feelings—not that we necessarily do, but

if we did . . ."

"Then we're good."

"Oh, Wyatt. We've been dancing around this, each of us knowing . . . wondering if the other knew . . . why?"

"Because we were protecting each other."

"And maybe ourselves too."

"From hurt?"

"That, yes, but also out of fear."

"Fear?"

"Fear of losing you forever." I said, softly, "Better to pretend we'd parted willingly and might someday return as friends but knowing that wouldn't work because..."

"Because we've always been more than friends."

Wyatt leaned in, putting his arm around me. I wanted to respond in kind, but first, I held up my hand. "Tell me, did Mitch know?"

He shook his head. "No. It was a surprise to him. Bella only told you. In her own strange way, she may have been trying to warn you. I mean, who would know how to deliver news like that? I certainly didn't."

Wyatt touched my cheek. He turned my face toward his gently. "Jayne, I hope you're planning to hang around. Not planning any trips to France right now?"

"Not France. I've been there. Maybe somewhere else, but not right now. For the time being—at least for the next six months, I'll be right here." I laughed. "Not necessarily on this rock. It's rather hard. But on Hope Road. So long as you're willing to allow me to rent the Berry house."

"I'm sure we can work something out."

"Besides," I said with a lazy shrug, "there are debts to be paid, and per my reckoning, you owe me a dance."

I laughed again. He didn't. Instead, he kissed me.

After a brief, surprised hesitation, I kissed him back.

There were no fireflies or dragonflies, but only the two of us and a jarful of silver dollars.

EPILOGUE

I sat in the wicker chair on Ruth Berry's porch, sipping tea as I waited for the day to arrive. The dragonfly pendant was cool against my flesh. I placed my hand over my t-shirt and felt the solid shape of the dragonfly beneath.

Face your fears.

Oh yes, that sounded good, didn't it? But it didn't mean there wouldn't be more fears to face, any more than being blessed with one happy ending meant you'd never have another.

Sounded like a bit of wisdom that Ruth Berry might've suggested adding to my toolbox. Right along with her advice to be careful what you wish for because you just might get it. There was a time when I'd believed Ms. Ruth knew everything. When she died, the bright light that had been my friend was extinguished. It was as if someone had cut my education short.

One of the many things she told me was to take care of today and the future will arrive on schedule, bringing both good and bad, whether you're ready or not, so you might as well laugh and enjoy the ride. This early morning, when the rest of the world was sleeping, I let the laughter bubble inside me. It tickled.

The sun was still behind the trees and only just tinting the sky when I saw a figure move, sort of detaching itself from the shadows. I straightened, setting my cup on the table, and I was preparing to stand when he said, "Jayne."

"Good morning, Wyatt." I went to the porch door and pushed it open. "Trouble sleeping?"

He stopped outside just short of the steps. "Missing you."

"We saw each other a few hours ago."

"After eighteen years apart, I'm reluctant to take anything for granted. Wanted to see for myself that you're still here. Why aren't you sleeping?"

"I woke early."

"A lot on your mind?"

I smiled. "Past and present, all at once. Memories have a way of pulling you in."

"Past and present? What about the future?"

"I'm ready for it." I took his hand, and together we crossed the yard to the fence. The solid hulk of the barn was beyond it, and above us the last bits of night were still holding out against the arrival of the new day.

As I leaned against the top rail, I said, "I was wondering about something. Do you think that Ruth knew about the affair? That my dad might be yours too?" I sighed. "I trusted her absolutely. Maybe too much."

Wyatt touched my hair. "I don't think so."

"You don't know?"

"I know you trusted and loved her, and you were smart to do that. As for whether she knew about the misdeeds of others and the possible result? I don't know for sure, and yet I absolutely do know. She loved you, Jayne. She loved you as if you were her very own child. If she'd known that letting us hang out together—other than concern for the obvious boy-girl stuff—she wouldn't have allowed us to be exposed to such potentially devastating heartache." He added, "She was a romantic at heart, and I think she wanted us to end up together. That wouldn't have been the case if she knew we might be half siblings."

I touched his hair too. "I think you're right."

"My grandmother didn't know everything, but she knew what mattered. Love."

Softly, I laughed. It was a happy sound and straight from my heart.

"Six months, huh?"

I said, "Six months. I'll be free, and I'll start my life over again."

"What do you call what you're doing now?"

"Now? Right at this moment, I'm standing within the circle of your arms. Over the next six months, I'll be tying up loose ends with Justin. I'd like to end that relationship on reasonable terms that are fair to both of us, and I'll also be getting the business of my life lined up and ready to roll on day one of the next iteration of Jayne Highsmith. This edition is going to be the best one of all."

"I like the one that's with me right now. What do you have in mind for the new version?"

"The next Jayne Highsmith is going to be herself. Not a girl dancing around her mother's temper, and not the Jayne who tried so hard to be someone else that she took that person's name and left a big part of who she was behind. This Jayne isn't going for perfection, but for authenticity in all its imperfections. In other words, occasional chaos and a little dirt can be managed, and might even add spice to the mix."

"Do you think the new Jayne will want to be

authentically imperfect along with me?"

I put my hands on either side of his face and looked him straight in the eyes. "I suspect we'll be better together than we ever were apart. From now on—whether by starlight, sunlight, or inner light—we'll find our way in this world and we'll do it hand in hand."

"Will we find happiness, Jayne?"

He was teasing me. I took his hand. "We won't even be looking for it. We already have joy. If happiness wants to join us, it's welcome to come along for the ride."

The End

ACKNOWLEDGMENTS

Thank you to everyone who contributed to *A Light Last Seen*, especially my amazing beta readers, Jill, Amy and Amy for being so generous with their time, talent and feedback to improve the story, and sincere thanks to editor, Jessica Fogleman for making the manuscript shine.

Thank you for reading A LIGHT LAST SEEN. I hope you enjoyed it! If you did, I recommend checking out THE MEMORY OF BUTTERFLIES or THE WILDFLOWER HOUSE SERIES (WILDFLOWER HEART) or CUB CREEK next.

QUESTIONS FOR DISCUSSION

1. Mothers are people too. They have heartaches and disappointments. They struggle. We like to believe that every parent puts their children ahead of their own fears and disappointments, but we also know that isn't always true. However, in the case of Jaynie and her mother, Jaynie's memory seized on the bad and forgot much of the good. If Jaynie's mother hadn't died, do you think mother and daughter might've found forgiveness and reconciliation?

2. We all want to fit in. To belong. Even if we are all different—unique—we crave that sense of belonging. But the quest to belong comes with a cost. In Jaynie's childhood she began making those alterations to her behavior without even realizing it. What are some of those instances? What are ways in which we each hide our unique light?

3. What role did Ruth play in Jaynie's life? Ruth was a flawed character, but pivotal in Jaynie's growth. What sort of person might Jaynie have become if she'd grown up without Ruth's support and encouragement?

4. In what ways do people chase happiness, and even happy endings? How does joy figure into it?

ABOUT THE AUTHOR

Photo © 2018 Amy G Photography

Grace Greene is an award-winning and USA Today bestselling author of women's fiction and contemporary romance set in the countryside of her native Virginia *(The Happiness In Between, The Memory of Butterflies, the Cub Creek Series, and The Wildflower House Series)* and on the breezy beaches of Emerald Isle, North Carolina *(The Emerald Isle, NC Stories Series)*. Her debut novel, *Beach Rental*, and the sequel, *Beach Winds*, were both Top Picks by RT Book Reviews magazine. This newest release, *A Barefoot Tide*, represents the merging of two worlds—that of Cub Creek and Emerald Isle, through the eyes of a new character, and continues in the sequel, *A Dancing Tide* released in October 2021.

Visit www.gracegreene.com for more information or to communicate with Grace and sign up for her newsletter.

BOOKS BY GRACE GREENE

BEACH RENTAL   (The Emerald Isle, NC Stories Series ~ Novel #1)

RT Book Reviews – TOP PICK
"No author can come close to capturing the awe-inspiring essence of the North Carolina coast like Greene. Her debut novel seamlessly combines hope, love and faith, like the female equivalent of Nicholas Sparks. Her writing is meticulous and so finely detailed you'll hear the gulls overhead and the waves crashing onto shore. Grab a hanky, bury your toes in the sand and get ready to be swept away with this unforgettable beach read." —*RT Bk Reviews*

Brief Description: *On the Crystal Coast of North Carolina, in the small town of Emerald Isle…*

Juli Cooke, hard-working and getting nowhere fast, marries a dying man, Ben Bradshaw, for a financial settlement, not expecting he will set her on a journey of hope and love. The journey brings her to Luke Winters, a local art dealer, but Luke resents the woman who married his sick friend and warns her not to hurt Ben—and he's watching to make sure she doesn't. Until Ben dies and the stakes change.

Framed by the timelessness of the Atlantic Ocean and the brilliant blue of the beach sky, Juli struggles against her past, the opposition of Ben's and Luke's families, and even the living reminder of her marriage—to build a future with hope and perhaps to find the love of her life—if she can survive the danger from her past.

CUB CREEK (Cub Creek Series #1)

__Brief Description__: *In the heart of Virginia, where the forests hide secrets and the creeks run strong and deep ~*

Libbie Havens doesn't need anyone and she'll prove it. When she chances upon the secluded house on Cub Creek in rural Virginia, she buys it. She'll show her cousin Liz, and other doubters, that she can rise above her past and live happily and successfully on her own terms.

At Cub Creek Libbie makes friends and attracts the romantic interest of two local men, Dan Wheeler and Jim Mitchell. Relationships with her cousin and other family members improve dramatically and Libbie experiences true happiness—until tragedy occurs.

Having lost the good things gained at Cub Creek, Libbie must find a way to overcome her troubles, to finally rise above them and seize control of her life and future, or risk losing everything, including herself

THE WILDFLOWER HOUSE SERIES

WILDFLOWER HEART (Bk 1)

~ Love and hope, like wildflowers, can grow in unexpected places. Kara Hart has been tested repeatedly during her first thirty years. She's recovering, but is she resilient enough to start her life over yet again? When her widowed father suddenly retires intending to restore an aging Victoria mansion, Kara goes with him intending to stay until the end of wildflower season.

WILDFLOWER HOPE (Bᴋ 2)

~ Kara is building a new life at Wildflower House - but will digging in to restore the old mansion not only give her a sense of belonging, but also restore her heart?

WILDFLOWER CHRISTMAS (A Nᴏᴠᴇʟʟᴀ)

~ Kara is expecting a quiet Christmas ~ just like she'd always known ~ but if she's lucky she'll have a very different Christmas experience ~ one worth building new traditions to treasure.

Please visit www.GraceGreene.com for a full list of Grace's books, both single titles and series, for descriptions and more information.

BOOKS BY GRACE GREENE

Emerald Isle, North Carolina Series
Beach Rental *(Book 1)*
Beach Winds *(Book 2)*
Beach Wedding *(Book 3)*
"Beach Towel" (A Short Story)
Beach Walk *(Christmas Novella)*

Barefoot Tides Two-Book Series
A Barefoot Tide *(Book 1)*
A Dancing Tide *(Book 2)*

Beach Single-Title Novellas
Beach Christmas *(Christmas Novella)*
Clair *(Beach Brides Novella Series)*

Cub Creek Novels ~ Series and Single Titles
Cub Creek *(Cub Creek Series, Book 1)*
Leaving Cub Creek *(Cub Creek Series, Book 2)*
The Happiness In Between
The Memory of Butterflies
A Light Last Seen

The Wildflower House Novels
Wildflower Heart *(Book 1)*
Wildflower Hope *(Book 2)*
Wildflower Christmas *(A Wildflower House Novella) (Book 3)*

Virginia Country Roads
Kincaid's Hope
A Stranger in Wynnedower
www.GraceGreene.com